ACCOUNTABLE

E.V. Stephens

PAGE PUBLISHING, INC.
New York, NY

First originally published by Page Publishing, Inc. 2016

ISBN 978-1-68348-009-9 (Paperback)
ISBN 978-1-68348-922-1 (Hard Cover)
ISBN 978-1-68348-010-5 (Digital)

Printed in the United States of America

To M, D & B with love—*finally!*

ACKNOWLEDGMENTS

First and foremost, I need to thank my family and my BFFs for their love and support. Coexisting with an author is not always easy, as writing is a solitary endeavor, but when I do pop my head out of my cave, I am so grateful to find you there for me. I also want to express my appreciation to V and E for their examples of courage and strength—I only wish they were here to celebrate this accomplishment with me.

Thank you to Kali Hammond, Brian Droste, and the entire Page Publishing team for helping to make my dream a reality. Thank you to Kristen Weber for her insight and guidance on improving *Accountable*. And thanks also to the Cornell University ILR School for sharing information on its website about the tragic Triangle Waist Factory Fire.

Space does not permit me to personally name everyone who has influenced or supported me along the way, and even if it did, regrettably, I'm sure I would fail to mention someone. If you've inquired about my progress or given me a kick in the *#% to try to end my procrastination, then you know who you are and should also know my gratitude is meant for you as well.

I began to write as a hobby, but over time, I realized I'd found my passion. I tried to create a "real" protagonist and supporting cast of characters who sometimes fail, but continue to strive to do right and be kind—people you'd like as friends and would want in your corner as you deal with life's challenges. I'm so fortunate to have people like that in my life and I wish it for you, my readers, as well. Thank you for spending some time getting to know Val and her friends.

EV
Chicago, January 2016

—— CHAPTER 1 ——

Traffic inched along on Lakeview Drive as drivers craned their necks for a peek at the police cars and medical examiner's van in front of the condo development just south of the river. Whether it's a wreck on the highway, fire trucks down the block, or a crime scene crawling with cops, tragedy is fascinating...when it strikes someone else.

The all-news station resonated through the speakers in my Escape and I got lost in the hypnotic pulse of blue lights on the roof of the squad ahead of me until the anchorman said, "Bedford Police are still searching for a homeless man in connection with the murder of a local bank executive. Gary Noonan is wanted for questioning in the death of David Lukas, director of operations for Lakeview Bank, who was gunned down last week at the construction site of the bank's new branch on Mission Street. In other news..."

I cut my eyes to the stereo. *That's it? Where's the part about Dave being funny, kind, and compassionate? That his life ended after only thirty-four years. Or that he was buried yesterday, leaving a wife, parents, and friends behind whose lives will never be the same.*

I switched off the engine but the horrible details of that day droned on in my head.

An electrician witnessed an altercation between Dave and Noonan at the branch around eight o'clock that morning. Noonan entered the building through a back door that workers propped open to unload supplies. In loud, slurred speech, he told Dave he wanted his house back because if the bank could afford to build a new branch, it didn't need another foreclosure. Dave calmed him down and gave him a number to call for assistance and Noonan staggered out.

Eleven hours later, my husband was dead.

The security cameras weren't online yet, and there weren't any witnesses because no one who'd willingly talk to the police ventured out in that neighborhood once the sun started to set. The contractor was a half block away when he heard what he thought were gunshots, but by the time he drove back to check things out, the shooter had fled. Noonan's status changed from person of interest to suspect after his black Ford pickup was spotted on a traffic cam two blocks from the branch within the timeframe of the shooting.

It's still hard to comprehend Dave was killed over a foreclosure. He had no responsibility for loan decisions, so how the hell could he become collateral damage in the mortgage mess?

Blood drummed in my ears and I put my head against the rest and closed my eyes.

Maybe I should've taken the week off like Mom and Dad and everyone else urged me to do. But why? So I could sit around and brood? Like I'm doing now?

I drew in a deep breath, held it, and let it escape slowly through my mouth.

Four-out-of-five mental health professionals would say the best way to cope with a critical incident is to return to a normal routine as soon as possible, and that's exactly what I'm doing. Of course, they might change their recommendation if they knew my routine but...

With a few more deep breaths, the thumping subsided and I opened my eyes. "Who cares what the shrinks would say?" I said aloud. "This is just another day at the office so I need to haul my ass out of this car and go to work."

I wiped my palms on my thighs, crawled out of my SUV, and started to weave my way through the gawkers clogging the sidewalk.

I didn't recognize the uniform posted at the door, and he assumed I lived in the building because he stopped texting and his eyes followed my low-rider jeans down to my shoes and then drifted back up to the center of the V-neck tee under my blazer. He adjusted his Bedford PD baseball cap and flashed a smile that would get him laid if he were in a bar.

The smile slid from his face when I parted the left side of my jacket to expose my shield. "Benchik. Homicide."

He slipped the phone into his pocket. "Fifth floor, Detective. Unit five-ten." I nodded and he entered my name on the crime scene log.

My heart rate climbed along with the elevator and I repeated *Just another day at the office* in my head until the doors parted on the fifth floor. Several men and women spoke in hushed tones as they huddled at one end of the hallway bordered by twelve units. I flashed my shield again to the uniform posted outside 510 and he handed me a pair of paper booties. I tugged them over my shoes and paused in the doorway to examine the frame and latch for jimmy marks or scratches. Both looked clean, so either the victim opened the door or the killer had a key.

I entered the loft and stood in the living room. Voices echoed from the end of the hall on the right and I looked toward them— toward the spot where the victim lay and to where I should go because I always meet the victim first. Except today I needed a little extra time to work up to it, so I pulled a pair of latex gloves from my pocket, snapped them on, and surveyed the room.

The top of the desk along the left wall was neat and the drawers were closed. Abstract paintings hung straight on several walls. The leather couch was parallel to the entertainment center/fireplace on the wall to the right, and matching chairs sat at right angles to the couch. Tiffany lamps were centered on end tables. There were no wrinkles in the Oriental rug or broken vases on the floor.

I turned toward the dining area and kitchen behind me to the left. Four chairs stood upright around the empty pub table.

I walked over to the end table on the far side of the room and stooped over for a closer look at a photo in a crystal frame. A woman in her mid-fifties, with a round face and shoulder-length black hair, stood with her arm around a younger version of herself, dressed in a black cap and gown. The frame next to it held a more recent photo of the young woman huddled around a small table with a brunette who was about the same age. They were toasting with green drinks— probably appletinis. I had a picture just like it taken with my best friend, Connie Warren, when we celebrated our thirtieth birthdays in Vegas two years ago. Of course in my picture, Connie and I were hoisting beers.

I scanned the room again and concluded that if a struggle occurred, it didn't happen out here. And I had stalled long enough, so I followed the voices and found Detective Greg Payton in the bathroom, his back to the door, as he watched Deputy Medical Examiner Leilani Norris tend to her patient in the porcelain bathtub.

Leilani had been at the bank Wednesday night too. When she arrived, she promised to take good care of my husband, and it took everything I had not to cry out when she kneeled beside him to do what I'd seen her do to so many victims before. Payton had been the one to persuade me to stand back and allow her to work. He walked me to the cruiser, propped me against the front fender, and remained at my side like an overprotective Labrador.

Though it's been two years, I could still picture his embarrassed smile the day we became partners and I told him he reminded me of an actor on *Judging Amy* named Richard T. Jones—partly because of his clean-shaven head but mostly due to his kind eyes and soft-spoken nature. My heart ached for him because he'd seen too many bodies even before he joined the force. First, those claimed by the gang violence that besieged Chicago's Cabrini-Green housing project where he grew up, and then his fellow soldiers killed by snipers or IEDs during his Army Reserve unit's deployment in Iraq. But in spite of the horrors he'd witnessed, his faith remained strong. I knew he'd been in church when he got the call this morning because he was wearing a jacket and slacks rather than his off-duty uniform of jeans and a T-shirt.

I suspected the call interrupted Leilani's Sunday routine as well—an hour at the gym followed by her weekly Tai-Chi class in Veterans Memorial Park. Her petite frame often fools people into believing she survives on yogurt and salad, but we've eaten together enough for me to know that while she favors her Native Hawaiian mother's physical appearance, she inherited her French father's love of food, and she depends on disciplined exercise to maintain a healthy weight.

Leilani had planned a career in orthopedics, but as a third-year med student at Columbia, her path veered sharply in September 2001. She volunteered to help catalog victims' remains from the Twin Towers and subsequently switched to forensic pathology. Her first week as an ME three years ago coincided with my first week in Homicide and we grew up on the job together.

She could've dispatched one of her staff MEs to the bank that night, but instead she skipped a night at the ballet and worked clear into Thursday morning to finish Dave's autopsy. And Payton forfeited sleep and precious time with his family to chase every lead with the rest of the squad. Like Connie, they both hovered close to me at the wake and funeral, ready to lend whatever support I needed.

But please don't let me need it here and now. I squared my shoulders, stepped across the threshold, and said, "What have we got?"

They pivoted toward me like targets on the academy's practice range.

"Val!" Leilani's perfectly plucked dark brows arched and the pitch of her voice reminded me of someone who got busted planning a surprise birthday party.

"What are you doing here?" Payton asked. The pitch of his voice didn't change. It seldom did. Always clear and calming. Like a hypnotist.

I pointed at the tub. "Homicide." I swung my finger toward my chest. "Homicide cop."

"You were supposed to take some time," Payton said.

"I did. Three days."

His eyes cut to Leilani, pleading with her to talk some sense into me, but she knew it would be futile to try. "We both know she's lolo," Leilani said and she tossed her head to reposition her long black ponytail down her back before leaning into the tub again.

"Crazy is right," Payton said. "How did you even find out about this?"

"I heard the traffic report on the radio. They mentioned delays due to police activity and the medical examiner's van on scene, so I called Dispatch, and after a bit of badgering, Bevin gave me the address. Do we have an ID?"

"Adriana Ortiz," he said. "Twenty-eight. Single. Lived alone."

I clenched and released my fists to ease some tension before I stepped up to the tub and looked down to see the young woman from the photos. My stomach flopped at the sight of the punctures peppering her flesh. "It looks like he used her for a dartboard."

"I counted twenty-seven stab wounds," Leilani said. "The wound to her chest is likely the cause of death, but the odd thing is the other twenty-six wounds were superficial. Deep enough to cause considerable pain but not enough to kill her."

"She was tortured," Payton said.

Their voices sounded muffled, as if I were underwater and they were poolside.

"You have a time of death?" Payton asked Leilani.

"Best estimate right now is between three and five Friday afternoon."

The wounds looked so tiny compared to a bullet hole.

Even from twenty feet away, I saw the blood soaking the front of Dave's white shirt, and I winced, as if the bullet had struck my own heart. Which in a way, it had.

I squeezed my eyes shut and fought to push the image into the place in my mind where I try to compartmentalize the job, but it was too soon and the image was too vivid.

I ran across the parking lot and dropped to my knees on the pavement. His hand still felt warm when I grasped it in both of mine, and I closed my eyes, convinced that I'd open them to find it was all a horrible nightmare.

I opened my eyes and the punctures on Ortiz's body pulsed upward like some 3D horror movie. A hot wave washed over my body and my legs wobbled. I reached out and braced my palm against the tiled wall above Ortiz's bathtub to keep from falling over.

Keep it together! I shouted in my head, and I breathed slowly, deeply until the faintness passed. When I felt steady, I moved my head around a little, pretending like I'd propped my hand against the wall for a better look at the wounds. I pushed back and asked, "Any guess on weapon?"

The awkward silence told me I'd failed to fool them, but they graciously let it go.

"Entry points are clean, indicating a sharp point," Leilani said. "And given the small diameter and smooth edges, my guess would be an ice pick or an awl."

I turned to face them. "What the hell is an awl?"

"It's a tool used to punch holes," Payton said.

"In what and by whom?"

"Wood or leather," he said. "Belts. Custom woodworking. That sort of thing."

I walked over and opened the cabinet above the vanity. Ortiz kept an assortment of over-the-counter pain and cold meds, as well as four toothbrushes in the boxes. Either she changed her brush every three months like the box advises or she had frequent overnight guests. And one of them could be our killer.

I surveyed the vanity. She kept a brush and hot rollers in the corner, along with her makeup, for which she showed no sign of brand loyalty. The cabinet under the sink housed cleaning supplies. I closed the door and looked around.

"What's wrong?" Payton asked.

I shook my head. "It feels like something's missing." I scanned the vanity again but couldn't put my finger on it. "Who found her?"

"Maintenance guy," Payton said. "Name's Dwayne Stuckey. Our vic called earlier in the week to report a problem with the garbage disposal. She scheduled the repair for Sunday because she'd be out all day. He didn't know where she was supposed to be."

"I noticed there were no signs of forced entry. I assume Mr. Fix-it has a key?"

"He does," Payton said. "Said he was replacing the faucet in three-twelve on Friday afternoon so we'll have to verify. He also told me he saw a guy with a ponytail hassling our vic Thursday evening. Guy was Hispanic. Under six feet. About one hundred and fifty pounds."

"Maybe Fix-it had a thing for her but he's too blue collar so she wouldn't give him the time of day," I said. "He decided to take a shot anyway but things got ugly and she got dead. Then he made up the story about the work order and the mystery harasser to cover his tracks."

"Theories are good." Payton studied the body. "Her lipstick's smudged. Maybe the killer covered her mouth with his hand and we'll get DNA."

"She has abrasions on her wrists indicating restraints," Leilani said. "I can't see any fibers, but they could be very small, or he could've used something smooth. Like an electrical cord."

I snapped my fingers. "A hair dryer. That's what's missing."

"She probably kept it on the vanity," Payton said. "Killer grabbed the first thing he saw."

"I doubt she had an ice pick or awl lying around the house," I said, "which means the killer brought a weapon with him but had to improvise to tie her up."

"Probably figured the weapon would be enough to intimidate her but she turned out to be scrappier than he thought."

I glanced back at the tub. Dried blood caked around the drain like the caramelized surface of crème brulée. "I suppose all the trace evidence was washed away."

I heard a thump and rattle and turned to find Officer Todd Argus, our best evidence technician, unlatching his case. "Off for three days and you already forget who you're dealing with, Benchik?" Argus tsked at me. "I can find anything."

A lot of guys on the force look like their head sprouts from their shoulders with no neck in between, but not Argus. He has a relatively small head on a longish neck and long, thin fingers. His appearance is sort of unfortunate because within the department, an evidence tech is referred to as an ET.

He focused his digital camera on the bathtub. When the flash fired, I flinched. Argus had been on call Wednesday night, and when he snapped his first picture of Dave, I lunged at him and tried to rip the camera from his hands.

"Come on," Payton said. He slipped his strong hand under my arm and swung me around toward the door. "Let's go do our job and let the doc do hers."

—— CHAPTER 2 ——

Payton had called dibs on Ortiz's desk, which left me with the bedroom.

The first thing I noticed was that Ortiz was a better housekeeper than I am. To me, the bed is made if I smooth out the sheet and blanket, but she'd taken time to fix her queen-sized bed with a floral spread.

The latest issue of *Cosmopolitan* sat on the nightstand under *The Notebook*, so she was liberated but still a romantic at heart. I opened the drawer and found a tube of hand lotion, a jar of moisturizer, and a box of condoms—the romantic was smart enough not to leave it to the guy.

The jewelry box on the dresser held some simple gemstones and turquoise. Nothing flashy, but the chains were probably 14K gold and sterling silver and would've scored a few bucks on the street. I went through the drawers and found an assortment of hosiery, jeans, sweats, T-shirts, and tank tops. And all of her lingerie came from Victoria's Secret.

I slid the closet door open and flicked on the light in a walk-in that ran the length of the room. Dresses, blouses, and casual pants filled half of the left clothes bar. Suits filled half of the right. I shifted a few hangers to read the labels—all Donna Karan. The shoeboxes on the shelf over the suits were organized alphabetically by Blahnick, Choo, Ferragamo, and Magli. A Kate Spade purse hung on a hook just inside the door. I unhooked it and riffled through the contents—a hairbrush, some cosmetics, and tampons, but no wallet. We'd probably find another purse somewhere in the condo. I hung it up, turned out the light, and returned to the living room.

Payton had pulled back the vertical blinds over the balcony doors to allow some natural light into the room as he searched the desk. I scanned the DVDs on the entertainment rack shelves. The titles included *An Affair to Remember, Sleepless in Seattle,* and the Zorro movies with Antonio Banderas.

"Mostly chick flicks," Payton said.

"There's more to cinema than explosions and car chases," I said.

"I can't tell you the last time I enjoyed an action flick." He closed the top drawer. "When Matthew and Erin aren't fighting over the remote, Pam is grabbing it to switch to some cooking show where she's going to"—he raised his voice—"get this great new recipe."

"Has Pam ever heard your impersonation?"

He cocked his right eyebrow as if to say *What do you think?*

I laughed and squatted next to the chair facing the windows. Ortiz had kicked off her black patent leather four-inch stilettos and I hooked my index finger through the heel strap and held it up for a closer look.

Leilani walked into the living room and her face lit up like a techie at an electronics show. "Those are Jimmy Choos!"

"Do I detect shoe envy, Doctor?"

She made an inch sign with her fingers.

I set the shoe down and stood, giving me five inches over her five-foot-four frame. "Can't blame you for wanting high fashion after wearing coveralls or scrubs all day."

She smiled. "That's what I tell myself whenever I buy a new pair." She snapped her fingers. "We should go buy some."

I turned up my palms. "Where would I wear them? They're a little dressy for court and I sure as hell couldn't chase a suspect. Of course if we ever have a killer who turns out to be a vampire, the heel could double as a stake."

Leilani shook her head as if I were a lost cause. "I should be able to do the autopsy about eleven tomorrow if you're planning to grace me with your presence."

I felt a flutter of anxiety in the pit of my stomach. I'd barely worked up the nerve to come in here. The odds were slim to none that I'd be able to deal with seeing a body on an autopsy table, but I told her we'd be there and then watched as she and her assistant, Danny Gallagher, wheeled the gurney into the hall. It rattled as it bumped over the threshold, just like it had when Leilani wheeled

Dave's body across the parking lot to the ME's van. Every muscle in my body contracted and I wondered if the oxygen had been sucked out of the room because I couldn't breathe. I cast an uneasy glance toward Payton. Fortunately, he was too absorbed in riffling through Ortiz's mail to notice.

I crossed to the sliding doors, flipped the lock, and stepped out onto a balcony large enough for two forest-green plastic chairs and a matching table. The loft faced north and afforded a spectacular view of Lake Wellington and the bluffs of Paradise Mountain. Despite eighty-degree temperatures and humidity to match, the breeze off the lake felt cool, and I gripped the railing and sucked in fresh air until Payton appeared next to me.

He bent his six-foot-one frame over and propped his forearms on railing. "How you holding up?"

"I'm okay." Sunlight flashed on the waves like cameras on the red carpet at a Hollywood premier, and I watched a sailboat glide across the water. I'd never gone sailing. I wondered if Ortiz had. Or my partner. "You ever been sailing?"

"Not that kind," he said. "Pam and I took a cruise on a nice big ship for our first anniversary"—he squinted as he did the math—"eleven years ago. She thinks we should go again next year for my fortieth birthday."

I smiled weakly. "When Dave and I went for our fifth anniversary last year, we got up early our first morning at sea and went up on deck to watch the sunrise. There was no one else there, and we stood by the rail, gazing at the ocean. It felt like we were the only two people in the only place on earth. No worries. No stress." *Nothing*, I thought, *compared to the overload of images buzzing around in my head like a swarm of yellow jackets since Wednesday night.* I sighed. "I wish I could've bottled the feeling because ever since Pritchard rang our doorbell…"

Jeremiah Theodore Pritchard worked Narcotics, but we'd partnered for three years in uniform. During our first year together, he'd badgered me to go out with his roommate from the University of Illinois until I finally caved in and agreed to dinner and a movie with my future husband.

The first uniform to respond to the contractor's 911 call had played basketball with Dave and Pritchard a few times. He recognized Dave and called my old partner. Pritchard had been there when my life with Dave began, and he'd been the one to break the news it was over.

I knew I'd be exhibiting some very un-cop-like emotion if we didn't move on to a new subject so I said, "Judging from the designer suits and shoes in her closet, our vic was either a fantastic bargain hunter or she had some serious money."

"What is it with those fancy clothes?" Payton asked.

I raised my palm. "Don't ask me. Levi Strauss is the most famous name to touch my ass."

He laughed. "You check out the plasma?"

"What is it with guys and big TVs?"

"Genetics," he said. "I found a couple cups from Mugga Java in the trash. Smelled like caramel something. And she either survived on salad or ate out a lot. Fridge was full of lettuce, carrot sticks, and alfalfa sprouts." He wrinkled his nose. "What more does a successful young woman need?"

"Chocolate," I said.

Payton tugged on my ponytail. "Do you dye your hair?"

"Why? Are you planning to let yours grow back and you need styling tips?"

He shook his head. "I was just wondering if the milk chocolate shade is an accident of birth or if you engineered it to match your obsession."

"Genetics," I said. "You find an address book?"

He rolled his eyes. "No one uses address books anymore."

"I do."

"You don't count. You don't even dye your hair or wear designer rags."

I looked back out at the water. "Murder is often about money or sex."

"She's got nearly thirty grand in her checking account," Payton said. "Money does not seem to be a problem."

"Detectives," Argus called out. "If you're finished slacking, I found something."

I locked the balcony door, and when I turned, Argus held up a red leather purse.

"It doesn't go with your shoes," I said.

"Who cares?" Argus said. "It's a Birkin bag."

"A what now?"

He looked at me as if I had snot hanging from my nose and slowly repeated, "A Birkin bag."

I shrugged my hands and shoulders.

"Come on, Benchik! There's a waiting list for these. Every woman wants one."

I wagged my finger. "You should be careful about generalizations, Todd."

"Are you telling me you wouldn't want one if you could afford it? It's Hermes. You have heard of Hermes."

I thought for a moment and then snapped my fingers. "The store that refused to stay open later to accommodate Oprah."

Argus's face filled with pity. "Sometimes you worry me."

I flexed my hands as I fought to harness some patience. "Please tell me you called us in here because you found something other than a ten-thousand-dollar purse."

"Ha!" Argus shot his finger at me. "You have heard of them."

I'd heard of them because Connie and I love *Gilmore girls* and Logan Huntzberger gave one to Rory Gilmore as a gift. But I kept that little secret, crossed my arms, and stared at him.

"Okay! Jeez, Benchik." He held up a wallet. "Besides the purse, her credit cards are still here, along with over two hundred bucks in cash and a very nice smart phone, so you can rule out a home invasion robbery."

Payton snatched the phone from Argus's hand and started to scroll. "Her call log shows nine messages from the same number between 9:00 PM Thursday and 1:00 AM Friday."

"Nine! Sounds like a friend with relationship trouble."

He scrolled some more. "The number isn't in her contacts so we don't have a name."

"Forget a friend with relationship trouble," I said. "Make that someone who used to be a contact and got deleted. Like an old boyfriend who wouldn't let go."

.V. STEPHENS

"Just the sort of guy who could commit murder in a fit of rage," Payton said.

"Check her speed dials while you're at it. Highest-ranked woman is probably her sister or best friend. She may be able to shed some light."

Payton scrolled through the entries. "Number one is Anita Zamora." He held up the phone.

I recognized the face on the screen and pointed toward the end table. "She's the same woman in a picture with Ortiz."

"She lives on Third," he said and I wrote down the address and phone number as he read them off. "I'll have TRU run the name and address for our mystery caller," he said as he dialed the number for the Technical Response Unit. After he finished the call he asked, "Best friend or neighbors first?"

"If Zamora had reason to believe Ortiz was in danger, she probably would've been the one to find the body," I said. "Let's ask around here first."

—— CHAPTER 3 ——

It's a funny thing about witnesses. Some are eager to be interviewed but others—like our victim's neighbor—scatter like cockroaches when you turn on a light. When we stepped into the hall, he jammed the key into his lock and practically dived through his doorway.

I looked at Payton. "Does he honestly think we didn't see him go in there?" Payton chuckled and I rapped on the cockroach's door. When he didn't answer after a second knock I said, "Bedford Police! We saw you enter the unit!"

The deadbolt clicked back, the door opened the width of the chain, and Cockroach peered through the space. I motioned for him to remove the chain. The door closed, the chain slid back, and the door opened again.

"Is it true she's dead?" he asked.

"Yes," I said. "Mister..."

"Unger. Walter Unger." He wore his brown striped polo buttoned at the collar and his khakis hiked up a little too high. If he boxed, he'd struggle to make welterweight class.

"Are you aware of any problems Ms. Ortiz may have had?" I asked.

Unger shook his head and pushed his black plastic glasses back up the bridge of his nose.

"Have you noticed anything suspicious or someone hanging around?" I asked.

He shook no again. "But I thought I heard a scream Friday afternoon."

We waited but when he didn't elaborate I asked, "Did you go next door or call to see if everything was all right?"

"No," he said with a dismissive shrug. "I figured it was the TV. Considering what we paid for these units, the walls are pretty thin."

I nodded slowly, feigning empathy for his situation. I swung my head toward Payton and shrugged my brows toward Unger to signal my partner he'd better take over. If I continued to look at the guy, I'd probably slap him or shake him, which would complicate my life in a way I didn't need right now.

Payton said, "The maintenance man told us he saw—"

"I'd check Dwayne out if I were you," Unger said.

"Why?" Payton asked.

"Because he hits on anything in a skirt."

"Dwayne said Ms. Ortiz had requested some work be done today because she was going to be out," Payton said. "Any idea where she was supposed to be?"

"Nope."

"You normally home on Friday afternoons?" Payton asked.

"I work from home." Unger shook his head. "It's creepy to think she was being killed just yards away, on the other side of that wall."

"Yeah." I looked him in the eye. "Creepy."

Payton handed Unger a card and asked him to call if he thought of anything. I waited until Unger closed the door before I said, "When we run background, we're starting with him."

Payton nodded, "Let's check with three-twelve. See if Mr. Fix-it left the unit at any time Friday afternoon."

Like Unger, the neighbor in 312 couldn't believe there'd been a murder in his building. Unlike Unger, 312 wasn't squirrelly. He confirmed Dwayne Stuckey worked in his unit between two and five o'clock Friday afternoon. Stuckey never left, but 312 confessed he almost walked out because he was getting tired of listening to Stuckey swear at the pipes.

We moved on to canvass the other residents. Only twenty-nine of Ortiz's neighbors answered their doors. When we showed them her driver's license photo on our phones, several didn't even recognize Ortiz as someone who lived in the building.

"Whatever happened to being neighborly?" Payton asked on our way to the car.

"Well, gee, Barn, we're not in Mayberry."

He held up a hand. "I'm just saying I don't understand how people don't speak to their neighbors. On the elevator. On the way to their cars. Somewhere. Even in Chicago, the people on my block knew each other."

"I hear you," I said. "I was five when my family left the Windy City, but I remember our neighbors hugging us and telling us how much they'd miss us." We crawled into the sweltering car and I clicked my seatbelt. "If my family hadn't moved, do you think we still would've met?"

Payton clicked his own seatbelt. "Sure. Assuming we both joined the Chicago PD."

I nodded. "Let's try the best friend."

He reached for the ignition but stopped and dug his phone out of his pocket and answered. I watched a thin woman with short legs patter along the sidewalk with her dachshund until Payton ended the call. "The BFF will have to wait," he said. "Cassidy's got something and he needs us to bring Ortiz's phone."

We found Colin Cassidy in his usual position—eyes glued to his flat-screen monitor in the Technical Response Unit on the third floor of police headquarters. Our resident computer whiz preferred science to sports in high school but would've easily deflected any bully's attempt to stuff him into a locker. A polar opposite to the computer nerd stereotype, he owned a dee-jay business with a buddy from college, and his goofy enthusiasm enabled him to coax even the most self-conscious partygoers onto the dance floor to let loose—including Dave and me at a department recognition dinner last fall.

"What's so urgent?" Payton asked.

"They got a nine-one-one call in the Bunker I thought you should hear," Cassidy said, referencing Bedford's new Emergency Services control center housed in a sub-level of City Hall. He punched a few keys and queued up the call.

"Nine-one-one," the operator said.

"Please help me." The voice was soft, female.

"What is the nature of your emergency, ma'am?"

"He's kill…killing…me."

"Who is?"

Silence and then the dispatcher again. "Ma'am. Ma'am, are you there?"

Cassidy stopped the playback. "That's it. Call came in at 3:29 PM Friday."

"Dr. Norris put the kill zone between three and five Friday afternoon," Payton said.

Ortiz's wounds flashed in my head. "The caller said, 'He's killing me.' Not 'He's going to kill me' like a victim might say when she's first confronted with danger. She must've gotten free to make the call sometime after the attack started."

"We weren't able to trace the number," Cassidy said. "Probably a disposable cell. Have you got the vic's phone?"

"Yeah." Payton handed Cassidy the evidence bag. "But it's no burner."

Cassidy initialed off before opening the bag. "I figured I can run a voice comparison between the vic's greeting and the nine-one-one call." He queued up both samples, punched a few buttons, and graphs danced up and down on his screen. "On the left is the recording from the nine-one-one call." Cassidy traced the red line on the screen with his finger. "And on the right is your vic's voicemail greeting." The lines didn't seem to match. "Damn!" Cassidy ran his hands over his close-cropped dark hair. "The sample's not long enough to make a definitive match. Doesn't mean your vic didn't make the call but it doesn't prove she did."

"What are the odds another woman placed a call like that within our kill zone?" Payton asked.

"And it fits if Ortiz was tortured like Leilani thinks," I said. "Ortiz managed to get free long enough to make the call but the killer regains control and finishes the job."

"Can you upload the nine-one-one call to our phones?" Payton asked. "Maybe we can play it for someone who knew Ortiz and they'll be able to make a positive ID on the voice."

Cassidy clicked away on his computer. "Done. You both have it. And I traced the number for your persistent caller. It's listed to Dylan Henry. Lives on Walnut. I sent the address and his driver's license photo to your phones too."

"You're the man," Payton said. He headed for the door but I hung back.

Cassidy looked up at me. "You need something else?"

I shook my head. "I just wanted to…Payton told me you're the one who spotted Noonan's pickup on traffic cam footage. You *are* the man, Colin. Thank you."

His face flushed a little. "I'm glad I could help."

I patted his shoulder and followed Payton out.

Our illusion of making a quick arrest dissolved when we arrived at Dylan Henry's townhouse and a neighbor told us Henry was in San Francisco and wasn't due back until around 6:00 PM.

With three hours to spare, we decided to try the best friend, Anita Zamora, but she wasn't home either.

"Maybe Zamora and Henry were having an affair," I said. "Our Vic found out and they killed her before leaving for a tryst in the City by the Bay."

Payton frowned. "That's a dark thought."

I shrugged and dialed the number for Zamora that Payton found on our victim's phone. After three rings, it kicked to voicemail. I left my name and number and asked her to call ASAP.

On the way back to stake out Dylan Henry, we stopped at a sandwich shop on South River Road to pick up subs, and we ate them camped out within view of the townhouse.

I finished my turkey sub first and stuffed the wrapper into the empty bag. "So do you think Mr. Henry is a stalker or simply very much in love with Ortiz?"

"Nine calls in four hours say drunk dials to me," Payton said.

I saw movement on the left fringe of my peripheral vision and I looked over at a white male, five ten, 180 pounds, wearing a black T-shirt and jeans, walking east on Walnut. I sat up straighter. *Is that Gary Noonan? Could that be Dave's killer? This guy's hair is shorter and he's clean-shaven but…*

"It's not him," Payton said softly.

I relaxed against the seat. I glanced at him and then looked back at the man in the T-shirt. "Yeah. I know." *Wishful thinking.* "Do they have any new information?"

Payton stopped chewing for a second then chewed fast and swallowed.

"What aren't you telling me?"

He seemed to wage an internal debate as he gazed out the windshield. "Last Saturday, unis responded to a complaint from a concerned citizen about a suspicious pickup truck parked behind Lincoln High School. They found Noonan asleep inside and woke him up. He seemed intoxicated but consented to a Breathalyzer™, which put him under the legal limit. They decided to search the truck anyway—without asking for permission—because they figured if they found a bottle, they could run him in for having an open alcoholic beverage container in the vehicle. They didn't find any bottles, but they did find a registered .38 automatic in the glove box."

An ache started in the pit of my stomach.

"They arrested him for carrying a concealed weapon," Payton continued, "but the case got kicked at arraignment. The weapon was not in plain sight, and Noonan's public defender argued the unis didn't have probable cause to search given Noonan passed the Breathalyzer™."

I closed my eyes. If the search had been legal, Noonan probably wouldn't have made bail and Dave would be alive. I breathed slowly until I felt like I could speak without my voice cracking. "Are there *any* leads on where he might be?"

"When he lost his house, he lost his permanent address," Payton said. "Since the foreclosure three weeks ago, he's either crashed with a friend or slept in his car. There's an APB on him and a BOLO on his car, and we've got a uni watching the friend's apartment, but if Noonan has seen the news, he knows he killed the husband of a police officer, so he also knows every cop in the state is looking for him. Either he's lying very low or he left town." He blew out some air in frustration. "Donovan and Garcia are working their asses off—everyone is but..." He crumpled up the wrapper from his veggie sub and stuffed it into the bag. "Are your parents going to stay for a while?"

"They wanted to but I managed to talk them out of it. Put them on a flight back to Vegas first thing this morning." I drained the last of my root beer from the cup.

"Why didn't you take more time off?"

"How much time, Greg? Three weeks instead of three days? Or maybe three months?" I sighed. "If you're worried about whether my head is in the game—"

"Hey! No!" He waved me off. "That's not what this is about. I just want to be sure you take care of yourself."

I nodded and gazed out the windshield at nothing in particular. "It's just…hard to explain." I looked at him. "When you were little and you got sick, did your mom ever sit with you all night, holding your hand and stroking your head?"

He nodded.

"That's how I spent Thursday night." I shifted my gaze out the driver's window. "My mom made breakfast and my dad did some little jobs around the house and it felt…safe. Too safe. Like it would become too comfortable having them around and I wouldn't want them to leave. It wasn't reality." I looked back at Payton. "This is what I'm good at, but if I stay away too long, I don't know if I'd be able to come back."

He nodded once. "Message received. And just so you know, I'm cool with whatever you need. Like, say you feel the need to sit in the car and scream at the top of your lungs. I'm good with that. Just let me know ahead of time so I can get out."

I chuckled in spite of my grief. "Thank you. For everything."

He held my gaze for a beat before turning his attention back to the street. "Pam said to tell you you're always welcome for dinner. No invitation needed. Just show up when you're hungry."

"Will you be there?"

Payton kept his eyes on the street but I still saw his smile from the side. "I have been known to show up when my pain-in-the-ass partner isn't dragging us off at the end of shift to check out one of her off-the-wall theories about a case."

Thank God for cop humor. "In that case, I respectfully decline but thank Pam for me." I watched a gray Jetta as it angled into a parking spot a few cars ahead of us. A twenty-something guy with longish blond hair got out. "The boyfriend's back and we need to do an interview," I sang in a cadence mimicking the old Angels tune from the sixties.

Payton grimaced. "Do me a favor."

"Anything, partner."

"If we ever go to a bar that does karaoke…don't."

"But I sound better when I'm drunk."

"That's what they all think," Payton said before he crawled out of the car. "Besides, we don't know if he's the boyfriend."

"The stalker's back works too," I said.

Henry wore a blue plaid camp shirt over a white T-shirt, navy Bermuda shorts, and flip-flops. Not my footwear of choice when driving, but I suppose it made the TSA shoe search a breeze. He unlocked his trunk and reached in.

"Dylan Henry?" Payton called out.

Henry glanced our way as he hauled a black carry-on duffle out of the trunk. "Who wants to know?"

Payton held up his shield. "We need you to come with us."

— CHAPTER 4 —

The only sound in the interview room was the swish of the heavy-weight paper cup Dylan Henry was spinning between his fingers and thumb.

"Adriana's phone records showed nine messages from you Thursday night into early Friday," I said. "What was so important?"

He shrugged. "I just wanted to talk. See how she was doing."

"Your neighbor said you were in San Francisco," I said.

"Yeah." He started to shake his head. "This is all my fault."

He couldn't be confessing. We hadn't even brought out the rubber hoses yet. "How is it your fault, Dylan?"

His eyes briefly met mine before drifting back to his coffee. "I cheated and Adriana found out about it." He sighed. "If I'd have been faithful to her, this wouldn't have happened."

"What are you talking about?" Payton asked.

"Adriana should've been in San Francisco with me. I had to go for a trade show and we'd planned it as this big romantic getaway. But then I screwed up and…" He sipped some coffee and his hand trembled a little as he lowered the cup.

"When did you see her last?" Payton asked.

"Memorial Day weekend. When we broke up."

"Where does Adriana work?" Payton asked.

"She's an associate at Smithfield, Royce, and Foley."

"That's the top law firm in the city," I said, "but if she was an associate, how could she afford that condo?"

"It was a foreclosure," Henry said.

"When did you leave for San Francisco?" Payton asked.

"Monday after work," Henry said. "The show was Wednesday and Thursday but we had to be there Tuesday to set up."

"About the phone calls," I said.

"Drunk dials." He rubbed his fingers over the stubble on his chin. "I took Friday as a vacation day. If we were still together, Adriana would've done the same thing. She would've flown out Thursday and we would've had a late dinner. I didn't even want to stay but I'd booked the hotel and the weekend rate was nonrefundable. The trade show wrapped up early so I went back to the room and drank every bottle of vodka in the mini-bar. I got to missing her and... started dialing."

"We're going to need the flight and hotel information," I said.

Henry looked at me, then at Payton and his eyes got big. "I didn't kill her if that's what you're thinking."

"Is that what we were thinking?" I said to Payton without taking my eyes off Henry.

Henry shook his head. "No. I didn't. I couldn't."

"Flight and hotel information." I wrote down what he told us and said, "And the name of your fling."

"Why?"

"Because she may have seen Adriana as a threat," Payton said.

Henry swallowed hard and gave us her name and told us she worked at the Natural History Museum. "But there's no way she would've hurt Adriana."

"You ever see a guy with a ponytail hanging around Adriana?" I asked.

Henry shook his head.

Payton took his phone out of his pocket. "We know this may be difficult but we have a recording of a nine-one-one call we couldn't trace. We think it was Adriana but we need confirmation."

Henry nodded and Payton played the recording. Henry grimaced as he listened. "Oh, God." He put his face in his hands and started to sob.

I jerked my head toward the door. Payton told Henry to sit tight and we headed to the squad room—an artificially illuminated rectangle with six laminate-topped, double-pedestal desks paired off in the center. Just like kids in class who don't want to sit near the teacher, cops don't like to sit outside their commanding officer's office. When I joined Homicide, the other detectives had switched desks, leaving the one outside the captain's office as my only option. Payton sits opposite me, Donovan and Garcia sit in the middle, and the two unassigned desks in the back remain empty unless some crisis warrants extra help.

"Those sobs seemed real," I said as we sat down at our desks. "I don't think he did it."

"I don't either," Payton said.

But we had to be sure. I volunteered to call the airline.

"Bless you," Payton said.

The customer service automaton thanked me for calling and informed me the wait time was approximately five minutes, then it kicked over to a recording of discounted fares. I reached for a pen, but in my absence, someone had appropriated every one from my Grand Canyon mug that serves as a holder. I opened my center drawer to get another and saw the tab on the file folder I've kept in that drawer since I moved into the desk. *Fiorello, A.*

Annie had been my first friend when my family moved to Bedford. The summer we were ten years old, a maintenance worker in Veterans Memorial Park found her body in a wooded area by Prescott Pond, twenty hours after she'd been abducted, molested, and strangled.

I always think of her at a new crime scene because the reminder of the horror she suffered helps drive me in the investigation, but the image of Dave lying on the asphalt hijacked my thoughts and I squeezed my eyes shut, as if that could banish the memory. *I'm so sorry I forgot, Annie.* I took a long, slow breath and exhaled. *Take care of him for me, okay?*

An agent came on the line and I grabbed a pen and closed the drawer. I jotted down the information the agent provided and ended the call. "Airline confirmed Henry's flights," I told Payton.

"Ditto for the hotel," Payton said. "The manager e-mailed a copy of Henry's bill. It shows he accessed the mini-bar eight times between 7:00 PM Thursday and 2:00 AM Friday."

"That supports the drunk dial claim," I said.

Payton stood. "I'll tell him he's free to leave."

While my partner cut our only person of interest loose, I started background on Ortiz. I was in the middle of entering her information on the search screen when "Girls Just Want to Have Fun" started to play on my cell. I knew Connie was calling to check up on me because my parents had gone home, but I answered anyway.

"Where are you?" she asked. "We drove over to your place but…"

A lie would save her from blowing a gasket, but then I'd have to make something up and I was too tired to be creative. "I'm at the station."

"What!"

I cringed and moved the phone away from my ear but I could still hear the chatter. We've been best friends since our first day at Northern Illinois University fourteen years ago, though our first five minutes were a little rocky. We'd both tossed gym bags on the bed nearest the window to stake our claim. After screaming at each other about who was there first, we'd settled the dispute the only way adults could. My rock crushed her scissors and the bed was mine.

I'd been her maid-of-honor when she married Kevin eight years ago and she returned the favor. I knew her innermost thoughts, fears, and secrets, and she knew mine—at least to the extent I share. She's much better at opening up about her feelings, though at the moment I wished she wasn't. Her volume seemed lower and I eased the phone back toward my ear.

"…were supposed to take some time," she said.

"I did," I said, "but unfortunately the criminal element in Bedford has other plans."

"The department could manage without you for a week."

"It could but I couldn't handle being cooped up that long. This is the best thing, Connie." I heard her exhale and pictured her chewing on her left cheek as she formulated her strategy.

"I did have a reason for calling other than to get on your case," she said.

"I hope so."

Payton came back in and sat down.

"Your goddaughter wants you to come over for popcorn and a movie," Connie said.

"Putting this on a five-year-old. Have you no shame?"

She chuckled. "It really is Emily's idea."

I loved her and her family as much as my own, but I wasn't in the frame of mind to hang out tonight. "I appreciate it, but there have been people around since…" I sighed softly. Connie and I had finished our pizza and were in the middle of *Message in a Bottle* when Pritchard rang my doorbell Wednesday night. She stayed, and she was waiting at the door with a hug when Pritchard dropped me off around midnight. And she insisted on staying until my parents arrived on Thursday. I rubbed my forehead. "I just need a little time to myself."

"I get it," she said. "Guess I'll have to settle for pizza and a DVD on Wednesday."

"Yeah," I said. *If I'm in the mood by then*, I thought. I told her to give Emily and Kevin a kiss from me and shoved my phone into my pocket. "Let's get out of here," I told Payton.

"I'm with you," he said. "Why don't you come over? I'll grill us up a few veggie burgers. Pam and the kids are at a cookout at Pam's cousin's so—"

"You should've said something earlier. I could've staked out Henry's place alone."

"Not a chance," he said.

"Not a fan of Pam's cousin?"

"The woman lives to shop and throw parties to show all of it off."

"I appreciate it, partner, but I meant it when I told Connie I need the time alone."

He nodded. "Okay. I'll see you tomorrow."

"Yes, you will," I said.

—— CHAPTER 5 ——

At the last census, Bedford's population registered at just over 214,000 people, and I seemed to encounter half of them on my drive home—cruising in their cars, peddling their bicycles or sauntering in the crosswalks—as they reveled in their final hours of freedom before the start of another work week. It was after 8:00 PM when I finally backed into the garage, and when I pushed the button on the garage door transmitter, the door started down but the light didn't come on. For the past month, I'd pestered Dave to change the bulb. I'd offered to trade household chores for sex and even threatened to hold the remote hostage before the Sunday games once football season started but he'd been so busy he...

My bottom lip quivered and I sucked it in. He couldn't wait for the pre-season to begin and had talked about booking a weekend in Chicago with dinner at Ditka's and tickets to a Bears game. But it was one more thing we wouldn't do.

I crawled out of my Escape and slammed the door, but on my way out, I paused behind his '67 Mustang and ran my hand over the buffed red trunk. He only drove it in perfect weather, and his desire to protect it from the elements forced him to park his Explorer on the street, which meant scraping windows and digging out of snowdrifts in the winter. "Boys and their toys," I said into the darkness before I locked the door and shuffled up the back sidewalk.

The faint aroma of onion from the meatloaf my mother baked for dinner last night still lingered in the kitchen when I opened the back door. I kicked off my shoes and flicked on the forty-watt light over the stainless steel sink before I hauled myself upstairs to the master bedroom.

When I opened the closet door to hang up my blazer, the sweet scent of Stetson pounded me like surf slamming into the shore and I stepped back. My eyes drifted across the suits and shirts he'd never wear again. I snatched a hanger off my bar, hung up my jacket, and shut the door.

I showered and went back down to the kitchen. My mother hadn't been able to sleep much either, and despite my protests, she'd spent a fair amount of time cooking. She'd stocked the freezer with containers of vegetable soup and the leftover meatloaf. I stood staring into the freezer, trying to work up a taste for something, but when I couldn't, I grabbed a container of soup, nuked it, and ate, standing by the sink.

I went back upstairs to the spare bedroom we use as an office, and the quiet grated on me worse than nails on a chalkboard, so I turned on the boom box before I logged on the computer to check e-mail. The first message was from a cousin I seldom saw, apologizing because she was out of town for the funeral. The next seven messages expressed similar sentiments.

"Amazed" started to play and my fingers froze over the keyboard. It was the first song we'd slow-danced to at Shooters on our first date. I turned the boom box off, closed my e-mail, and logged off. I went back downstairs to the living room and sat in the recliner. I reached over to the end table between the recliner and couch to pick up the 8" x 10" photo from our wedding. He'd balked at wearing a tux but damn! He was *so* handsome. I traced my right forefinger over his wavy dark brown hair and then down his left cheek, across his square jaw and over the dimple in his right cheek. Then I looked at his eyes. Those warm brown eyes where I always found peace and strength.

I moaned and clutched the frame to my heart. I doubled over and rocked until it felt like all of the air had escaped from my lungs. I sucked in a quivering breath and leaned back. *I've got to do something—anything—to stop thinking!* I set the frame on the table, snatched the remote from the coffee table, and turned on the TV. I clicked through several channels until my thumb froze over the UP button.

Dave clicked through ten channels as we snuggled on the couch after making love.

I laughed at him. "If you went head-to-head with a kid texting in algebra class, you'd crush him." He stopped on a PBS nature show where some guy—who was obviously insane—wrestled with a six-foot alligator, and I said, "You couldn't pay me enough."

"You mean like the kind of money you make for being a walking target in this city?"

"You've got a point." I angled my head back and we kissed.

He motioned toward the TV with his beer bottle. "Maybe we should try that."

"Alligator wrestling?" I glanced at the TV. The camera shot had shifted to a dolphin giving birth. I looked up at Dave and he flashed the grin I'd fallen in love with the first time he used it on me on our second date.

"I was referring to giving birth," he said.

I would've been less shocked if he whacked me in the head with his beer bottle. We'd revisited the topic of children last Christmas after watching Emily Warren rip into her presents, but he said we were too committed to our jobs to think about it. I shifted so I could face him. "Come again."

"That would certainly improve our chances." Again with the grin.

I held up my finger. "Let me rephrase." He rubbed the back of his hand along my arm and I swatted it away so I could focus.

"I know we've hedged on the child issue," he said, "but I've been thinking about it a lot and…I don't want to have kids when we're too old to keep up, so I think we need to start taking some action." I fidgeted a little and he lifted my chin and said, "You still want kids, don't you?"

"Yes!" I wanted to kick myself for answering so quickly and I added, "I think so."

He cocked his head. "You think so?"

"I do. It's just…" I blew out some air, desperate to slow my racing thoughts. "It's just that with everything I've seen on the job…I don't know if I have the courage to bring a child into this…mess."

"Is that all?" He slipped his arm around me and kissed the top of my head. "You're the strongest person I know, and together we can raise a considerate, responsible person who might be able to figure out a way to stop some of the bullshit."

A distant thump drew me back to the present and I realized the air conditioning kicked on. Goosebumps prickled my skin as the cool air drifted over me and I crossed my arms and focused on the TV. Adriana Ortiz's face displayed onscreen over the Channel 3 anchor's left shoulder. They reported her name, age, and the fact she'd been murdered in her home. They also pointed out we didn't have a suspect at this time. A litany of other violence and political misdeeds followed her story so I changed the channel but the news stayed the same.

"Fat chance of anything stopping the bullshit," I muttered. I turned the TV off and silence enveloped me like fog. Maybe time alone wasn't such a good idea after all.

I considered going out to cruise the streets around the branch to try to find Noonan, but Payton was probably right. The bastard was probably long gone. And after four straight nights of fitful sleep, I was too damned tired.

I hauled myself back up to the bedroom and took the Yellowstone National Park T-shirt Dave had worn Tuesday night off his valet stand. I buried my face in the shirt and inhaled the faint scent of Irish Spring and Dave. I peeled off my tank, slipped into his shirt, and lay down on his side of the bed. I ached for the comfort of his arms around me and tugged his pillow from under my head. His scent lingered on the cotton and I was glad I didn't feel like changing the sheets yesterday. I hugged the pillow tightly and closed my eyes.

"Val," Dave whispered in my ear.

I rolled onto my side and he looked at me with his beautiful brown eyes—always so full of understanding, empathy, and love that I sometimes get lost gazing into them. I reached out and touched my fingers to his stubbly cheek. His skin felt cool, and when I looked back into his eyes, they were fixed and vacant.

My eyes flew open and I found my palm resting on the cold, empty sheet next to me. I pushed myself into a sitting position and pulled my knees up to my chest. I ran my hand through my hair and breathed deeply to slow my heart rate. I felt the coolness of perspiration on the nape of my neck and I ran my hand across it.

I glanced at the clock and the display glowed 4:47 AM. I knew there was no way I'd fall back to sleep, so I hauled myself out of bed, got dressed, and headed to work.

—— CHAPTER 6 ——

On the drive in, I wondered what the tone would be in the squad room on my first official day back. I knew I wouldn't face a bunch of sad sacks because cops don't do emotional displays, but the guys could avoid the usual banter out of concern over my state of mind and I couldn't handle that. And as icing on the cake, our new captain started today.

I bounded through the main entrance like it was any other day and found John Porter, our barrel-chested duty sergeant, sitting behind the front desk where he'd probably sit every morning until they carried him out. I offered a cheery "Morning, Sarge" as I passed by.

"Good to have you back, Detective," he said. Like most every other cop in the department, he'd taken time to pay his respects. "Oh, hey!" he called after me. "I got paperwork on your vic from yesterday." He pulled two folders from a stack and handed them to me.

My nerves hummed with nervous energy so I took the stairs to the sixth floor to burn some of it off. I swiped my key fob and crossed the hall to the squad room to drop the files on my desk and grab my mug before heading to the break room to start a pot of coffee. A few minutes later, I settled in my chair, ready to start the day, but when I swiveled to face the computer, my eyes landed on the five-inch replica of the Statue of Liberty I bought when Dave and I visited New York City two years ago and I froze. We'd had a great time but we hadn't booked a summer trip this year because we'd both been too busy. We planned to take a week at Christmas but...

Tears blurred Lady Liberty and I closed my eyes. When I opened them, Payton was standing at his desk, looking concerned. "Hey." I forced a smile. He said "hey" back and I sensed him watching me as I typed in my username and password. I heard laughter in the hall and a moment later, Carlos Garcia and Shawn Donovan walked in.

"Benchik! You're back," Donovan said.

"I guess this means you'll have to return her chair, man," Garcia said.

"If you messed with the height, Donovan." I aimed my finger at him.

"Relax!" he said. "Your chair never left your desk."

Donovan is a nine-year veteran with two years in Homicide. He reminds me of a fire hydrant because he has reddish-blond hair, a long torso with short legs, and though he's only five eight, he weighs nearly two hundred pounds, thanks to his perpetuation of the cops and donuts myth. And he likes to piss around. Garcia, on the other hand, could be a health club spokesman. He's five ten and one hundred sixty pounds of pure muscle, and I've never seen him eat a donut. With only eleven months on the squad, our rookie hadn't picked up any bad habits, thanks to the discipline instilled by the United States Marines.

Garcia moved in slightly, like he was going to share a secret, and quietly said, "We're going to get the guy, Val."

"I know," I said with a single nod.

An awkward silence hung in the air for a beat before Donovan said, "So what do we know about our new boss?"

"Victoria Morgan has sixteen years on the job," Garcia said. "She's fifty-three and has a bunch of commendations. Saved a kid from a burning building when she was in uniform."

"That's the bio," Donovan said. "I'm talking gossip, rumor, and innuendo. How about it, Benchik?" He raised his mug. "What's the word in the women's john?"

I turned to my computer. "Even if I knew something, I wouldn't tell you."

And I did have the sort of information Donovan was fishing for because when Morgan paid her respects on Friday, she confided we had more in common than our job. Twelve years ago, her husband was shot to death after he pulled a car over for blowing a red light. The occupants had just robbed a liquor store and the passenger fired a round before Roger could react. He'd died in the street. It took courage for Morgan to share those details—especially before taking command of my squad—but her story was personal and it wasn't mine to tell. I stood up and headed for the door. "I need more coffee."

"Come on, Benchik," Donovan urged.

I stopped and turned. "I've got nothing, Shawn. And the truth is, I'm fine with anything as long as she's not wearing an eye patch and carrying a parrot on her shoulder."

"Argh mateys!" a female voice called out behind us.

Garcia's gaze dropped to the floor. Donovan pressed his lips together, and when his eyes met mine, he snorted a laugh, lowered his head, and focused on whatever nonexistent spot had Garcia's attention. And my partner looked like he'd eaten bad shellfish.

I took a deep breath, smiled, and turned on my heel to face our new commanding officer. Without a patch, both of Captain Morgan's green eyes were visible and fixed on me.

She cocked her head. "Relieved, Detective?"

I extended my hand. "Welcome to Homicide, ma'am."

"Good to see you, Benchik," she said and she returned my firm handshake. Morgan was built like a roller derby defender but she had the poise of a plus-size runway model. Not a strand of her auburn hair was out of place. Light foundation coated her fair skin, along with some eyeliner and a flattering shade of lipstick. And her tan twill suit provided an air of professionalism, balanced with enough functionality to chase a suspect if required.

I noticed she still wore a wedding band when I also noticed a bandage on her left hand that wasn't there Friday. I wagged my finger toward the bandage. "Kitchen mishap?"

"Boating mishap," she said, "but it's fine." She introduced herself to everyone with a handshake and then turned to address our small group. "I've had a chance to review your jackets, and I'll be reading the current files today to get up to speed on your caseloads." She nodded once and walked to her new corner office but she paused by the door. "Oh, and in case anyone's wondering, the parrot's in his cage at home."

Covert glances shot around the room.

"She serious?" Garcia mouthed at me.

"Like I would know," I whispered.

"You obviously met before today," Donovan said. "So let's have the scoop."

"No scoop," I said. "She paid her respects before anyone else arrived."

They both clamped their mouths shut and diverted their eyes. Nothing like the mention of death to make people—even homicide cops—uncomfortable.

Morgan called my name from her doorway and crooked her finger.

Donovan chuckled. "Five minutes and you're being called into the principal's office."

I pointed at the red splotch on the front of his pale green polo shirt. "Weren't you wearing the same strawberry stain last week?"

Donovan looked down and then he looked back at me with a smug face. "If you were a better detective, you'd recognize this one is raspberry."

I turned toward Morgan's office and let out a little sigh of relief at knowing it was business as usual. I entered the office and Morgan closed the door and told me to have a seat. I settled in the chair affording a peripheral view of the door.

To my surprise, she came around her desk and sat next to me. "What are you doing here, Benchik? You've got time coming. Why not use it?"

"Most people get three days bereavement leave and are expected back at work producing results on day four," I said. "I've had my leave. It's time for me to get back to work."

"Most people do not deal with what we do."

"There is nothing to do at home except think. At least here I can be productive." I looked her in the eye. "Please, Captain. I need to work."

She regarded me for a moment. "Just to be sure we're on the same page, you understand that work cannot include any involvement in your husband's case."

"Yes, ma'am," I said softly, but I glanced at my lap when I said it.

"Not very convincing," she said. I sighed deeply and met her eyes and she wagged her finger toward the window with a view into the squad room. "What do you think of this team?"

"They're the best, ma'am."

"That's what I hear. And that's why you need to trust Donovan and Garcia and leave it to them to bring your husband's killer to justice. Understood?"

"Yes, ma'am."

She nodded once. "Dismissed."

I stood, straightened to attention, and walked out of her office.

Payton looked over the top of the file he'd been reading. "Everything okay?"

"Mm-hmm." I walked over to the whiteboard in the back corner of the squad room, erased the hangman's noose, and wrote our victim's name and vital statistics in black dry erase marker. I also wrote "Ponytail?" and "Client?" under the Suspects column.

Payton walked over and held up two folders. "Financials or background?"

"Background," I said. He handed me the folder and I scanned the report. "She was an only child. Her father died when she was five and she lost her mother last year. Looks like she'd park wherever there was an open space downtown—whether it was legal or not. Had fifteen citations in the last year. And she was a regular *Speed Racer*. Got stopped by a state trooper last month for doing seventy-four in a construction zone, but there's no other record of any kind." I flipped to the next page. "This is interesting. Phone records show an incoming call at twelve nineteen from the same burner number used to place the nine-one-one call."

Morgan walked up and crossed her arms as she scanned our entries. "Old school. I'm surprised you don't have an electronic board."

"The cap—Captain Ryker wasn't a fan of technology," Payton said, "and with the budget cuts, we'd never get one now anyway."

"I like the board," I said.

"Me too," Morgan said, "though this one would look better with some suspects."

"It's a work in progress," I said.

"Work faster," Morgan said. "I just got off the phone with Deputy Commissioner Moraz."

Cal Moraz spawned from a long line of police officers, but unlike his relatives—who'd paid their dues with a combined seventy years on the street—he rose to the top like pond scum, landing a cushy administrative assignment immediately upon completion of his requisite year in uniform, spent at the lowest crime district in the city.

"Probably made that call while he was sipping his latte in a *very* public place," I said under my breath, eliciting a glare from my partner.

Morgan stooped slightly in my direction. "What was that, Detective?"

"I'm guessing the deputy commissioner wants this to go away ASAP, ma'am."

"Good guess." She straightened and walked to her office.

I felt Payton's eyes glued to the back of my head as I added "Burner Phone" to the board. "What?"

"For all you know Morgan and Moraz could be best friends," he hissed.

"Please!" I spun to face him. "Moraz's only friends live under rocks."

He groaned.

"You want me to be a kiss up like Donovan?"

He opened his mouth but snapped it shut.

"I thought so." I wagged my finger toward his file. "Find anything useful in there?"

"No large withdrawals to indicate drug or gambling problems," he said. "We've got grocery and gas purchases, and the two hundred bucks in her wallet came from an ATM withdrawal on Friday morning." He continued to scan. "Whoa. She got a ten-thousand-dollar direct deposit a month ago. The memo indicates it came from Smithfield, Royce, and Foley. There was another payroll deposit from the firm a week later, but it's smaller than the others. And there were two payroll entries since then but they came from Legal Aid."

"She quit the most prestigious law firm in the city to work for Legal Aid?"

"Quit or got fired," he said.

I snapped the cover onto the marker. "I think we need to troll by the law offices of Hammerhead, Tiger, and Bull and do some chumming."

— CHAPTER 7 —

"Do you have an appointment?"
It was one of two programmed responses from the diminutive blond receptionist behind the gigantic black desk. The other was "Good Morning. Smithfield, Royce, and Foley. How may I direct your call?"

We spent several minutes trying to persuade her to grant us an audience with Smithfield, Royce, or Foley, while she kept insisting that without an appointment, none of the three could speak with us unless she knew the nature of our visit.

I turned my back to her, rested my elbows on the counter and mouthed, "Stepford receptionist."

Shock registered on Payton's face. "Whoa! If you could see the look she just gave you, you'd arrest her for attempted murder of a police officer."

I forced what I hoped was an engaging smile and turned back toward her. "I know you're simply doing your job, but either we get in to see one of the partners or you go to jail for obstruction of justice."

Her eyes got very big. "You couldn't."

I met her eyes and narrowed mine slightly.

Behind us, a rich baritone said, "Is there a problem?"

Stepford Receptionist snapped to attention in her chair. "No, Mr. Smithfield."

"Partner number one." I turned to face him.

"These police officers were just inquiring about speaking with you," Stepford said.

"Police?" Smithfield looked about sixty, and his golf-induced tan made his white hair seem whiter. His dark gray pinstripe suit screamed tailor-made, and his yellow power tie with tiny gray diamonds probably cost as much as my off-the-rack linen suit and cotton blouse combined.

Payton introduced us and said, "We're here about Adriana Ortiz."

Smithfield frowned. "Ms. Ortiz is no longer employed by this firm."

"She's no longer employed anywhere," I said. "She's dead."

Impossible as it would seem, his tan skin paled. "Good Lord." He motioned toward the hallway on his left. "Let's go to my office."

We followed him down a short hall and into an outer office. A middle-aged woman in a crisp navy suit sprang to her feet the moment Smithfield appeared. She gave a terse "Good morning, sir" to her boss and regarded us with the wariness of a gatekeeper unaccustomed to being out of the loop.

Smithfield told her to hold his calls, and we followed him through a carved-wood door into a corner office twice the size of my living room. He settled heavily into an oversize black leather executive's chair positioned behind a monstrous mahogany desk with a finish so polished I could've used it to apply eye makeup.

"I can't believe it." Smithfield shook his head. "What happened?"

"She was murdered," I said.

"Why? By whom?"

"We're hoping you may have some information to help us figure it out," Payton said.

I scanned the photo array on the credenza behind Smithfield. In one shot, Smithfield smiled broadly while shaking hands with the governor. In another, he and a woman I presumed to be his wife posed with another couple. All wore formal attire so it was probably a charitable benefit.

"Pat shot a three-under par that day," Smithfield said, pointing toward a picture of himself with Mayor Foley on a golf course, their mouths clamped on cigars.

"Cubans?" I asked.

Smithfield smiled. "I'll never tell and the evidence seems to have gone up in smoke."

"Tell us about Ms. Ortiz," Payton said.

Smithfield folded his hands on his stomach. "She was very competent and was being considered for a junior partnership when she tendered her resignation. Very bright girl."

I tensed slightly like I always do when a man in a position of power refers to a capable woman as a girl. "Law students would give anything to be in Ms. Ortiz's position," I said, "so why did she tender that resignation?"

"She wanted to…give back," he said, as though the notion were absurd. "Adriana had an idealistic streak. I thought she was making a terrible mistake and told her so, but she'd made her decision."

"What types of clients did she handle?" Payton asked.

"Mostly our smaller accounts. Contract work. Negotiation."

"Any of those clients feel as if she didn't live up to her end of the bargain?" Payton asked.

"If there had been, she wouldn't have gotten the chance to tender her resignation. In fact, her work was so exemplary that we—the partners—gave her a well-deserved bonus."

"Ten thousand dollars," I said and his brows arched. "Cops prep for cases too. How about the people she went up against on behalf of your clients? Any problems there?"

"Not that I'm aware of." He eased forward in the chair and shifted his folded hands to the desktop. "Far be it from me to tell you how to run a case, but it seems more plausible her death is related to her new position. Perhaps you should focus your energy in that direction."

"We're pursuing every lead," Payton said.

Smithfield reached over with a perfectly manicured finger and pressed a button on his phone and summoned the gatekeeper. "I'm sorry but I'm late for a meeting," he said as he stood. "Feel free to speak with anyone here."

"Thanks for granting permission," I said, "but we already intended to."

Gatekeeper appeared and Smithfield asked her to show us to the conference room before he walked out.

We cooled our heels in the conference room for twenty minutes until Gatekeeper popped her head in to inform us Mr. Royce had arrived.

"We'd better not keep him waiting," I said. "What's his time worth? Ten bucks a minute?"

Gatekeeper's face showed no hint of amusement. "Follow me, please." She popped back out.

"She could be a beefeater at Buckingham Palace," I whispered to Payton as we fell in behind Gatekeeper. "Maybe they get fired if they laugh at lawyer jokes."

Gatekeeper introduced us to partner number two, and compared to Smithfield, Edward Royce looked downright pasty. He was about twenty years younger, with sandy brown hair. His gray suit lacked pinstripes, and squares accented his pale yellow power tie.

He greeted us with a firm handshake and a warm smile, and after we were seated, Payton motioned to a photo on Royce's desk of a girl wearing a powder blue jersey. "How old is your daughter?"

Royce smiled. "Eight."

"Same age as my daughter," Payton said. "Erin's a soccer nut too."

The smile faded from Royce's face. "This news about Adriana is quite a shock. I worried about her but I never thought something like this would happen."

"Why did you worry?" Payton asked.

"She put in a lot of hours," Royce said. "That's part of being a young lawyer but—" His intercom buzzed and he excused himself and picked up the receiver. After a moment he thanked the caller and hung up. "I'm sorry but we just got a call from one of our biggest clients and—"

"They'll have to wait," I said. "I'm sure you can find a way to count it as billable hours. Why did you worry about Adriana?"

"She wanted a partnership in the worst way, and I think when she started out, she thought she'd convinced herself she would be capable of doing whatever it took to win."

"But?" I prompted when he failed to elaborate.

Empathy flashed on Royce's face. "But she was a very kind young woman. Unfortunately, the bottom-line mentality that drives a business decision is often in direct conflict with compassion." He checked his watch. "I'm sorry. I do have to go, but I would be more than happy to speak with you later." He stood and so did we. To his credit, Royce personally escorted us to Timothy Foley's office instead of getting Gatekeeper to do it.

Smithfield obviously represented old money and connections, and Royce was the poster boy for family values, but Timothy Foley's demographic was difficult to pinpoint. There were no pictures of him hobnobbing with high society or tossing it around with the wife and kids. His photo gallery consisted of shots of him. Reeling in the big one off the stern of a fishing boat. Dangling from a rope over the edge of some cliff.

"You're quite the outdoorsman," Payton said.

"Money isn't much fun when it's sitting in a portfolio earning 5 percent," Foley said.

"Where do you get 5 percent?" I asked.

"Very true," Foley said. He was dressed in what I was beginning to think were the firm's official colors, but instead of a suit, he wore a pale yellow Izod golf shirt and gray slacks.

I noticed a photo of Foley in a tux, standing with his arm around the mayor, and the connection finally clicked in my head. "Foley."

Foley flashed a publicity-perfect smile. "He's my big brother." He shifted a cardboard file box from his desk to the floor. "Forgive the mess. I'm trying to catch up. Just got back from Africa. The Serengeti is pretty airtight as alibis go."

Poker faces are an asset for cops but Foley's comment caught us both off guard. "Why would you need an alibi?" Payton asked.

"Preparation, Detective. As an attorney, I spend a lot of time on defense, but the only way to earn a partnership at the most prestigious law firm in the city is by playing an excellent offense."

"Or sharing DNA with the mayor," I said.

Another blinding white smile. "That too." Foley settled into his chair with a sigh. "Terrible news about Adriana."

"What can you tell us about her?" Payton asked.

"She was a very competent attorney but not everyone is cut out for corporate law."

"She had a conscience," I said.

A wry smile curled Foley's mouth. "No profession is so maligned as mine, but just wait until someone files a frivolous lawsuit and sues you for everything you're worth."

"Maybe if there were fewer lawyers, we wouldn't have all those frivolous lawsuits," I said.

"About Adriana," Payton cut in.

"In my opinion, she lacked the killer instinct it took to succeed at this firm," Foley said. He stopped to sip from a bottle of performance water. "She needed to learn about people. Take time to get the lay of the land. Little things like finding out how the court clerks take their coffee can mean the difference between a quick trial and a continuance that'll take them into retirement."

"Anything else?" Payton asked.

He thought for a moment. "Except for Tuesday nights, she worked her ass off."

"What was so special about Tuesdays?" I asked.

Foley shrugged. "I don't know, but she always left at five."

"Your partners didn't mention that," Payton said.

"I'm sure they didn't know. Carter plays golf on Tuesday afternoons, and Ed is out by four thirty on most days to go to some activity or another for his kid."

"Any theories on why someone would want to kill her?" Payton asked.

Foley shook his head. "I wish I could solve the case for you but I really don't know."

We found our way back to the main entrance, and as we waited for the elevator, Payton said, "So what was so special about Tuesdays?"

"Yep," I said. "And was it something that could get her killed?"

CHAPTER 8

The morgue is located on the lower level of County Hospital's complex on Vermont Street, just west of the expressway. We parked in the restricted area off California and walked down the ramp to the ambulance bay, where an attendant buzzed us in through the single door.

Our footsteps echoed on the tile as we made our way along the pale blue corridor. My anxiety mounted with each step, and ten feet from the door to Autopsy Suite One, I stopped as if I'd plowed into an invisible barrier.

Payton stopped and turned. "You okay?"

"Yeah." I looked down and raised my right foot as a cover. "I just got a cramp in my foot." I rotated it around a little and then gingerly transferred my weight. "All better."

Payton pressed the button and the door swooshed open. I drew in a deep breath and slowly exhaled as I followed him in.

Leilani Norris was wearing her customary floral-print scrub top that served as a reminder of her island heritage and also provided a splash of vibrant color in this cold and sterile environment. Unlike the coveralls she wore at crime scenes, the scrubs revealed her muscles, toned mainly through lifting dead weight all day. She always stood on a small stool to get a better look at the body from above, and she turned when we entered.

"Sorry we're late," I said.

"Don't be. If any of us had any sense, we'd have chosen different careers."

I'd seen dozens of corpses at a variety of crime scenes in my ten years on the force, but somehow the victims seemed more vulnerable when they were lying naked on the cold, shiny table. Maybe it was the irony that to catch their killers, we had to subject them to even more mutilation.

Leilani placed her left hand on Ortiz's pallid skin, pressed a scalpel into the flesh over her left shoulder, and ran the blade to the middle of Ortiz's chest, slicing through layers of skin like a knife through a tomato.

Ortiz's face dissolved into Dave's and my stomach flipped, launching a tidal wave of bile up my throat. I dug my phone out of my pocket, glanced at the blank display, and said, "I've got to take this," as I bolted for the door. I ran across the hall and barreled through the bathroom door, not thinking someone could be on the other side preparing to exit. I bent over the synthetic marble sink and punched the COLD faucet with my palm. I splashed several handfuls of water over my face, and then I cupped my hand and rinsed the sour taste from my mouth.

I stood there for a moment with my forearms resting on the vanity. I'd never gotten sick at an autopsy before. Not even as a rookie. But I'd never attended an autopsy four days after my husband's murder either. I stared at my reflection.

I have to hold it together or else Morgan will put me on leave. And I have to work if I want to survive this nightmare.

I shook the excess water off my hands and snatched three paper towels from the dispenser to dab my face dry.

Payton and Leilani both looked toward the door when I rejoined them. Concern pinched their faces but they didn't say a word.

"Sorry," I said.

"It's okay," Leilani said. She tossed a glance toward Payton. "I was just telling Detective Payton your vic died from a direct wound to the heart, and based on the size of the wound, the weapon is an ice pick."

"What else?"

"No defensive wounds," Leilani said. "And if there can be good news in such a case, the rape kit was negative."

At least Ortiz had been spared one horror, though she'd probably feared it was the killer's intention.

"There was residue of adhesive tape on and around her mouth," Leilani said. "I sent it to the lab. And the blood alcohol was zero."

"DNA?" Payton asked.

"Not yet but I'm hoping. And I'll keep you posted on the tox screen."

We thanked her and left her to the details of her work.

We were uncharacteristically silent as we drove until Payton finally said, "Fake phone call was a good cover but I still think you came back too soon."

"I'm fine."

"Look, Val—" Payton started but my phone interrupted him.

Saved by the bell. Or in this case, the theme song from *ET.* Argus's number flashed on my caller ID and I answered with, "Give me good news, Todd."

"I don't know how good it is," Argus said. He sounded tired, which wasn't surprising given he'd been pulling double-duty with Jill Talbot on maternity leave. "I found a lot of prints in Ortiz's place that aren't hers. I'm still running them through AFIS but it's going to take awhile. I also found several male brown hairs in the bathroom, so I'm running those against the DNA database. And I was able to determine that the varnish found embedded in the vic's carpeting was of the marine variety, so that should help some."

"Right," I said. "I'll put out an APB on Jack Sparrow."

"Nice reference," Argus said.

"Glad you liked it." I thanked him for the information, ended the call, and recapped the conversation for Payton.

"Dylan Henry's hair is blond," he said. "She must've been seeing someone else."

"Let's hope Ortiz's new boss at Legal Aid will be able to shed more light than her old bosses," I said.

We entered the storefront office on Vermont and waited several minutes for our victim's supervisor to finish with a client. Elizabeth Bauer offered us coffee before she refilled her own mug and settled back in at her wooden desk, marred with nicks and spill rings.

"What prompted Adriana to take this job?" Payton asked.

"Because no one with options would chose this, right?" Bauer had picked up a file but she slapped it down on the desk, frustrated by having to defend the legitimacy of her office.

Payton shook his head. "Not at all. I've got a lot of respect for people who take this route because if everyone worked for big firms, my little brother would be doing twenty-five to life."

I thought his little brother was in the Army. I looked at him but he was looking at Bauer.

The beleaguered attorney sighed. "All Adriana told me was that life at the firm was not what she expected. A lot of young attorneys take a position here just to get some face time in court to put on their resumes. We tend to get the ones who barely passed the bar or the ones who are one step from disbarment because of personal issues. I was very impressed with Adriana's credentials. Skeptical? Sure. I don't mean to sell my staff short. Some of them are very talented and very dedicated, but some are hacks who've reached the end of the line. Someone like Adriana walks through the door, it's truly a gift."

"Any problems with her clients here?" I asked.

Bauer sipped some coffee, mainly to stall while she considered whether or not to divulge information. She set the mug down. "She was helping a young mother get a restraining order against the baby's father, who was abusive to the mother. From the way she dealt with the client, she was either extremely empathetic or she'd had some personal experience with domestic abuse."

"We're going to need a name," I said.

Bauer scoffed. "I can't violate privilege."

"How about giving us the name of a guy who would cause you concern if he came in here," I said. She mulled it and then tipped her head slightly. I took it as a concession and asked when she saw Ortiz last.

"About eleven thirty Friday," Bauer said. "I was coming back from court and she was headed out to meet with some potential witnesses in a negligence case."

"Would we be able to get those names?" Payton asked.

Bauer tapped her pen on the desk and then sighed heavily. "I'll check the file."

"So you had no contact with her after that?" I asked and Bauer shook no. "We were told Adriana had a standing appointment on Tuesday evenings. Any idea what that was?"

She shook no again. "I'm sorry I can't fill in more of the blanks but she hadn't opened up much about her personal life." She stood. "I'll get those names you asked for."

I scanned the list on our way to the car. "One of these people had to be the last person to see her alive other than the killer."

"Unless they're one and the same," Payton said. "Maybe one of them had something to hide." He popped the locks. "I wonder if she had her Tuesday appointment in her calendar."

"Let's find out." I called Cassidy and asked if he'd been able to access Ortiz's calendar. He told me he had and I asked if it showed any recurring appointments for Tuesdays.

"Uh, let me check," he said. I heard clicking and he said, "She had a recurring weekly appointment from 7:00 to 9:00 PM with someone whose initials were M.E."

"Does it link to any names in her contacts?"

Another pause filled with clicking. "Nope."

"Does it show any appointments on Friday afternoon?"

More clicking. "Sorry," Cassidy said.

I thanked him, ended the call, and told Payton about the mysterious M.E.

"I doubt she's having drinks with Dr. Norris," he said.

"I really want to talk to Anita Zamora. If anyone knows about Tuesday nights and why our vic left the firm, it's the BFF." I scrolled through my Placed Calls log and dialed Zamora's number again but it still kicked to voicemail. I left another message and then I turned my attention to Payton. "What was that about your brother?"

"Gangs ran the Projects," he said, "and as far as the cops were concerned, all black males in my neighborhood were bangers. A little mom-and-pop store near the high school got robbed and the perp shot the clerk. A couple of uniforms saw Ricky walking home and picked him up because he was wearing a Chicago Bulls cap. They found his fingerprints on the door—because he stopped there for a soda and chips—and the owner ID'd him as the shooter. All black kids look alike, you know. They didn't find a gun but they said he ditched it. If my mother hadn't called Legal Aid, and if the lawyer hadn't taken time to find reliable witnesses to refute the evidence"—he made air quotes—"they would've moved him right through the system."

"So was the Army his idea or yours?"

"It wasn't like I dragged him to the recruiting office," Payton said. "It was an option and he was smart enough to take it. He's a major now. A good man." He nodded to himself, satisfied with how his brother's life had turned out. "Hey, didn't Dylan Henry tell us his little fling worked at the museum?"

"Uh-huh."

"That's only a half mile away from here," he said.

I smiled. "What do you say we surprise her at work?"

Payton hung a left onto Twenty-Sixth and headed for the museum. We found Henry's girlfriend at her desk in the group sales offices and learned she hadn't spent any time pining for Dylan. Two days after they broke it off, she met a stockbroker in a bar and spent the weekend of the murder with him in Cancun, which I confirmed with calls to the airline and hotel while Payton drove to the home of the first witness on Adriana Ortiz's list.

As it turned out, Ortiz had only met with two of them. The second one told us Ortiz received a phone call around noon, and when she disconnected, she apologized and cut the meeting short.

"Noon is close to the time Ortiz's incoming log showed the call from the burner phone," Payton said as we walked into the squad room a little before 5:00 PM.

"Mm-hmm," I said. "Mystery caller is looking better for murder all the time."

"What do you say we call it a day? Come at it with renewed energy in the morning."

"I think I'll stick around for a while longer. Run background on the neighbors and that abusive husband Ortiz's boss told us about." Payton frowned and I added, "I won't stay too late."

"Uh-huh." He held up his hand and walked out.

I left an hour later, but instead of going home I drove to Tombstone—the neighborhood where Dave died. The area got tagged with its unfortunate nickname several years ago after a rash of street shootings led one reporter to reference the O.K. Corral.

I cruised the streets looking for a black F150 pickup and asking around to see if anyone had seen Noonan. It was nothing that

Donovan and Garcia hadn't already done, but at least I felt a little less helpless.

When I finally headed for home, I used the drive to try to figure out how what we'd learned fit together, but so far the pieces of the puzzle failed to form a coherent case. Adriana Ortiz left her boyfriend because he cheated, and she left her job because it failed to live up to her expectations. But what had happened to turn her dream job into a nightmare? Is the reason she left related to why she was tortured? Or was the torture personal? Or maybe connected to her standing Tuesday date?

And where the hell was her best friend?

— CHAPTER 9 —

Ortiz's building didn't have security cameras but Cassidy down-loaded footage from the surrounding businesses, and we settled in at our desks Tuesday morning to review everything recorded between noon and 6:00 PM the day of the murder.

"If you don't switch to decaf soon, I'm going to have to scrape you off the ceiling," Payton said without looking up from his monitor when I sat down with my fourth…or fifth mug of coffee.

"I'll get you a putty knife," I said. "By the way, did I tell you background on Ortiz's neighbors came back clean?"

His eyes narrowed. "You ran all of them last night?"

I raised my mug in a toast. "Behold! The power of caffeine."

He shook his head at my dependence but couldn't help smiling. He stretched and wagged his hand toward his monitor. "I've seen guys with hats, guys with long hair, guys with short hair, and guys with no hair at all, but so far, the only ponytails I've seen were on women."

"Me too." I rocked my head from side to side and one of my neck muscles snapped.

"Hey, Benchik," John Porter called out from the squad room doorway. He jerked his thumb toward the hall. "There's a young woman out here to see you. Said you've been trying to get a hold of her. The name is—"

"Anita Zamora?"

"Right. She's in your visitor's room."

I popped up from my chair. "It's about time."

The small room next to Morgan's office is decorated with a love-seat, two easy chairs, a coffee table, and an end table with a lamp. Designed to look more like a living room than a squad room, we use it whenever we need to meet with victims' relatives.

Except for less makeup and a more modest blouse, Anita Zamora looked the same as she had in the Vegas photo in Adriana

58

Ortiz's living room. I made the introductions and offered her something to drink but she declined.

"I'm sorry I didn't get back to you before this," she said. "My boyfriend and I went to Aruba for a long weekend and we left our phones here. We really wanted to get away, you know? It was great, but I was so tired when we got back last night that I didn't bother with my messages until this morning." She waved her hands. "I'm sorry, you really don't care. What is this about?" She folded her hands in her lap and arched her brows, questioning why she'd been summoned.

There is no easy way to deliver news that will shatter someone's world, so I try to be direct but compassionate. "We're sorry to have to tell you this, Ms. Zamora," I said. "Adriana was killed Friday afternoon."

She let out a nervous little laugh. "What? No. She...she can't be." She stared at me with the mix of horror and disbelief I'd seen on the faces of every friend and relative I notified. Then her lower lip began to quiver.

Had my face looked like that when Pritchard broke the news to me?

"You're...uh...you're sure it was Ana?" Her voice begged us to tell her there'd been a terrible mistake.

"We're very sorry for your loss," I said.

She squinted as she held my gaze. "How? What happened?"

"She was stabbed in her loft," I said softly.

"Oh my God!" She clamped her hand over her mouth. She squeezed her eyes shut and started to rock in the chair. After a time, the rocking slowed and then stopped and she lowered her hand and looked up. "Why? Who would...?"

"We don't know yet," I said. "We're hoping you may be able to fill in some of the blanks. When was the last time you spoke with her?"

Zamora's forehead pinched as she forced herself to recall. "Thursday night. I wanted to touch base before we left Friday morning."

"Was she anxious about anything?" Payton asked.

Zamora shook her head slightly. "She was...she was looking forward to the weekend."

"She requested for some repairs to be done in her unit on Sunday because she wouldn't be home," Payton said. "Do you know what her plans were?"

"The beach," Zamora said. "She said she wanted to veg out on the sand all day."

"Did her family have money?" I asked.

Zamora looked confused for a moment and then realized why I'd asked. "The clothes, right?" She flashed a smile. "She knew every outlet store and resale shop in town and she waited for sales."

"There aren't many sales on Birkin bags," I said.

Zamora frowned. "That was a gift from the guy she was seeing."

"We spoke to Dylan Henry," Payton said. "He told us they broke up because he cheated."

"It was too bad," Zamora said with genuine regret, "because he actually treated her well. And Ana was in no position to cast stones."

"Are you saying she was seeing someone else too?" I asked.

Zamora nodded. "Back in April, I called her one night and heard a guy's voice in the background, but it wasn't Dylan. I confronted her the next day and she didn't even try to deny it."

"Who was the guy?" Payton asked.

"I don't know. She wouldn't tell me. But he's the one who gave her the bag."

So he had money.

"Several people at the firm told us she made it a point to leave on time every Tuesday," Payton said. "What was so special about Tuesdays?"

"It was her meeting night," Zamora said. "She's in...she *was* in recovery. Drug abuse. She liked the group session at St. Andrew Church."

It finally made sense why we couldn't find anyone with the initials M.E. in her life. "The appointment in her calendar wasn't with someone whose initials were ME," I said to Payton. "It stood for 'me'. She blocked out the time for herself."

"She said it was time she took responsibility." Zamora sucked in a choppy, deep breath and let it out. "Ana had an obsessive personality. In college, it was alcohol at frat parties. Then in law school, she started using coke. Ana never does—" Her voice caught and she bit her upper lip. "She never did anything halfway."

"We spoke to the partners at her old firm," Payton said, "and they all seemed to think she had a very bright future. Why did she leave?"

"I asked her the same thing but she never told me." Zamora got a distant look in her eyes as she recalled her best friend's failure to confide. "All she said was she left because it wasn't how she wanted to spend her life, which is strange because she was so excited when she graduated from law school and got one of only three open spots at the firm."

"When did she first start talking about leaving?" I asked.

Zamora rubbed her forehead. "Uh…she seemed really happy until…I don't know…it was a few weeks before the Fourth of July. We went to a cookout and I knew something was bothering her, but she wouldn't tell me what was wrong."

"Is there any chance she was using again?" Payton asked.

Alarm flashed on Zamora's face. "No. At least I don't think so." She ran her hand through her hair. "One night when she was still using, she called me, all freaked out. Her heart was racing and she was feeling really bad, but it was the best thing that could have happened because it finally hit her the drugs could kill her. The next day she asked me to go to a meeting with her for moral support, and she's been clean ever since. I really don't think she'd go back to it."

I thought the same thing when my parents told me my kid sister was in rehab, but Kelly had relapsed twice that I knew of and—Zamora sniffled and I refocused. "You said Dylan actually treated her well. Was that unusual for her boyfriends?"

"Sometimes I think she substituted men for alcohol and drugs," Zamora said. She picked at a chip in the lavender nail polish on her thumb. "She always fell for bad boys. Motorcycles, fast cars, and no clue about respecting women. She'd let them treat her like dirt. They'd break up, but the minute they'd show up with flowers or tickets for some hot concert, she'd take them back and the whole cycle started again." She looked up and flushed with embarrassment and shifted uneasily in her chair. "I shouldn't be saying these things. I loved Ana and…"

I nodded, trying to assure her we understood. "Ms. Zamora, what you tell us could help us catch her killer. Were any of them abusive?"

She sighed. "She never admitted any of them hit her, but a few times I noticed a bruise on her arm…or around her eye." She rubbed her upper arm with her left hand. "I was always telling her to be more careful. I insisted she call me when she got home so I wouldn't have to worry." Her bottom lip started to quiver again. "Maybe if I had stopped her from going out with them in the first place instead of just telling her to call me…" She put her hand over her mouth.

I reached over and put my hand on her forearm. "This isn't your fault, Ms. Zamora. You were a good friend. You looked out for her." She slowly raised her eyes to meet mine. "Would you be able to give us the names or contact information for any of them?"

She sniffled. "Uh, I don't know some of the last names but I'll give you what I can."

"Did Adriana know any Hispanic guys around thirty," Payton asked. "He wore his hair in a ponytail and—"

"They let that son of a bitch out?" Zamora looked incredulous. "I don't know why I didn't think of him before. I guess I just thought he'd stay in jail this time."

"Who?" Payton asked.

"We were in junior high the first time he was arrested," Zamora said. "Every time he got out, he'd come around. Ana didn't want to have anything to do with him, but he just wouldn't accept she'd moved on."

I touched her arm. She flinched and looked at me. "Who are you talking about, Anita?"

Her eyes grew hard. "Cesar Rivera."

Payton shot me a glance. Looks like we finally had a suspect.

We took Zamora to the conference room and left her with a legal pad and pen to write down whatever she could recall about Ortiz's former boyfriends, and we ran background on Cesar Rivera, a.k.a. Ponytail.

"Rivera was fourteen when he first hit the system," Payton read from his screen. "He's been in and out of jail ever since. Was released in early June, after serving eighteen months on a weapons charge, and his current address is a halfway house on Mission and Pershing."

"Let's see if Cesar is home," I said.

We got to the halfway house a little before eleven o'clock, and when I crawled out of the car, I couldn't stop myself from looking east down Mission. The branch was a little over a half mile away—not visible from here—yet I could picture the parking lot as if I were standing in the middle of it. And worse, I knew it would be etched in my memory forever.

"Val?"

I looked at Payton, and from the apprehension on his face, I knew he knew I was thinking about our close proximity to the bank. I held my palm up toward my partner. "I'm okay."

He nodded. "Okay."

We went inside and the counselor told us Rivera hadn't been there since the first week he was out. He'd apparently checked in after meeting with his parole officer, stayed a week, and never returned.

We went back to the car and sat with the windows down as we plotted our next move. Payton called the parole officer and found out the two were supposed to meet yesterday but Rivera never showed.

"There's a shock," I said. I exhaled hard and it was the only air to move in the car. "Burner phones are popular among drug dealers and other nefarious individuals like Rivera."

Payton smiled. "Nefarious?"

"Would you prefer lowlifes?"

"No," he said. "I like nefarious. It lends an air of class to our otherwise low-rent job."

"So Rivera calls Ortiz Friday afternoon while she's meeting with her witness," I said. "He manages to talk our vic into meeting with him and they end up at her place. Things take a bad turn and she manages to get her hands on his burner phone to call nine-one-one before she ends up dead." I wagged my finger toward Payton. "What was the number used to call nine-one-one?"

"Cassidy sent the message to both of us."

"Yeah, but you're better with the techie stuff."

He shook his head and started to scroll through his messages for Ortiz's 911 call. I dialed the number as he read it off and he craned his neck. "What are you doing?"

"Phone records can't tell us who's on the other end but maybe the owner will," I said.

"You think a *nefarious* individual like Rivera is going to ID himself when he answers?"

"Sometimes they're analog in a digital world," I said.

"You should talk, Ms. I-Still-Use-An-Address-Book."

I made a *Shut up* face at him as I waited. The number rang once before the canned message played. I pressed END. "Caller is out of the service area."

"Really," Payton said. "What would you have said if someone had answered?"

"I would've told him I got his number from Adriana and had a business proposition for him." I shrugged. "It was worth a try." I gazed out the window. "Connie knows things about me I've never told anyone else, so why did Ortiz hide her lover's identity from her best friend?"

"Maybe it's not a him."

"That could cause her to keep quiet." I clicked my tongue. "Or maybe she reconnected with Rivera and she knew Zamora would disapprove. She realized she'd made a mistake getting back with him and broke it off again. He calls her Friday morning to invite her to lunch but she blows him off and he shows up at her place and kills her."

"He's certainly capable," Payton said.

"And what changed at work to make her leave her dream job?"

"Maybe the lover's identity and the reason she left the firm are connected."

"You think she was seeing a partner?"

"Could be," Payton said with a shrug. "Maybe by choice. Or maybe she was being sexually harassed. With the clout those three guys have, she figured it would be easier to quit than file charges. Royce reads like the consummate family man, so I think we can rule him out. My money would be on Foley because of the implications for his brother's campaign."

"That would be a motive." I drummed my fingertips on the roof. "Then again, she lost her father when she was five, and she made some bad dating choices. Smithfield could've been a father figure. Stable. Mature."

Payton started the car. "Let's go straight to the top and work our way down."

— CHAPTER 10 —

W e arrived at Smithfield, Royce, and Foley and breezed past the gatekeeper's desk without asking for permission to see the most senior of the senior partners. I knocked once on Smithfield's door and opened it before he invited us to enter.

Smithfield popped up from his chair. "What the hell? What do you think you're doing, barging in here like this?"

"Our apologies, Mr. Smithfield," I said, "but the back nine will have to wait."

Payton and I settled into the plush chairs across the desk from him.

He sank back down into his chair. "I hope this means you've made progress on Adriana's murder."

"We have," I said. "Why didn't you tell us you and Adriana were having an affair?"

Skilled at controlling his emotions for court, Smithfield didn't bat an eye. "That's absurd. Who made such a ridiculous accusation?"

"That's not important," Payton said.

"The hell it isn't," Smithfield said, "because I'm going to file one hell of a slander suit."

"Comments have to be false to make it stick," I said.

"Watch me."

"Does your wife know?" I asked.

"No!" He aimed his index finger at me. "And if you—" He clamped his mouth shut and let his hand drop to the desk.

"We didn't come to sew a scarlet letter on your yacht club blazer," I said. "You withheld information in a homicide investigation and it's time you shared."

"How long were you seeing each other?" Payton asked.

Smithfield worked his jaw a little as he waged his internal debate. To lie or not to lie? That was the question. After a few seconds he said, "Almost three months. It started in April."

I asked who ended it.

"She did."

"Even after you gave her a Birkin bag," I said.

He glanced at me sideways and his nostrils flared. He was still fuming over that decision.

"When was the last time you saw her?" Payton asked.

"The day she ended it and walked out of here." He failed to keep the resentment out of his voice.

"So what happened, counselor?" I asked. "She start pressuring you to leave your wife, and rather than risk having her go public, you killed her?"

He smiled ruefully. "While it was quite an ego boost to think she was truly interested, I knew she wasn't in it for love or money."

"She was using you to get a partnership," Payton said.

"Until she decided she didn't want one." He spread his hands. "So you see, I had no motive to kill her."

I stared at him in awe. Did he truly expect us to believe him given he twists the law and essentially lies for a living? "Unless her bonus wasn't really a bonus," I said. "She could've threatened to go public with your affair, and one blackmail payment turned into the gift that wouldn't stop giving, so you found another way to make it stop."

Smithfield seemed amused by our theory.

"You want to tell us again why she left the firm?"

He drew in a deep breath as he tried to summon the patience to deal with the exasperating civil servants before him. "As I said before," he said slowly, as if he were talking to a couple of three-year-olds, "she wanted to give back."

"Where were you Friday afternoon?" I asked.

"Spent the weekend on my boat." He tugged a little at the edge of his shirtsleeve to slip it back over his Rolex. "We shoved off sometime after one o'clock and didn't dock again until around 5:00 PM Sunday."

"Who's 'we'?" Payton asked.

"Just a federal judge, the mayor, and a congressman." Smithfield's lips curled into a smirk. "I think this conversation is over, don't you?"

If he knew how much I wanted to slap that smirk off his face he'd have me arrested for attempted assault. "Old boys club, huh?"

"Our wives don't share our penchant for the water."

"Where was Mrs. Smithfield while you were bonding with the boys?"

His nostrils flared. "Leave my wife out of this."

I scoffed. "We can't do that. She may not have been as oblivious as you think."

He slammed his fist onto the desk. "Listen, Detective—"

"Does your cool, calm, and collected veneer desert you often?" I asked.

He took a moment to calm down. "Vivian does a lot of charitable work. She had fundraising dinners the entire weekend."

"And we should take you at your word because you've been so honest with us to this point," I said. Smithfield shifted slightly in his chair. "Would your wife be at home right now?" I jerked my thumb over my shoulder. "We can swing by on our way back to the station."

He held up his hand. "I'll call her." He scribbled a few notes as he spoke to his wife in hushed tones and then he hung up. "She had a salon appointment at 9:00 AM Friday before an afternoon benefit luncheon and fashion show. Beautify Bedford is raising funds for a new fountain in Veterans Memorial Park."

"Another fountain. Great," I said. "At least the homeless will have a shiny new place to clean up."

He smirked as he tore the sheet off the pad and handed it to me.

"You ever see a guy with a ponytail hanging around Adriana's place?" Payton asked.

Smithfield thought for a moment. "As a matter of fact, I did. The last time I was at her place. I'd just gotten off the elevator and he was walking away from her door. He left by the stairs. I asked Adriana about him but all she said was he was someone from her past."

"You're an officer of the court," I said. "Why would you withhold information in a murder investigation?"

"I wanted to come forward," he said, "but I hoped someone else saw him and you'd get the ID without my involvement."

In spite of his earlier lies, his eye contact and the tone of his voice led me to believe he was sincere, but we drove straight from the law offices to the marina to check his alibi.

A parking valet, the guy in the harbormaster's office, and a dock-hand all confirmed Smithfield, Mayor Foley, Congressman McLeod, and some appellate court judge cast off at about two o'clock Friday afternoon and didn't dock again until Sunday night. And the chair-man of Beautify Bedford confirmed Vivian Smithfield attended their Friday shindig and stayed until the bitter end at five o'clock.

"The hair Argus found was brown, so we knew it wasn't Smithfield's," I said as we walked to the car.

Payton held up his finger. "On the upside, we probably found the source of the marine varnish from Ortiz's carpet."

"Smithfield's crew mates aren't exactly poster boys for integrity," I said. "Foley is up for re-election next year, and his conservative sup-porters would get bent out of shape if word got out his little brother's married partner was having an affair with an associate. Maybe—"

Payton vigorously shook his head.

"You don't think the mayor or someone on his staff is capa-ble of…"

He tugged his sunglasses down the bridge of his nose and glared at me.

I held up my hand. "Okay, I'm grasping at straws."

He pushed his sunglasses back into place. "You know, I wanted to ask you after we talked with Anita Zamora. How is Kelly doing?"

He knew my sister's history, and apparently he'd noticed my lapse in concentration when Zamora talked about our victim's battle with substance abuse.

"She's okay, I guess. She called to—she called last Thursday."

"From where?" Payton asked.

"I don't know. It was noisy. Probably a bar."

"I meant what city."

"She didn't say. For all I know she could be in rehab. It would explain why she couldn't come in for the funeral."

"Wouldn't your parents have told you?"

I shook my head. "They would've figured I had enough to deal with." I crawled into the car and slammed the door.

We spent the remainder of our shift entering background requests on Ortiz's bad boys from the list Anita Zamora created. Payton headed home and I felt a twinge of guilt for telling him I would do the same. Instead, I drove to St. Andrew Church. I figured I could chat with the coordinator of the substance abuse session and be long gone before any attendees arrived.

I parked on the street and entered through the side door to the Fellowship Hall. A man setting up folding chairs in the middle of the large room turned when he heard the door close behind me. I was surprised to see it was Dr. Jeremy Konrad, a psychiatrist who is part of the referral network for the department's Victims' Services Unit.

"Hey, Doc," I said.

"Detective." He extended his hand and his condolences, and he apologized for not being able to pay his respects.

I thanked him with a smile and quickly changed the subject by asking if he was there to facilitate the substance abuse counseling session.

"I am," he said. "The regular coordinator had to take a leave of absence, so all of us in the network have been covering his sessions." He signaled for me to have a seat and asked what brought me there.

"My partner and I are investigating the murder of Adriana Ortiz." I handed him a photo and I knew he recognized our victim when his shoulders drooped. "Let me start by saying I understand the need for confidentiality, but we don't have a lot of leads at this point, and her best friend told us Adriana attended this session."

He gazed at the photo some more but he was only stalling as he tried to decide whether to confirm or deny her attendance. He finally said, "She does...did."

"Did she seem particularly upset or worried about anything?"

"Everyone who comes here is worried about something, and you know I can't say anything specific." He held the photo out to me.

"Please keep the picture and show it to the other group members. Tell them if they saw anything suspicious—maybe someone hanging around or someone who followed her from the church—to please call our tip line with no questions asked. Or they could tell you and you can relay the information to us anonymously. I realize it's out-of-the-ordinary but—"

"I'll mention it." He slipped the photo into his shirt pocket.

I thanked him and stood.

"How are you holding up, Detective?"

I tensed. I did not want to discuss my state of mind with anyone, especially a licensed mental health professional. I turned and looked directly into his eyes. They were pale blue and conveyed kindness and understanding, which had to be invaluable in his line of work. I forced a smile. "I'm okay."

"Yeah?"

I nodded once and shifted my gaze over his shoulder to a bulletin board covered with neon-colored flyers announcing upcoming events. I wondered if Kelly was attending a meeting.

"My granddaughter would've turned nine on July twenty-second," he said softly. I cut my eyes from the bulletin board to him and to answer my unasked question, he said, "Like Dave, her death came as a shock."

So maybe he understood more than I gave him credit for. "My condolences."

He nodded in appreciation and his gaze drifted toward the floor. I wondered if the random gray strands scattered through his brown hair had been there for years or if they'd appeared as a result of his recent tragedy.

His shoulders heaved with a deep sigh and he looked up. "With the miracles of modern medicine, the thought of someone dying from complications following an appendectomy is almost ludicrous and yet…" He cleared his throat. "When she first complained of a stomachache, my daughter and son-in-law thought it was a virus, so they waited a few hours. Colleen kept saying, 'We should've taken her to Emergency sooner.' The if only can be a real bitch."

Tell me about it. "Dave shouldn't have been at the branch," I said. "He should've been playing basketball with his buddies like he did every Wednesday, but the contractor called about some problem, and it was his responsibility to ensure the branch was ready in time for the grand opening after Labor Day. If he hadn't gone over, maybe Noonan would've been happy to just shoot out the windows and…"

I sucked in some air, surprised by how much I shared. I must've opened up because of what Konrad had shared, which was probably his goal and I fell for it.

"It's called Magical Thinking, Val," Konrad said. "If only that car hadn't blown the red light. If only they'd taken a later flight. If only he'd have let that call go to voicemail and gone to play basketball with his buddies instead." He looked at me for a moment. "I've always remembered one story of a 9/11 survivor. Normally, he would've been at his desk by the time the first plane hit, but he'd worn new shoes and felt a blister forming, so he stopped in a drug store to buy a box of bandages. Those who believe in fate believe we are where we're supposed to be, when we're supposed to be there. Our current situations are very similar. I have to listen to people talk through their grief while I'm grappling with my own. You have to investigate a murder while trying to come to terms with your husband's."

I caught myself picking at a hangnail on my thumb. It's a nasty, nervous habit I've had since I was kid and I could hear my mother's voice telling me to stop so I did.

"This may seem a little self-serving," he said, "but it might help if you attended one of the grief counseling sessions through Victims' Services. You don't have to participate. At least not right away. You can just listen to what others have gone through and how they reacted and dealt with it. And when you're ready, you talk."

"Depending on circumstances, I'm sure some of the members vent their frustration and maybe even talk about how they want to kill whoever did it."

"Uh…sometimes," he said with a nod, "but it's part of the process."

"I'd hate for the presence of a cop to hamper their recovery, but thanks for the offer."

"You've got my number," he said. "Don't hesitate to use it."

Like that's going to happen. I thanked him again and left.

— CHAPTER 11 —

I felt sluggish when I entered the station's underground parking garage Wednesday morning because for the second night in a row I'd spent hours driving around Tombstone. I shifted into PARK and reached to shut off the engine when the DJ said, "Happy hump day!"

I slouched against the seat. Dave had been gone a week.

Last Wednesday had started like most other days. We ate breakfast together—Fiber One Honey Clusters cereal—and we kissed good-bye. I'd spent the day in court and he called at 4:11 PM to say there was a chance he'd be late for his game because he had to meet the contractor to resolve some issues. Then the doorbell rang at 7:27 PM and changed my life.

I felt a hand on my left shoulder and spun around.

Payton raised an apologetic hand. "Sorry, I thought you were ignoring me for some reason. Everything okay?"

We were standing at the counter in the break room, though I didn't recall walking in. I nodded. "Everything's fine. You need water for tea?" Payton shook his head so I filled my mug with coffee and we headed to the squad room.

"Maybe we'll get something from Ortiz's Tuesday night counseling session," I said, trying to sound more hopeful than I felt as I logged on my computer.

"I don't know how when it's confidential," Payton said.

"Jeremy Konrad said he'd ask the group members to let us know if they saw anything."

Payton leaned forward. "How does Dr. Konrad know we're even looking?"

"I…uh…on the way home last night I stopped by St. Andrew's and—"

"You barged in on her group counseling session!"

"I did not! I got there before it started and I only spoke to Dr. Konrad."

Payton narrowed his eyes. "Okay. First of all, St. Andrew's isn't on your way home. Secondly, does the concept of confidentiality mean anything to you at all? For some people, those sessions are all they have. If they feel they can't speak freely, it's like you cut off their lifeline."

"You know Kelly's history," I said, "so don't tell me how important those sessions can be, okay? I get it. That's why I told the doc if someone has information, they could tell him or call the tip line. No questions asked."

He sucked his teeth. "Run down any other leads on the way to work this morning?"

"No." I opened the pouch from the ME's office that someone had left on my desk. I pulled out the enclosed folders, and my heart skipped a beat when I saw "Lukas, David K." on one of the tabs. My hand trembled slightly as I opened the file, and my breath caught when I saw the enlarged copy of Dave's driver's license photo paper-clipped to the left cover. I shifted my eyes to the right-hand page. The autopsy report was on top, and images of Y-incisions and skullcaps flooded into my mind, but I pushed them back and flipped to page two.

What the hell am I doing? I shouldn't be reading this.

I scanned the page anyway and stopped on Cause of Death.

Cardiac tamponade.

"Hey, partner," Payton said.

I snapped the folder shut and looked up, armed with a new understanding of how felons felt when we caught them in the act. I damn near messed my pants.

Payton's eyes dropped to the file and he pounced across the desk to snatch it from my hands. "You're a glutton for punishment, aren't you?"

"I guess whoever said 'ignorance is bliss' knew what they were talking about."

"How did you even get this?"

I pointed at the courier pouch. "I thought it was Ortiz's preliminary report."

He shoved the file into the middle drawer of his desk and closed it. "I'm going to talk to Dr. Norris about the idiots working over there."

"They're not idiots and they didn't do anything wrong. I'm a big girl. I knew what I was doing." I straightened the stack of folders.

Argus burst into the squad room with a cheery "Good morning, Detectives!" and strutted up to our desks.

Payton said, "Hey, Todd" without looking up and I didn't say anything.

Argus frowned. "Not much of a greeting for the man who's going to blow your case wide open." We both locked eyes on Argus and he smiled. "Now that I have your attention, do you remember all those prints we found at your vic's place? Well, I finally got a hit. They matched a lawyer named—"

"Carter Smithfield," I said.

Argus stared at me. "How did—?"

"He was having an affair with the vic," Payton said, "so finding his prints in her condo doesn't do us much good."

"What about his—?"

"White hair," I said. Argus looked like a balloon popped by a pin. "Thanks anyway, Todd."

"Yeah, sure," he muttered and he shuffled out.

My hands were poised over my computer keyboard when Captain Morgan bellowed our names. We both looked toward her office and she jerked her thumb, signaling for us to join her. We traded curious glances, went in, and stood at ease before her desk.

"I just got a suggestive call from Mayor Foley," Morgan said.

"He didn't seem like the type," I said, eliciting a cough from Payton.

Morgan nodded, egging me on. "Keep it up, Detective, and you may get a chance to perfect that stand-up routine you've got going." She went from smiling to somber in a blink. "My officers are to cease and desist from harassing one of his closest friends."

"That didn't take long," I said.

"I'm sure the mayor is just trying to protect the reputation of one his largest sources of campaign revenue," Morgan said, "but do you really think Carter Smithfield is your guy?"

"We were hoping," I said, "but his alibi checked so…"

Morgan nodded. "You're the reason for the drawer full of antacids, aren't you, Benchik?"

I felt a little offended. "Captain Ryker had a touchy stomach, ma'am."

"Uh-huh." She waved her hand at us as if she were shooing a fly. "Go."

"We need to talk to Rivera's known associates," I said as we walked out of her office.

"Guess we're going back to Tombstone," Payton said.

I drove for a change, and though I'd been spending a fair amount of time in the neighborhood, darkness had cloaked much of the decay. In the sunlight, it was impossible to overlook the transformation the farther east we drove on Mission as the new, red-brick townhouses and gleaming condos along South River Road were replaced by rows of frame homes with boarded windows, peeling paint, and sagging gutters.

"Lee. Sherman. MacArthur." Payton shook his head as he gazed out the passenger window. "You think it's a coincidence the most dangerous streets in the city are named for generals?"

"Are you saying it's prophetic?"

"Pathetic is more like it," he said.

I pulled into an open spot on Mission. We checked in again at the halfway house, and then dropped in at a nearby bar and liquor store, but Rivera was still AWOL.

"So if you were a low-life drug dealer, where would you crash?" I said as we walked out of a Laundromat and into the blazing mid-day sun.

"Girlfriend," Payton said. "Too bad we don't know who that is."

I reached for my phone. "We know someone who may."

J.T. Pritchard answered after three rings with, "Hey, darlin'."

I was so irritated when he'd first called me that because I thought he was patronizing his little lady of a partner. But after riding with him for a while, I observed the respect he had for women, and I realized it was his term of endearment—no different than when Connie called me "sweetie" or when I call Emily "peanut."

I told him I needed a favor.

"Oh, okay…Uh…What do you need?" he stammered. "Fix a faucet? Cut the grass?"

I smiled, partly because I could cut the grass myself and partly because it was strange to hear apprehension in the voice of someone who'd regaled me with stories of rattlesnake hunting during his teenage years in Texas. "Not that kind of favor," I said, "although I'll be sure to call when the time comes to rake leaves. I need you to rattle a few cages. See if you can shake Cesar Rivera loose."

"You want me to use my carefully cultivated network to find a dirt bag like Rivera?"

"Yes, please."

He sucked his teeth a bit and then asked, "What's in it for me?"

"Oh, I don't know, Pritchard. Maybe the knowledge you helped take a killer off the street."

"Homicide is your gig. I do drugs."

I chuckled. "Yeah, that explains a lot."

"Uh…that didn't come out—" He blew some air into the phone. "I'll sniff around and see what turns up."

The line went dead and I stared at my phone. "I don't know how I survived three years in the same car with that man."

"It was the Lord's way of teaching you patience," Payton said.

Guess that lesson needed some work.

—— CHAPTER 12 ——

We figured someone in the neighborhood must have seen Rivera around, so we started our canvass on Mission, flashing his mug shot to everyone we encountered, hoping we'd get a lead. We didn't, but even lack of progress works up an appetite, so we drove over to the Paretti's near County Hospital to grab some lunch.

Though Chicago is only a hundred miles east, Bedforders have a different concept of what makes a good hot dog, and we don't consider it sacrilegious to use ketchup instead of diced tomatoes. In fact, we insist on it, and Paretti's served the best dogs and beef sandwiches in town. Their locations are always packed, but it was only eleven thirty, so we beat the lunch crowd.

Payton wanted to sit outside and chose an isolated table along Ninth Street. He quickly unwrapped his hot dog, with everything, and took a huge bite. "These are the best."

"Except for one thing." I peeled back the waxed paper on my own lunch. "Yours lacks chili." I bit into my chili-cheese dog and gazed over Payton's shoulder as I chewed. A young woman walked up to a man sitting at a table for two and hugged him from behind.

I ran my hands down Dave's chest from behind the couch. He looked up at me and we kissed.

A car horn blared and I was back outside Paretti's. I folded two fries into my mouth but stopped chewing when I caught Payton watching me. He asked if I was okay and I shrugged my head and swallowed. "I'm amazed by the human brain. How the smallest gesture or smell can send memories flooding back."

"Hits you when you least expect it?"

I nodded and we ate in silence for a bit. Payton seemed to be deep in thought as he chewed and I asked what was on his mind.

"Smithfield told us Ortiz left the firm because she wanted to give back," he said, "and that's admirable, right?" I nodded and he

78

nodded along with me. "So why did she tell her best friend she left because the job wasn't what she expected?"

I sucked down some soda. "I think it all comes back to that ten grand, and if it wasn't blackmail, then I'll bet it has something to do with a client. Maybe something upset her so much she threatened to violate client privilege and the old boys figured they could shut her up if they tossed some cash her way. And it worked for a while, but it wasn't enough because guilt started keeping her up at night and she decided to unburden her conscience."

"Unburden her conscience?" Payton rolled his eyes.

"Just"—I wagged my finger at his hot dog—"eat and learn. Winning a case is one thing, but if Ortiz were complicit in some sort of cover-up, then she'd walk a line between what's legal and what's right. Maybe she thought she could live with herself, but the ghosts started talking to her and she was afraid she'd relapse, so she quit to do something socially redeeming. But her resignation concerned the partners and/or the client and they killed her to keep her quiet."

"Wow!" Payton said. "That's quite the conspiracy theory."

"You've got something better, I'm listening."

He opened his mouth then closed it.

"Uh-huh. That's what I thought." I motioned to his lunch. "You finished?"

"Yep." He crumpled his paper.

We tossed our trash and were walking back to the car at a leisurely pace when Pritchard called.

"Word is your boy's been staying with an old girlfriend," Pritchard said. "Nineteen fifty-seven South Iowa Street. Apartment three B. And you owe me one, darlin'."

"Oh, please," I said. "You owe me so many you'll be paying me back until we're drawing our pensions." I pressed END before he could argue and I told Payton the location.

"Cesar's not a nice guy," he said. "We knock and announce and he may do something stupid."

I agreed and Payton popped the trunk release so we could retrieve our vests. He slipped his on but I stared at mine, unable to force the visual of the hole in Dave's chest from my mind.

"What's wrong?" he asked.

"It's just…when Dave felt anxious about my work, he'd tell me there were ways I could make a difference without putting myself on the line. And I would respond with something about people in perfectly safe jobs dying every day and…" I sighed. "How twisted is it that I'm the cop and he got shot at work?" Sympathy filled Payton's eyes and I slipped my vest on, fastened the flaps, and slammed the trunk door. "Let's go arrest a homicidal drug dealer."

Payton found an open spot on the corner of Twentieth Street with a view of the front door of the three-flat apartment building. He lowered the windows and we settled in to wait for backup. A half block away, someone had removed the cap from the fire hydrant and jammed a board in to create a spray. About a dozen kids laughed and yelled as they splashed around in the water.

"We really should shut that thing off," Payton said.

"Shut it off? I'm about ready to join them. All we need is an overweight guy wearing nothing but a towel and this sauna experience would be complete." I swabbed my temple with my fingers to catch a drop of sweat before it rolled down to my ear. I glanced at Payton. His tan shirt remained buttoned at the neck and the knot of his brown-and-green geometric-print tie was still pushed into place. "Are you even warm?"

"After spending a summer in Iraq, this is balmy, partner." He watched the kids frolic for a while before he said, "Pam's parents called last night. They want to do this big family trip to Disney World. Make it a combined Thanksgiving and Christmas celebration."

"Sounds like fun."

"Yeah, it'll be nice. I'll probably take a week starting—" He sat up straight. "Heads up."

Rivera had emerged from the apartment building and he cupped his hand to his mouth to light a cigarette.

"Where the hell is our backup?" Payton said.

Rivera scanned the street and paused when he looked in our direction. He took another drag, looked around, and flicked the butt.

"He's going to rabbit!" I snatched the portable radio from the console, flung my door open, and bolted from the car. Payton shouted my name as I sprinted across Twentieth without even checking for traffic.

Rivera veered into the gangway next to a sea foam-green house, and by the time I turned up the gangway, he'd hopped the fence into the alley and headed south. I paused when I saw the "Beware of Dog" sign dangling from the chain link, but Rivera would be getting mauled if the dog were out, so I stuffed the radio into my back pocket, grabbed the top of the gate, and scrambled over the fence. I had my shield on a lanyard around my neck, and it pounded my stomach as I landed on the pavement. I dashed through the yard and vaulted the back gate in time to see Rivera disappear around the corner garage.

I took off south, and I had to breathe through my mouth to avoid smelling the pungent air emanating from the garbage cans. I emerged from the alley and heard the roar of an engine just in time to pull up before propelling myself into the path of a white Expedition moving west on Twentieth. The SUV passed but distracted me long enough to lose sight of my suspect.

I scanned west. Nothing. I scanned east and zeroed in on Rivera a split second before he disappeared into another alley. I crossed the street at full speed and yanked my Glock from my holster as I approached the alley entrance. I took cover by the corner garage and then popped my head around the wall for a quick look.

The alley dead-ended at the Roosevelt Expressway. A junkyard ran along the left side and houses lined the right. I pivoted back and flattened against the garage. Sweat trickled down my temples, and when I pulled the radio from my pocket, I gripped it tightly so it wouldn't slip out of my sweaty hand. "Six-oh-seven portable," I panted into the handheld. "Suspect is in the alley…between Wisconsin and Ohio…two thousand block."

"Ten-four," Payton's voice crackled in response.

I shoved the radio back into my pocket and rounded the corner, staying low along the garage wall until I ducked behind some garbage cans. I moved deeper into the alley, zigzagging out from behind one can and then dropping down behind another. The cans were plastic and wouldn't do jack to stop a bullet, but Rivera would have to see me to know where to aim.

I'd reached the middle of the alley when I heard something scurry across the concrete. Could be a rat. Or it could be Rivera. *Same thing*, I thought, which eased my tension slightly.

I peeked around the can and saw Rivera scaling some cartons stacked along the fence behind the junkyard. If he cleared that fence, we'd need dogs to sniff him out.

Leading with my gun, I darted out from behind the cans and ran straight at Rivera. I stopped in front of a garage ten feet away from him, raised my gun, and aimed at his center mass. "Police, Rivera! Let me see your hands!"

Rivera froze.

"Show me your hands now!"

Rivera slowly lifted his hands as he started to turn.

Dave raised his hands.

Had Noonan said something first, or had he opened fire the moment Dave exited through the back door?

Dave must've been so scared. Facing that bastard alone. With a gun pointed at his chest.

Focus, damn it!

I blinked in time to see the muzzle flash and *boom!*

The bullet slammed into my left side. The force threw me back and I bounced off the garage door and landed in a heap on the concrete.

— CHAPTER 13 —

Once, when I was about eight, I'd gone to the playground near our house and saw some boy I didn't know playing on the parallel bars. Instead of swinging from one rung to the next, he'd stand on the ladder and leap out to grab the rungs in the middle. It looked like fun.

After successfully jumping to the fourth rung three consecutive times, I got cocky and tried for the fifth. I missed and landed flat on my back. I'd never had the wind knocked out of me before, and as I lay staring at the bright blue sky, gasping for air, I remember thinking how angry my mom would be if I never came home.

Fast-forward twenty-four years and my mom would still be pissed to hear I didn't make it home. I tried to breathe but couldn't get any air.

Maybe the bullet collapsed a lung.

I looked down but didn't see any blood on the concrete or my vest.

I got the wind knocked out of me, that's all. Just relax! Relax and breathe!

Pain jabbed my side when I finally managed a ragged gasp, which also sucked in the acrid smell of cordite hanging in the humid air. I struggled to raise my right arm—my gun—but it was as if my nerves had shorted out and left every muscle in my body useless. I watched helplessly as Rivera scrambled over the fence into the junkyard.

My head pounded. Like when I was a kid and we'd have contests to see who could hold their breath the longest. I heard tires squeal, the roar of an engine, and then tires screeched again.

"Officer down!" Payton barked into the radio. "We need a bus in the alley of the two-thousand block of Wisconsin. Roll additional units!" I tried to push myself up but then Payton kneeled beside me. "Easy, Val." He put his hand on my shoulder. "Is he gone?"

I nodded slightly. "Over the...fence."

He raised the radio to his mouth. "Six-oh-seven to dispatch. Suspect in officer shooting is Cesar Rivera. Male Hispanic. Five feet, seven inches. One hundred fifty pounds. Twenty-eight years old. Last seen in the vicinity of Twentieth and Wisconsin."

The spasm started to subside and my breathing evened out, though it appeared the pain would be sticking around for quite a while.

"Let me take a look, partner," Payton said as he gently moved my right arm and leaned over. "Bullet's in the vest. Nothing got through. You're okay. Nothing got through."

I braced my left elbow against my ribs and used my right arm to push up into a sitting position against the garage door. After a few shallow breaths I said, "Next time, I'm driving."

"Fine by me," Payton said. "Maybe if you were driving today, you wouldn't have taken off after him. Alone. What the hell were you thinking?"

"If I didn't, he would've gotten away."

Payton jutted his chin out and spread his palms as if to say *Hello! That's what happened anyway.*

"Losing him wasn't part of the plan, okay?" I sat there a little longer and then held out my right hand as an invitation to Payton to help me stand.

"I think you should wait for the medics," he told me.

"I'm okay." I wiggled my fingers at him. He set his jaw and stared at me for a moment as he summoned his patience, then he took my hand and gave me a boost. I scanned the pavement. "Where's my gun?"

Payton reached back, yanked it from his waistband, and handed it to me, butt first.

I took it and jammed it into my holster. "Let's go."

Payton caught my arm. "Hold it, chief. The only place you're going is the hospital."

"I'm fine."

"Policy dictates you get checked out."

"Oh! Well, if policy dictates." I saluted and Payton's face looked a little like Jackie Gleason's just before he'd say *"To the moon, Alice!"* I felt guilty about mocking him and my shoulders sagged. "Fine. But cancel the bus."

"No way."

"You can drive me," I said. He shook his head. "Then give me the keys. I'll drive myself."

His eyes narrowed. "You're nuts."

"This is news to you?"

He exhaled forcefully and raised the radio to his mouth. "Six-oh-seven. Cancel the bus."

"Ten-four, six-oh-seven," Dispatch responded.

"Can we at least go to County?"

He smiled. "You're afraid Connie will be on duty."

"Damn straight." My best friend is a nurse practitioner and the day-shift supervisor in Emergency at Wellington University Medical Center. "I'm not in the mood for a lecture right now."

He pondered it for a second before he said, "Too bad."

Two hours later I was sitting on an exam table, wearing the latest in hideous hospital fashion. The doctor and an unnecessary dose of radiation had confirmed my diagnosis.

"The good news is there are no cracked ribs to contend with, but you've got some serious soft tissue bruising," Dr. Jason Kozak said. "We'll give you an elastic bandage you can put on or take off as needed to help minimize the pain."

"I'm fine," I said.

Kozak took a pad from his pocket. "I'll write you a scrip for some painkillers."

"I've got aspirin at home."

His eyebrows arched with a *Seriously?* sort of expression and he cracked a smile. It caused the only wrinkles on his face, casting doubt that he was old enough to be a board-certified physician. "You're going to want something stronger," he said. A lock of blond hair fell over his forehead as he looked down to scribble his indecipherable instructions. He ripped the sheet off the pad and held it out.

Legalized pill pusher. I could've told him my reluctance to take anything stemmed from my sister's addiction but I kept my mouth shut and took the prescription.

He told me I could get dressed and he pulled the privacy curtain around behind him as he left to fill out my release papers. I slipped the paper gown off my shoulders just as the curtain jerked back. Reflexively, I pulled the gown back up. The rapid movement felt like an upper cut from a heavyweight boxer and I grunted.

Connie scowled at me from the foot of the table, which wasn't easy to do with lively blue eyes as kind as hers. "If you didn't want to do pizza and a movie tonight, you could've just said so."

"What took you so long?"

"We had a multi-vehicle pile up on the Teddy—I just finished up with my last patient and saw Greg in the waiting room—what the hell happened?" She rattled off without taking a breath.

"I'm fine." I held up my hand even though it wouldn't stop her from saying what was on her mind.

"If you were fine, you wouldn't be here."

"I'm here because my partner is a walking rulebook." I reached for my T-shirt and threaded my arms through the sleeves, but when I reached up to pull it over my head, pain jabbed my side and I stopped.

"Need help?"

"No!" I sounded like a five-year-old. I slowly worked my way into the shirt and popped my head through the neck opening.

Connie was staring at me with her arms and disposition crossed. "What happened?"

I thought about staring back but that would've been tedious. "Technically, I got shot."

Connie cornered the market on cool, calm, and collected, but her five-foot-six frame stiffened. "Define technically."

"I was wearing my vest like a good little cop, so there's no hole. Doogie Howser said I'll have a bruise for a few weeks. No big deal."

"'No big deal.'" Her voice rose an octave with each word.

"It's going to be a long day if you repeat everything I say."

"Ugh!" She flexed her hands as if she wanted them around my throat.

"I'm a cop. It happens. This wasn't the first time. It won't be the last."

"You talk about it like your neighbor got your mail by mistake. How can you be so…someone shot you!" Her lower lip quivered.

What's this? A crack in her tough, professional veneer? I shimmied off the gurney, took her by the shoulders, and looked straight into her eyes. "I'm okay, Connie."

She teared up and looked down at the floor to buy some time to control her emotions. She shook her head a little and her dark brown ponytail slipped off her shoulder. Dealing with distraught relatives, screaming children, and hallucinating junkies had to be less frustrating than trying to reason with me. She finally raised her head, met my eyes, and forced a smile. "So how's the new CO? What's her name?"

Hallelujah. A new subject. "Victoria Morgan."

"Captain Morgan!" Connie hooted. "I'll bet the guys are going to milk that one."

If only it had been the guys.

Connie's jaw dropped. "Oh, Val, you didn't."

"Of course I did."

"You said something about an eye patch or a parrot."

I sucked some air through my teeth.

Her eyes grew wide. "Both?"

"Uh-huh. But I think she was okay with it. She made a crack about the bird being in a cage at home, so it's cool." A nurse walked in with a clipboard. "Finally!" I snatched it from her, signed off, handed it back, and she left. "Where's my partner?"

"Nurses' station," Connie said.

I moved as quickly as my ribs allowed and found Payton leaning on the desk, chatting with several nurses behind it.

He looked up as we approached and said, "How are you, partner?"

"Stubborn as ever," Connie said.

"The doctor said I'm just fine, thank you." I held out my hand. When we arrived, I'd given my gun to Payton for safekeeping. He handed it back and I clipped the holster on my belt. "Did they find Rivera?"

He shook his head.

Terrific. "Let's get back."

"Uh-uh." Payton shook his head more forcefully. "You're through for the day."

I glanced at my watch. "We still have an hour left on shift."

"Morgan said if you show your face in the squad room, she'll suspend you for insubordination."

"She couldn't do that...could she?"

Payton turned his palms up.

"She threatened to nail your ass to the wall if I come back, didn't she?"

"Maybe you wouldn't mind the black mark on your record, but I can live without it."

I exhaled sharply. "Fine. I'll go home."

"Guess again," Connie said. "You're spending the night with us."

"I don't need a baby-sitter."

"All evidence to the contrary. Look, Kevin is in Atlanta for a network installation so we can do our girls' night. You're coming home with me. No argument."

I didn't protest because convincing a member of Congress to listen with an open mind would be easier than talking Connie Warren out of something once she makes a decision.

—— CHAPTER 14 ——

Connie barely closed the door to the attached garage when Emily ran into the kitchen. "Auntie Val!" She threw her arms around my legs.

I put my hands on her head. "Hey, peanut."

"I've got something to show you," she said before she scampered down the hallway.

Connie motioned to the family room off the kitchen. I followed her in and sat down with a grunt. Emily had been playing school, and I stared at her little blackboard and the books stacked on a small desk. Annie and I both wanted to be teachers and we played school all the time, using our dolls and stuffed animals for the students. I sighed heavily with regret for what might have been.

"Hey," Connie said.

I looked at her.

"You were thinking about Annie," Connie said softly.

I nodded.

Emily ran in, carrying a piece of paper. "I made this for you today." She handed me a crayon drawing of two stick figures holding hands in the clouds.

I smiled. "It's beautiful, Emily."

She looked up at me with her mother's big blue eyes and took my left hand in both of hers. "I know you miss Uncle Dave, but you don't have to worry about him because he went to heaven, and my grandma's already there so she'll take care of him." Her voice brimmed with that innocent self-assurance of a five-year-old.

I forced a smile and sniffled as I stroked her hair. "I'm sure she will, peanut." I pulled her close and kissed the top of her head.

"Go get cleaned up for dinner, missy," Connie said. We watched Emily run out and then Connie stood. "I'll fix up the spare room."

I patted the cushion. "This'll be fine."

"You're not sleeping on the sofa bed," she said.

"Compared to the cots at work, this would be like sleeping on a cloud," I said. She arched her brows and set her jaw. "Spare room would be great," I said, "and I'd really like to take a shower ASAP."

"There are extra towels in the hall closet and you can help yourself to a tee and shorts or whatever. I'm going to start dinner."

I didn't realize how much the day's events had sapped my energy until I hauled myself up the stairs and my feet felt like they were encased in concrete. I grabbed the shorts and tee from the top of each stack in Connie's bottom drawer and carried them into the guest bathroom. I undressed and turned for the tub, but I froze when I caught a glimpse of magenta and purple in the mirror. I reached up and my hand trembled as I traced my fingers over my ribs. "It could've been worse," I told my reflection. "It could've been a hole. Of course if it had been a hole, there's a good chance I'd be dead."

And would that be a bad thing?

"What the hell?" I whispered. I braced my palms on the vanity. If Dave knew that thought even entered my head. I looked my reflection in the eye. "Shame on you for thinking it."

I washed the day's grime off and turned the hot faucet up as high as it would go, but the water still ran cool, so I got out, toweled off, and got dressed. I schlepped downstairs to the family room, settled on the couch, and put my head back to catch forty winks before dinner. The muzzle of Rivera's gun flashed in my mind and I flinched. Goosebumps rippled across my skin and I crossed my arms.

"Cold?"

I opened my right eye and found Connie looming over me. She'd changed out of her mauve scrubs into a yellow tank and denim capris. The tank exposed her well-toned upper arms that resulted from lifting patients, grocery bags, and a five-year-old rather than weights. "You better have Kevin check your water heater when he gets home. I had the faucet turned all the way up but it wouldn't get hot."

"There's nothing wrong with our water heater," she said. "I'll be right back." She stooped to pick up Emily's shoes on her way out.

I heard a step creak slightly as she climbed the carpeted stairs. A few minutes later, the step creaked again, a cabinet door thumped shut in the kitchen, and then Connie appeared, carrying a pink hoodie and a small tumbler filled with two fingers of amber liquid that I knew was Glenfiddich because she knew Scotch was my drink of choice when wine or beer weren't strong enough to smooth the bumps of the day. She tossed me the hoodie, and after I slipped it on, she handed me the glass.

I cocked a brow. "Medicinal purposes?"

"You won't fill the prescription Dr. Kozak gave you so…" She settled on the couch next to me. "I suppose you don't want to talk either."

I swallowed a mouthful of Scotch and the burn hit my throat. "Ahem…about what?" She bobbed her head as if I should know, and I did, but I didn't want to talk about it. I pointed at a purplish spot on the blue Berber carpet. "I see you've got a new stain. What is that? Grape juice?"

"Yes. And don't change the subject."

I drank more Scotch and followed along as it traced a warm path through my body. Connie kept her eyes on me and I dropped my head back and stared at the ceiling. "You want to help?"

"You know I do."

I rolled my head to look at her. "What is cardiac tamponade?"

Her face twisted up a little. "You reading medical books in your spare time?"

"Came across the term in a case file."

"Oh. I'm surprised the ME didn't explain it."

"We weren't able to attend the autopsy."

She nodded. "Well, basically it's a life-threatening injury where bleeding from a puncture or blunt force trauma causes the sac around the heart to fill with blood."

I thought about what she said, though Scotch on an empty stomach made it a challenge. "So the blood in the sac put so much pressure on his heart that it couldn't beat."

Connie started to nod but stopped. "Oh, dear God! You read Dave's autopsy report."

More Scotch.

"Why would—?" She pressed her lips tightly and drew a deep breath. God give her strength. "Why couldn't you leave it alone?"

I scoffed. "Maybe because it is my life."

"That's not what I..." She propped her elbows on her thighs and put her folded hands to her mouth. She was probably praying for me.

Dave would've done anything for anyone. Knowing his big heart was squeezed to a stop nearly stopped mine. The question I wasn't sure I wanted answered hovered in my mind. "Did he suffer?"

Connie tapped her hands to her mouth a few times, then lowered them and looked at me. "You've had relatives say they wanted the truth but you know it's not always better." I kept my gaze steady as her eyes pleaded with me to let it go. Finally, she said, "He...it..." She sucked in some air and blew it out. "It's not instantaneous," she said fast. Like it would hurt less that way.

My arms grew limp. I grew limp. I don't know how I didn't slide right off the couch. *Why had I thought knowing the horrific details of his last moments would make it easier to accept? My problem is I never know when to quit.* Connie grasped my forearm but I pulled my arm away, reached over, and set the glass on the coffee table. "It's been a tough day and...I think I'm going to head home."

"You're injured and you've been drinking. You're not going anywhere."

That's why she was so quick with the single malt. "Medicinal purposes, my ass." I glared at her.

"You don't want to talk, fine. We...you can just..." She inhaled deeply to clip her growing frustration. "Dinner will be ready in twenty minutes." She stood and walked quickly from the room.

We ate Connie's chicken casserole and salad, and she refused my offer to help clear the table. Emily insisted I read *Green Eggs and Ham*—six times unless I lost count—while Connie cleaned up the dishes, and then we settled in the family room to watch *The Little Mermaid*.

The muzzle flashed and the bullet slammed into my chest. My blouse grew wet and warm as blood oozed from the hole. I looked up and my parents were standing over me. Dad held Mom close as tears streaked down her face. Connie walked up beside them, looked down at me, and said, "Damn you, Val."

I tried to sit up but felt as if I were glued to the bed—which was very narrow—and made up with white, puffy sheets like the tufted satin in a—casket! I struggled to sit up as Cesar Rivera appeared. He reached into the casket, yanked my gun from my holster, and handed it to Gary Noonan. Noonan raised his hand and fired and Dave crumpled to the floor.

I gasped and sat up and it took a few seconds for me to recognize the Warrens' family room. Emily sat cross-legged on the floor, so absorbed in the movie she didn't notice anything. I looked at Connie. Concern pinched her face and she held my eyes for a moment before she slowly turned her head toward the TV.

CHAPTER 15

I barely slept because my encounter with Rivera played over and over in my head like a vinyl record with a scratch. I finally surrendered and got up at 5:20 AM.

In spite of kissing the concrete, my black pants looked okay, but my shirt smelled worse than a hamper, so I kept Connie's tee. I crept into the kitchen and tore a sheet off the magnetic pad on the refrigerator. I scribbled a note, thanking Connie and Emily for taking such good care of me, and I added a PS that I'd return Connie's shirt in a few days.

The Warrens live a convenient half mile from the Blue Line, so I walked to Forty-Third and Washington and hopped an inbound train. I got off at Polk and stopped in Mugga Java for a box of donuts. By the time I arrived at the station, I desperately needed caffeine, but I swapped Connie's tee for a spare from my locker before heading to the break room. I started a pot of coffee and took advantage of the pause-and-pour to intercept a cup.

"You were supposed to take the day off," Payton said over my shoulder.

I shoved the carafe back onto the warming plate and turned to face my partner. "If I took the day off, I would've done something dangerous like clean the refrigerator, which would've exposed me to toxic waste and the threat of dishpan hands. I'm much safer here."

Payton scoffed. "So much for my plan to call in sick to take my family to the beach."

"Yeah, right. The day Greg Payton plays hooky is the day I turn in my shield."

He grinned but it didn't mask his concern.

"Look," I said, "I'm tired and a little sore, but I wouldn't be here if I wasn't 100 percent." Payton's left brow arched and I said,

"Okay, maybe 90 percent, but don't worry. Anything happens, I've got your back."

Payton dunked his tea bag a few times. "Considering you usually function at 80 percent, this is a step up."

"*Snap!*" I said, toasting his zinger with my mug.

"What the hell, Benchik!"

J.T. Pritchard's deep voice startled me enough that I flinched and almost spilled my coffee. I set my jaw and turned. "Hey, Pritchard. You get a lead on Rivera?"

"How're the ribs?" he asked.

I backhanded Payton in the chest.

"You were partners," Payton said. "I figured he had a right to know."

I ignored them both and drank more coffee.

"Well?" Pritchard demanded.

Just to push his buttons, I gazed at him deadpan. He always needed a shave because he maintained a scruffy appearance for the street, and he'd need to get his close-cropped, sandy brown hair trimmed in a week. His jaw muscles bunched and I half-expected to see steam start to blow from his ears.

"Y'all should've taken a day off," he said, his southern roots sprouting like they always did when he was agitated.

"I'm sorry," I said. "Where was it you got your medical degree?"

He shoved his hands into the back pockets of his jeans. Probably the only way he could keep them from wringing my neck. His voice had an edge when he said, "Forgive me for giving a damn about my old partner and best friend's wife."

Pritchard is six-four, so I had to tilt my head back a bit to meet his intense green eyes, and when I did, I caught a glimpse of his pain before he bowed his head. To change the subject, I lifted the cover on the box. "Donut?"

He looked up with a quizzical expression and then laughed. "It's the least I can do to honor tradition." He selected a vanilla frosted and took a bite.

"In return..."

He stopped chewing and his shoulders drooped. "I'm not going to like this, am I?"

"I don't give a rat's ass if you like it or not. Payton and I need to talk to Cesar Rivera, and I'm sure you know someone who knows what rock he slithered under."

"I already gave you the girlfriend's address," he said. "It's not my fault he flew the coop." I flashed the *Don't mess with me* stare I usually reserved for the street and he said, "I'll see what I can find out."

I patted his shoulder. "Thought we could work something out."

"I've got to get downstairs." He paused by the door. "You be careful, darlin'."

"You too."

He left and we carried our mugs and donuts to our desks. A few minutes later, Sergeant Porter walked in, carrying a donut in one hand and some file folders in the other. "I heard," he said. "You okay?" I nodded and he said, "You take a round from a scumbag and you still stopped for donuts." He slapped a folder down on Payton's desk. "Better be worth it. I got one hell of a paper cut from the flap." He took a bite of his donut and moved on.

"Whatcha got there?" I asked.

Payton opened the folder. "Background on Ortiz's bad boy friends." He skimmed the pages. "We've got one possession charge, a few DUIs, and some speeding tickets but that's it."

"They could still be guilty of assault and battery but the women just never filed charges," I said. "Anything on Rivera?"

He shook his head.

"There are only so many rocks he can hide under."

"He shot a cop," Payton said. "If he's got an ounce of sense, he's in Rio by now."

"Probably took Noonan with him," I muttered and Payton tossed a sympathetic glance my way. Feeling a bit unsettled, I cleared my throat and said, "I'm really starting to like the political angle."

My partner's brown eyes drilled through me. "I wonder if Morgan would like to part with some of Ryker's antacids."

"Maybe you need to give up your herbal tea and go back to coffee."

"Tea is not going to give me an ulcer or cost me my job."

I put my palm over my heart. "Would I do that to you?" I felt the buzz of an incoming call and Connie's number flashed onscreen. Great. I considered letting it go to voicemail, but then she'd probably come to the station, so reluctantly, I answered.

"I was thinking I could pick up Chinese," Connie said. "I can be at your place around…twelve fifteen?"

"You could but you'll be eating alone."

"*Do not* tell me you're at work!"

"Okay."

After a beat she said, "You really are insane" and she ended the call.

I sighed and tucked the phone in my pocket.

Captain Morgan walked in, carrying a chocolate-frosted donut on a napkin, and she stopped when she saw me. Before she could chew me out I said, "Doc said I could come to work if I felt up to it."

"That's good news, but even though you were wearing a vest, the shooting was a critical incident, so you don't hit the street without a trauma debriefing."

A visit with a shrink was the last thing I wanted right now. "Do I get to choose who I speak with?"

"As long as he or she is on the department's list of mental health professionals who specialize in working with law enforcement." She continued to her office and closed the door with her foot.

"This can be a good thing," Payton said. "When I shot that kid last year, it really helped to talk with an objective third party."

"I prefer to talk because I want to, not because someone tells me I have to."

"Trouble is, you never want to," he said.

"I'll see you later," I said. "Unless I get committed," I added before I walked out of the squad room.

I wanted to get back to work ASAP, so I called Jeremy Konrad from my car to ask if he could squeeze me in. Lucky for me his ten o'clock appointment had cancelled. I drove to his office in the Physicians' Pavilion at Wellington University Medical Center and waited in my car until 9:55 AM.

Konrad ushered me into his office, so tranquil with its pale blue walls and potted green plants. He filled two mugs with coffee and handed me one, and we sat in the high-backed easy chairs in front of his desk. He looked tranquil too, in a pale blue shirt and tan trousers. I sipped some coffee and grimaced.

"Must be pretty bad for a cop to react like that," Konrad said.

"No. It's uh…now I know what battery acid tastes like."

He chuckled but quickly downshifted to serious. "I heard about your close call when I got in today. Any report of an officer-involved shooting is always disturbing." He sipped some sludge and swallowed it like water. "You're obviously okay physically or else they would've admitted you, but I'm surprised you're at work. You're entitled to a sick day."

"I'm a little sore but not enough to stay home."

"Any anxiety?"

"No more than any other cop on the street."

He nodded, though I got the impression it didn't mean anything except he heard me. "You know the first step in dealing with trauma is to acknowledge your feelings."

"Denial bad," I said like a caveman.

Konrad tilted his head slightly. "Have you always used humor to deal with emotionally challenging situations?"

"I thought I was demonstrating my razor-sharp wit." I smiled. He didn't. *So much for my razor-sharp wit.* I sipped some sludge just to be doing something.

He set his cup on the desk and looked at me for a moment, like he was establishing some sort of mental link. "So what happened out there yesterday?"

I pictured the alley. The muzzle of Rivera's gun flashed and I flinched slightly as I felt the bullet strike my vest. I looked at Konrad but his face failed to register any reaction. "Bad day at the office. I got careless. But, hey! I wore my vest so no harm, no foul."

He shook his head once and almost imperceptibly. "I realize I don't know you well, but 'careless' is not a word I'd associate with you."

"I wanted it a little too much," I said with a shrug. "You've worked with enough cops to know how it is. Something happens that could make you miss a step and it gets the rumor mill churning.

Hell, Donovan probably has a pool going on when I'll lose it at a crime scene."

"I doubt there's a cop in this department—Donovan included—who didn't put him or herself in your shoes at least for a moment," Konrad said. "And I have worked with cops long enough to know you're family."

"And we've seen how dysfunctional families can be. I just...It was my first confrontation since Dave's murder and...I charged in, hell-bent on proving myself, and I guess I hesitated long enough to give the suspect an opening."

"Why did you hesitate?"

The image of Dave facing that bastard's gun flashed in my head like it had when I confronted Rivera. I closed my eyes and pushed it back, and when I opened my eyes, Konrad was still looking at me. Still waiting patiently.

Maybe I should tell him. He's not my best friend, who's worried sick about me. And he's not my partner, who's trying to have my back. He's just a kind man with no vested interest who listens for a living, and maybe that's exactly what I need right now.

"I got shot because there were three of us in that alley," I blurted out. I looked at Konrad. If my startling revelation fazed him, he didn't show it. And saying it out loud wasn't nearly as scary as I thought it would be so I waded in deeper.

"My ability to concentrate has always been a strength, but these images and memories come out of nowhere and..." My heart was beating fast and I took a deep breath to try to slow it down. "Everyone thinks I should've taken time off because the job will remind me of what happened but..." I shook my head, frustrated by their inability to understand. "It doesn't matter where I am or what I'm doing because I feel my husband's presence everywhere. Our house. The squad room. My car. The shower." I shook my head again, this time in disbelief over my inability to focus. "In some ways, work is tougher than it's ever been, but I feel like I need purpose in my life right now, and this case gets me out of bed in the morning." I realized my racing heart had slowed and I felt calmer. I sighed. "I know my concentration isn't as strong as it was but I figure every day it'll get a little stronger."

"As will you," Konrad said.

I met his eyes. "So do I need to get fitted for a jacket with wrap-around sleeves?"

He smiled. "Hardly. If you sat here and told me you were fine, maybe. But you realize there are things to deal with and that's the first step." His lips parted slightly, as if he wanted to say something else, but he stopped himself.

"I can be a pretty good listener too," I said.

He smiled. "It was a little eerie to hear you talk about how the memories come out of nowhere because I just had one of those moments myself. During Earth Week, Caitlin's class learned about the effect of fossil fuels on the environment and she called and said, 'Grandpa, you need to get a hybrid' and I…" He paused and sighed. "I traded in my Navigator for a Toyota a week after the funeral." His brows pinched and his eyes drifted to the mug in his hand, and then he shifted slightly in his chair.

It was reassuring to know a psychiatrist could be uncomfortable discussing his innermost thoughts.

He lifted his eyes. "Sometimes when I get in my car it makes me think about how much we lost, but mostly it reminds me of the positive impact she had during her short life. Destructive behaviors aside, there's no wrong way to deal with grief, so don't put additional pressure on yourself by feeling as though you should behave in a certain way."

"That's actually…helpful," I said.

He smiled. "You sound surprised." I shrugged it off and he said, "The good news is we're honoring our loved ones by getting out of bed each morning and continuing to do what we're good at. It's what they would've wanted for us."

Our eyes met and he raised his brows, silently asking *Am I right?* I let out a tremulous breath and nodded. "Do I have to come back?"

He shook his head. "But my door is always open if you want to."

We shook hands and I left. When I sat at my desk fifteen minutes later, Payton asked how the visit went.

"You'll be relieved to know the good doctor has determined me to be sane."

"That makes one of us," Payton said. "I've got bad news. You want to hear it?"

"It's my second favorite kind."

"The abusive husband of the legal aid client is out as a suspect. He got arrested after a bar fight Thursday night and he didn't make bail until Saturday morning."

I rubbed my forehead. "You remember the space in the old Life board game where the tornado blows you back to start?"

"No kidding," he said. "Aren't you glad you came in today?"

—— CHAPTER 16 ——

We'd spent all of Thursday and most of Friday talking to Ortiz's old boyfriends, but all of their alibis checked, and we weren't enthusiastic about any of them as serious suspects. We also made the rounds to hardware and home improvement stores to find out if any had recorded a recent sale on an ice pick. Our inquiry elicited chuckles from the older sales associates and blank stares from the younger ones, but none of the stores had sold any ice picks in the past year. We were at a point where we had to accept the killer probably found the pick in his grandparents' basement or bought it at a garage sale. We were tired, hot, and sweaty by the time we returned to the station a little after three on Friday afternoon.

"You have any big plans for the weekend?" I asked Payton as I double-clicked to open the case file so I could transcribe our notes.

"Shopping for a lawn mower tonight and the zoo on Sunday."

"Ooo!" I wrinkled my nose. "With this heat, the Elephant House should be particularly pungent."

"Tell me about it." He thumbed through a few messages. "Hey, you should come. The kids would love it." I glanced at him over my monitor and he said, "It's not a pity invite."

"Sure it is, but thanks." My desk phone rang, displaying the number for the Bunker, and I felt a little flutter in my stomach as I answered because they typically don't call us directly.

"Detective, it's Rita Bevin," the 911 operator said. "I thought you should know that a man just called, begging for help. Maybe it's nothing, but…I took the call last Friday from Adriana Ortiz, and now I get this call at nearly the same time."

The flutter turned into a knot. "You did the right thing, Bevin. Do you have an address?"

Payton tossed a *What's up?* look at me and I held up my finger.

"The call ended before we could get a location," Bevin said.

"Forward the call to my cell and tell everyone in the Bunker to call Payton or me if you get another call."

"Don't even tell me," Payton said as I hung up.

I looked at him and my stomach roiled with the thought of another body in a bathtub. He got up and knocked on Morgan's door while I stared at my phone display, waiting for Bevin's message. Morgan came out of her office as the incoming messages icon flashed on my screen. I opened the message and switched my phone to speaker.

"Nine-one-one," Bevin said.

A weak male voice said, "I need…help."

"What is the nature of your emergency, sir?"

"He's…he's going to…k-kill…"

"Sir," Bevin said, but there was only silence.

I punched END, tossed my phone on the desk, and ran my hands through my hair.

"What the hell!" Payton said. "Are we looking at the start of a spree?"

"I've got to brief the brass," Morgan said. She went into her office and shut the door.

I chewed my cheek and stared at my phone, willing it to ring. Payton said something and I looked up. "Huh?"

"A watched pot never boils and all that."

"I know. I just…What are we missing? How do we find the victim?"

Morgan came out of her office. "There's no telling when we're going to get the call and it's going to be a long day—or night—when we do, so why don't the two of you get out of here. Grab some down time while you can."

I opened my mouth to protest but Morgan raised her left hand and then pointed at the door. I didn't have the energy to argue.

I couldn't remember the last time I'd gotten any exercise and figured it might help me sleep, so when I got home, I changed into an old T-shirt and shorts and headed to the basement to crank out some miles on the wind bike. Normally, when I work a tough case, I let the leads roll around in my head as I peddle, but we didn't have any real leads on this case, so I had nothing to occupy my mind. And allowing my thoughts to go where they wanted would be counter-productive to exercising for stress relief, so I put on a Dixie Chicks CD and forced myself to sing the lyrics in my head. I'd biked over nine miles before looking at the odometer, so I rounded it to an even ten, stretched, and climbed back upstairs to shower.

I padded down to the living room, clean but far from relaxed, and I flopped down on the couch and closed my eyes. A short time later, a swarm of mosquitoes started to hover by my ear. I brushed it away, but when it didn't stop, I opened my eyes and realized the buzz was really my phone, vibrating on the coffee table. I snatched it up and my heart leapt into my throat when I saw the number for the Bunker on the display. Except for the address, I knew what they'd say, and when I ended the call from Bevin, I immediately called Payton. He was still at the mall with his family and asked me to pick him up so Pam could keep the car.

As I drove, the images in my head bounced between Dave lying on the asphalt and Adriana Ortiz in her bathtub.

My partner was leaning against a tree outside Sears when I pulled up. I was accustomed to seeing him in a suit and tie, and I flashed a wide smile when he got in my Escape wearing a rumpled Chicago Bears T-shirt, faded jeans, and beat up gym shoes.

"Wow. You do relax."

He scowled at me. "If you can call shopping for a lawn mower relaxing. Erin wants us to get a manual push mower to protect the environment, and I'm all for it but I'm not sure if my back can take it."

"How old is Matthew now?"

He flashed a smile. "That's a good idea."

We hit some traffic on Olympic by the airport, and it was just before 7:00 PM when I pulled in behind the squad that was dou-ble-parked in front of the brownstone owned by Scott and Rachel Caruso. Neighbors huddled on the sidewalk and speculated about what had happened as we passed them and climbed the concrete stairs and entered the house.

The small entryway opened into a large living room on the right and a hallway to the kitchen in back. We climbed the polished wood stairs to the left and passed two bedrooms before reaching the master suite at the back of the house.

Officer Carl Willard stood in the bathroom doorway and he jutted his chin in our direction as a greeting. "Wife found him." He shook his head. "It's not a pretty sight." He stepped aside to make room for us to enter.

The closer I got to the black marble whirlpool bathtub, the harder my heart thumped in my chest. I peered into the tub and the bloody punctures covering Caruso's torso drew my eyes like magnets to steel. Abrasions on his wrists indicated he'd been bound, though the killer had taken whatever he used with him. My head spun and I quickly averted my gaze and scanned the checker-box tile floor. I've watched people hyperventilate but never experienced it personally. Maybe I needed to start carrying a paper bag just in case.

"Any sign of forced entry?" Payton asked.

"Nope," Willard said. "Now that the big guns are here, I guess I'll go keep the lookie-loos at bay." He winked at us and walked out.

"Odds are slim they were both able to get free to call the police," I said. "He forced them to call. He wanted them to think they had a chance…to believe we'd get here in time."

"Psychic horror," Payton said. "We've got one sadistic son of a bitch. He wanted them to know what was coming."

Had Dave known what was coming? I drew in a sharp breath and sucked my top lip as I waited for the wave of anger and the urge to cry to pass. Then I forced myself to look at the body again. Even with his legs bent, Caruso barely fit in the tub. "He's a big guy. How did the killer subdue him?"

"Hey," Todd Argus said as he walked in. "I see your guy iced another one."

"He's not *our* guy!" I glared at Argus. "And maybe you could find some evidence to point us to a suspect this time, huh? Mr. I-Can-Find-Anything!" I pushed past him and rushed through the bedroom.

"Should I help her yank that stick out of her ass?" Argus asked Payton.

"I'd watch it if I were you, Officer!" I called out as I passed through the bedroom door. I turned just in time to see Leilani or else I would've plowed into her.

"Everything okay?" she asked.

"We've got another dead body and an ET with a big mouth! Aside from that, I'm just peachy!" Leilani recoiled and my shoulders drooped. "Sorry."

"I heard it's just like Adriana Ortiz," she said.

I nodded. "Only he left a wife and child behind."

She leaned to her left to peek into the bedroom, and then she looked back at me. "Anything I can do?" She arched her brows in friendly encouragement.

"Yeah, there is. Find some DNA to match a perp in our database so we can nail this son of a bitch."

She frowned. "I meant for you."

My stomach twisted a little because the only thing I really needed was the one thing no one could give me. "I know and appreciate it, but right now, finding an angle on this case will do more for me than anything else so..." I jerked my head toward the bathroom. "You should probably get in there."

Leilani went off to meet her patient, and a few seconds later, Payton popped his head into the hall. "You okay?"

"Yeah," I said. "It's just—"

"Argus."

I nodded.

"Okay then." His head disappeared from the doorway.

I peeked into the middle bedroom and my heart sank at the sight of a canopy bed covered with stuffed animals. I moved on to the front bedroom. It had been converted to a den, with a TV in one corner on the outside wall, a computer desk in the other corner, bookshelves along the short wall next to the door, and a love seat opposite the TV.

A half-empty cup from Mugga Java sat on the desk next to a laptop, and to the left of the computer was a picture frame with a shot of Caruso's daughter. I opened the small center drawer and found a checkbook. The register showed a balance of just over fifteen grand, with payroll entries of a little over six grand every two weeks.

Payton walked in. "I found his cell phone on the dresser and checked the incoming log. Unlike Ortiz, there were no calls from a burner number. I had Cassidy check the home number too, but nothing there either."

"So the killer approached him in person," I said.

"Looks that way," Payton said.

I shook my head. "This may rule out Rivera."

"Not necessarily," he said. "Ortiz could've been personal and suburban soccer dad could've had a drug problem."

"And Rivera is what? Doing this to send a message to anyone who stiffs him?"

Payton frowned. "Okay. You're right. It doesn't make sense, so Rivera is probably not the killer." He shrugged his chin toward the desk. "You find anything?" I told him about the pay stub and account balances and he whistled.

I thought about the timing of the phone calls. "Does it bug you that both calls came in at exactly the same time?"

"You think three twenty-nine means something to the killer," Payton said.

"I do. Like maybe something happened at that time that's a trigger for the murders."

Payton considered it. "It could be a reference to scripture. Like the signs people hold up at sporting events."

"Well, then it's up to you to decode the message, partner."

He smiled. "I'll have Cassidy run some queries. Biblical and otherwise." He looked around, like he was buying time. "We should probably talk to the wife."

My muscles tensed.

"You going to be okay to do this?" he asked.

"Uh-huh."

"Okay." He gave a single nod and walked out.

I thought back to my own questioning—if you could call it that. I'd been at home with an alibi when Pritchard arrived to make the notification, so it was really just a formality. Donovan and Garcia had actually seemed more uncomfortable than I was as they posed the questions that had to be asked.

The same questions I'd asked dozens of times during my years in Homicide without realizing how incredibly insensitive and intrusive they felt.

I took a cleansing breath.

I hope I'm okay to do this.

— CHAPTER 17 —

We found Rachel Caruso perched on an overstuffed print couch with her hands jammed between the cushion and her thighs. Payton introduced us and she looked up with red-rimmed eyes that struggled to focus.

I felt my mouth go dry, as if I'd slept with it open all night, and I could feel my heartbeat in my throat. I hadn't felt this apprehensive about talking to a relative since the first time I made a death notification. I took a deep breath and said, "We're very sorry for your loss, Mrs. Caruso. We know this is difficult but we need to ask you some questions."

She sniffled and slowly nodded.

We sat in the chairs across from her. She'd probably spent fifteen minutes this morning styling her blond hair, which fell just below her shoulders, but the humidity had it drooping like a weeping willow.

"When was the last time you spoke with your husband?" Payton asked.

"This morning. Before he left for work."

"Where did he work?" I asked.

"Paragon Insurance. He was vice president of claims."

"Any problems you know of?" Payton asked.

"Not really," she said. "It's been crazy the past few years. So many people lost their health coverage when they lost their jobs, and Scott hated having to deny claims for people who were already struggling but..." She licked her lips, which looked puffy from crying. "He felt for them. He really did."

Just like Dave. His primary responsibilities involved overseeing the customer service center, transaction processing and facilities, but as a senior officer of the bank, he got weekly updates on the status of all loans. As the foreclosure rate increased, not a Tuesday passed without him coming home and talking about how nice it would be to chuck it all for a new line of work. Maybe if he had...

"But that was about the extent of it," Rachel Caruso said.

Extent of what? What did our victim's wife say?

"Was it normal for your husband to be home on Friday afternoons?" Payton asked.

She shook her head. "He usually worked until at least five thirty or six, but a big client was in from San Francisco this week and Scott..." She put her fingers to her mouth, as if she could hold back the emotions. "There wasn't one night this week that he got home before eight o'clock, so he planned to work only a half day today."

"Who knew his schedule?" I asked.

"Just the people at work, I guess."

"Do you know if he had any special plans for the afternoon?" Payton asked.

"He...uh...he was planning to work on the dollhouse for"— she inhaled sharply—"dear God! Beth. How am I going to tell our daughter?" She put her hands to her face and sobbed.

After she'd brushed the tears away and her breathing evened out, I asked, "Where is your daughter?"

She sniffled. "She's spending the week in Chicago with my parents. They're driving back Sunday."

"Do you work, Mrs. Caruso?" Payton asked.

She nodded. "I'm managing director of the Aleron Foundation."

"You do good work," Payton said of the organization, which supports dozens of local charities and community initiatives.

I nodded in agreement. Aleron's founder, Ridley Wellington III, was on Lakeview Bank's board of directors. Dave started to attend the board's monthly meetings after his promotion and I'd teased him relentlessly about rubbing shoulders with Bedford's elite.

"What time did you get home?" Payton asked.

She squinted as she tried to remember. "About six fifteen, I think. I'm usually home by five, but we're planning our fall fundraising event and the coordinator and I visited one of the venues we're considering." She gazed at her trembling hands for a moment before she slid them back between her thighs and the cushion. "I...I can't believe—" She shook her head. "He should be playing poker right now."

Just like Dave should've been playing basketball. I reminded myself to stay in the moment and asked, "Where did he play?"

She stared at me for a moment and blinked, her ability to process slowed by shock. "Uh…he and his friends got together the first Friday of every month. It was Ray's turn to host."

"It would help if we could get all the names and addresses," Payton said. "If your husband was having some sort of problem, he may have told his friends at the last game."

"Of course."

"Were there any financial problems?" I asked.

"Mm-mm." She shook her head.

"What about drugs or gambling?" Payton asked.

Her forehead pinched. "No. Nothing like that."

"We're sorry to have to ask, Mrs. Caruso," I said, "but how was the marriage?"

Mouth agape, Rachel Caruso squinted at me as she struggled to comprehend what sort of monster could ask such a thing at a time like this. "My husband was…how can you…?"

"We realize it's a difficult question but it's also relevant." My stomach churned as I watched her discomfort and I wished we could walk out and leave her to grieve.

She glared at me. "You spend all your time in the gutter dealing with murderers, so everyone you come in contact with is some sort of monster. Is that it?"

Her eyes darted between us, searching for some sign of humanity, and I did something I never do—something a good cop should never do during an interrogation or even an interview. I broke eye contact and allowed my gaze to drift to the floor.

"It's impossible for anyone to be happy, in a committed relationship, right?" She breathed heavily. "Well, just because you never see the good in life doesn't mean it's not there!"

I wanted to shout *For some it isn't! Not anymore!* And then I wanted to slap myself in the head or kick myself in the ass because I hate self-pity. I took a deep breath and it wavered a little as I let it escape. I knew Payton would give her time to compose herself before he asked another question so I stared at my note pad until I heard his voice.

"We are sorry, Mrs. Caruso," Payton said, "but we need to know."

I raised my head and cast a sideways glance at my partner. He arched his brows a little, silently asking *Are you okay?* I looked at Rachel Caruso but gave a tiny nod to let him know I was fine.

Rachel Caruso glared at both of us a little longer before she said, "Scott was faithful. I was faithful. Okay?" She bowed her head and rubbed her fingers across her forehead. "We had a wonderful marriage," she said to her lap. The rubbing stopped and she looked up at us. "We were very much in love. Scott is...*was* a wonderful husband and father."

Payton took his phone out of his pocket and brought up Adriana Ortiz's photo. He held it up for Rachel to see. "Do you recognize this woman?"

She studied the screen for a moment. "She looks familiar but I meet so many people through the fundraisers."

Payton asked if she had guest lists from the events.

"It depends," she said. "At some events, tickets can be purchased at the door so we don't have names, but for other events we have a list. Who is she?"

"Her name is Adriana Ortiz." He slipped his phone into his pocket. "She was murdered last Friday and the facts of the case are similar."

Suspicion clouded her eyes. "What are you saying? Are you insinuating they were having an affair?"

"No, ma'am," I said firmly, and the absence of emotion in my voice helped me relax. "We just need to determine if there is any link between them. She was an attorney and they may have crossed paths due to a lawsuit. Or maybe they stopped at the same place for coffee."

She shook her head. "I've never seen her before."

"Is there anyone who had an issue with your husband outside of his work?"

She sat wringing her hands as she searched her memory. The wringing stopped and she shifted slightly. "There was something last

Saturday. Scott got into an altercation with a man after Beth's soccer match in Garfield Park."

"What was the fight about?" Payton asked.

She shrugged. "I don't know. Beth and I had already gone to the car. I asked Scott about it when he got to the car but he said the guy was a jerk and to forget it." I asked if she could describe the guy and she shook her head. "I didn't see his face." She thought for a moment. "He was wearing a baseball cap, though. Black, I think."

"Do you have any sort of team roster?" Payton asked.

She nodded. "Scott was a coach. It should be on his computer."

"Would it be all right if I took a look?" Payton asked. She nodded and he excused himself to go upstairs.

We sat in silence for a moment before I asked if there was anyone we could call for her.

"My sister is on her way," she said softly.

Moral support or not, I knew the coming days would be some of the most difficult she'd ever face. I slipped a Victims' Services card out of my wallet, scribbled my cell number on the back, and handed the card to her. "Victims' Services provides assistance with a variety of issues, and my number's on the back."

Her hand trembled as she stared at the card.

"We're going to do everything possible to find who did this."

She nodded but I don't think she believed me. I stood and walked out of the room. I waited by the front door until Payton came down, and we removed our paper booties and left.

"Paragon Insurance is big," I said on the way to the car. "What law firm do you think they'd have on retainer?"

"That would certainly qualify as a link," Payton said, "but I doubt we'll be able to get a hold of anyone before 9:00 AM Monday."

I checked my watch. "It's not even eight o'clock. If they haven't heard what happened, Caruso's poker buddies could still be riding the river."

"And chances are good they've been drinking," Payton said, "so they're more likely to talk. Let's do it."

We found Caruso's five poker buddies gathered around a table with tumblers full of twelve-year-old single malt, shrouded in cigar smoke. They had a standing rule to turn off their phones, so we had to break the news. They emptied their glasses in a toast to Caruso and asked how they could help.

We learned they'd all arrived around six, and when Caruso wasn't there by quarter-after, they tried calling him, got his voicemail, and decided to carry on without him. They all swore Caruso was faithful, did not have a problem with drugs or alcohol, and with the way they played, not even gambling. None of them recalled seeing a guy in a baseball cap hanging around, and Caruso hadn't said anything during their last game to indicate he'd been concerned for his safety.

We left them to their stogies, Scotch, and reminiscences and shuffled back to our car.

"Baseball Cap Guy sounds like our best lead," I said, "if you can call it that considering half the men in this city walk around in baseball caps."

"Well, maybe we'll get lucky," Payton said, "because according to Caruso's team schedule, Lakeview Academy has a match at 9:00 AM tomorrow in Pasteur Park."

I told him I'd bring the coffee.

CHAPTER 18

I parked under a tree in the Pasteur Park lot and drank my coffee while I waited for Payton. I gazed at an eerily familiar blue sky and felt the same heat and humidity push down like a dry cleaner's press, and I wondered how many other reminders there'd be today of that first Sunday in August twenty-two years ago—the day of Annie's murder.

The parade of mini-vans started at eight thirty, dispensing kids with shin guards and parents lugging coolers. Payton pulled in just before nine and we began our canvass. Many of the parents admitted they'd signed a petition to remove Scott Caruso as coach due to his unsportsmanlike behavior, but no one noticed the altercation between Caruso and Baseball Cap Guy. And three quarters of the men and half the women wore baseball caps, so no one recalled seeing anyone who didn't belong hanging around the field. Our mystery man had managed to blend in.

We grabbed lunch and made it to the morgue on time for Caruso's autopsy. Leilani confirmed twenty-seven stab wounds inflicted with the same type of weapon used on Ortiz. And she set the time of death between three and five Friday afternoon.

"Didn't find anything in the preliminary tox screen either," she said as she removed what I think was his liver.

"Maybe Mrs. Caruso has the drug problem and Rivera killed him to set an example," Payton said.

I tensed at his suggestion the widow was the cause of her husband's murder, which was odd because I'm usually the first one to suspect the spouse. But if anyone had even considered I had something to do with what happened to Dave…"I don't think so," I said.

Payton swung his head toward me. "Why not? Soccer moms do drugs too."

I shook off the notion. "I didn't get that impression from Rachel."

His eyebrows rose. "Rachel, is it?"

I scoffed. "Oh, you've gotta be…Is there something you need to say?"

"I'm saying I found something here I didn't find with Ortiz," Leilani said sharply and we both looked at her. "Good. Now that I have your attention." She easily rolled Caruso's body slightly to the right to expose two small marks on the back of his left shoulder. "These marks are indicative of a stun gun."

"Explains how the killer controlled Caruso long enough to tie him up," Payton said.

"Yep," Leilani said. She looked at me and I could see the concern in her eyes.

"Mahalo," I said and I walked out, leaving my partner behind. I was halfway to the car by the time he caught up to me.

"You know I didn't mean anything back there," he said.

"I know."

"Okay. Good." After a few steps he said, "Stun gun is good news. It gives us another avenue to pursue."

"Hopefully it won't be another dead-end."

"The wife said Caruso's name appeared on all claim-denial letters to policyholders," Payton said, "and he received some pretty nasty letters, e-mails, and even phone calls in response, but he felt most were just venting their frustration."

I stopped walking. "What are you talking about?"

"That's what you missed when you zoned out yesterday."

"Oh." I felt my face flush and knew it wasn't from the heat. "It was just…when she told us how her husband empathized with the policyholders, it reminded me of how preoccupied Dave seemed on Tuesdays after their weekly loan reviews. He would've helped Noonan if it were up to him, so it makes Noonan's actions even harder to accept."

Payton popped the locks on the cruiser. "Victims' Services was good advice. Have you given any thought to—?"

"No," I cut him off, "but if it makes you feel better, when I had to get a shrink's stamp of approval after the shooting, Dr. Konrad and

I talked about more than just how I felt staring down the barrel of a drug dealer's gun."

"Good," he said.

Not really, I thought, *but I'll get there.*

We returned to the station and requested background on Caruso. We recalled seeing a lot of baseball caps when we reviewed the video from around Ortiz's building, so we reloaded the footage and printed screen shots of all the men wearing caps whose faces were visible. We were wrapping up to leave when we heard the elevator ding. A few seconds later, Connie walked in, carrying two cups from Mugga Java.

"Hey, Connie," Payton said.

"Hi, Greg. I didn't expect you. I would've brought you a tea."

He waved her off. "I'm actually leaving, so you ladies enjoy your coffee and girl talk." He told Connie it was good to see her and tossed me a wave on his way out.

"I figured you must be swamped since you haven't answered my calls," Connie said.

"Yeah, it's been pretty hectic."

"You've got time for a mocha," she said and she headed for the visitor's room. I followed her in, we settled on the couch, and she handed me a cup. "I just wanted to catch up and see how you're feeling since the…incident."

"I've got a very festive-looking bruise. Want to see?" I reached for the hem of my shirt.

Connie chuckled and waved her hand. "Pass." We both sipped some coffee and she said, "I caught the early news today."

Rather than make eye contact, I slid the corrugated ring up and down my cup.

"They said the police don't have any suspects in the murder of a man found stabbed to death in his home last night," she said. "And that the case is very similar to the murder of an attorney last week."

"Wow. For once they got it right." I sipped some coffee and kept my eyes on the cup.

"They also said he's survived by a wife and daughter."

My throat tightened. "Mm-hmm."

"How are you doing with that?"

*How am I doing with the fact the victim left a widow behind? Or how am I'm doing with being a widow? Probably not very well with either but…*I sighed. "Shit happens."

Connie choked on some coffee and I tensed, ready to help if needed. She stopped coughing and looked at me as if she expected me to say something else. When I didn't, she said, "That's it?"

I turned up my palm. "What else is there?"

"Aw, come on, Val. Don't pretend like this isn't affecting you. You're obviously not sleeping much and I doubt you're eating right. You're pushing yourself too hard."

"And you're sounding like my mother."

She spread her palms. "Call me crazy but I worry about you."

Maybe you should worry about me. Maybe I should worry about me. Apparently, I shut down the moment I arrived at the branch and saw Dave because it's only been two weeks, yet I'm back on the job as if nothing happened. And even though I almost fell apart at the graveside when everyone started filing past to place rose petals on Dave's casket, I blinked and breathed and swallowed my way through it. How can I be so unemotional?

I felt Connie's hand on my arm and looked at her.

"Talk to me. Please."

"About what?"

Connie got the same distant look in her eyes like I'd recently seen in the eyes of another best friend. The mix of sadness and regret that clouded Anita Zamora's eyes when she told us she never knew why Adriana Ortiz left the law firm. Connie sat back against her corner of the couch and rubbed her forehead. "Why do you do this?"

"Do what?" I drank some coffee.

"Refuse to show emotion like any normal human being."

"Just abnormal I guess." I crossed my eyes. Normally it would've made her smile but today she was stone-face all the way. "Do you believe in premonitions?" I asked, hoping to send her off on another tangent.

"I've seen enough at work that I don't rule anything out. Why?"

"I was just thinking about when Dave first told me he wanted to start a family. It was shortly after that guy he worked with crashed his motorcycle, and I thought he was just reacting to the shock, but now…" I shook my head. "I wonder if he sensed something."

"Like his own mortality?"

I shrugged.

"Look," Connie said, "I know you feel you need to be tough all the time because of the job."

I dropped my head. So much for another tangent.

"Being a cop is a lot like emergency medicine," she said. "If I didn't learn to leave work at work, every other case would tear my heart out and I'd be committed in a month. I know you've got to keep your distance to function, but there's compartmentalizing work and then there's you. You don't let anyone in. Like when we were in college and your grandmothers passed away. You pulled away both times then too. You're like a…turtle or a…a freakin' armadillo."

I snorted a laugh.

"It's not funny!" Her face flushed and her brows pinched. "And you know what I mean. When it feels threatened, an armadillo curls up in a ball"—she made a fist—"and it uses its shell to protect its soft, vulnerable abdomen. Only with you, it's not your gut. It's your heart." She pointed at her own. "You work so hard at controlling what you feel and what you say. But every once in awhile, something gets to you and then"—she made another fist—"you curl up with that shell around your heart and shut down."

She was right and I could pinpoint the moment I first crawled into that shell—that muggy Monday evening when my parents told me Annie was dead.

"You slap up your cool exterior," Connie said, "but I worry about what's inside the shell."

I smiled. "A cool interior."

She shook her head. "You can't bury this, sweetie."

I can't talk about it right now either because if I do, I may disintegrate.

She ran her hand through her hair. "Why are you even working this case? I'm sure if you told Captain Morgan you wanted off—"

I held up my hand. "I can't do that."

"Why not?"

"Because I won't let the son of a bitch who killed Dave take my work from me too!"

Connie gulped. I knew she was relieved I'd shown some emotion, but her eyes betrayed her concern.

"I've got a lot to do so..." I stood and walked to the door but I paused with my hand on the knob. "Thanks for the coffee and for your concern, but I'm okay." I opened the door and walked out. I sat at my desk, and a few moments later, I heard the elevator ding and the doors thumped shut. I stared at my monitor.

It hadn't been a conscious decision to pull away, but losing Annie hurt so much I always kept my distance a little afterward. I knew I'd never have a friend like her again anyway, so why bother? Of course I was ten, so what the hell did I know? At the time, I couldn't fathom meeting Constance Redmond who, in spite of my best efforts, would manage to insinuate herself into my life and my heart to the point where I cannot imagine getting through life without her.

Right now all I could do was hope she had the patience to hang in there with me one more time until I crawled out of my shell.

— CHAPTER 19 —

I got in very early Monday and found a file on my desk with the query results for 3:29 and March 29th that we asked Cassidy to run. Eleven crimes had been reported in Bedford at that time or on that date, including one rape and one DUI with a non-fatal injury. On the surface, there was no evidence of a connection, but without a solid suspect, we had to follow every lead, so I requested background on the parties involved.

"What are you up to?" Payton asked when he arrived a few hours later, mug of tea in hand. I filled him in and he told me I was industrious.

"Desperate is more like it and I already struck out on ten of them. The truth is, if the time of these murders is linked to some crime, the case could've happened anywhere." I sipped some coffee. "Oh, and uniforms got zip on the canvass of Caruso's neighbors so..." The results for the parties involved in the DUI accident displayed on my screen and there was no connection to Ortiz. "Make that eleven." In frustration, I threw my pen and it skittered across the desk onto the floor. And landed at Morgan's feet.

She stooped over, picked it up, and handed it to me. "Tell me you have a suspect."

"Okay, but I'd be lying."

"We do have a new angle," Payton said. "The killer used a stun gun on Caruso so we'll check purchase records. Of course if he paid cash we're screwed but—"

"We ran the MO," I said. "The closest hit we got was a woman who used a screwdriver to stab her husband in a domestic dispute."

"You run it through VICAP?" Morgan asked.

Payton nodded. "We've got a guy who uses a mountain climbing pick and a bunch who prefer various hunting knives, but no one who uses an ice pick and cleans up after himself."

Morgan sipped some coffee and I stared at the cup in her hand. Payton had found several empties in Ortiz's trash, and I found a cup on Caruso's desk. "They both went to Mugga Java," I said.

Morgan hoisted her cup. "I go to Mugga Java. Does that mean I'm the next victim?"

I also recalled Morgan's bandaged hand on her first day. "Maybe you're the doer," I said without thinking. "Argus found marine varnish in Ortiz's place, and on your first day, you had those rope burns you said you got from sailing but…"

Payton shot me a *What the hell did you say that for?* look.

Morgan smiled. "Are you taking pain meds for those bruised ribs, Detective?"

"I certainly hope so," Payton hissed through clenched teeth.

"No, ma'am. I'm just tired, frustrated, and grasping at straws."

"Well," she said, "to quell any suspicions you may have, Roger and I enjoyed sailing, and I'm still a member of a club that works with at-risk teens. The goal is to foster teamwork, but the group I was with that weekend…not so cohesive. One of the kids left his position, and I barely caught the rope in time to stop the boom from swinging around and taking out two other kids."

"So instead of a cold-blooded killer, you're actually a hero," I said.

Her nose crinkled. "Nah." She turned for her door.

"According to his wife, Caruso got some nasty e-mails and letters from pissed off policyholders but you know Paragon will stonewall when we ask," I called after her.

"Start typing the request," she said over her shoulder.

I looked at Payton. His jaw was hanging down to his desk. I spread my palms. "What?"

He shook his head some more, still unable to believe what I'd said, but he finally composed himself enough to ask, "Who's Roger?"

"Husband."

"She divorced?"

"Widow." I focused on my monitor. "We've got the Carusoes' financials. They were doing very well. Their combined retirement nest egg is worth over a million bucks. There's another four hundred thou in savings and investment accounts, and according to Paragon Insurance's annual report, Caruso recently received a half million-dollar bonus."

Payton whistled.

"No unusual activity or frequent cash withdrawals." I leaned back. "As much as it pains me to say this, I think we can rule Cesar Rivera out as a suspect."

"Maybe for the murders," he said, "but we're going to nail his scrawny ass for trying to take you out." I chuckled and he nodded his approval. "That's much better. What say we head over to Paragon?"

"Sounds like a plan."

We picked up our subpoena and drove to the Paragon offices, but Ross Danner, senior vice president of operations, had yet to arrive, so we spent the wait time talking to Caruso's assistant. She told us Caruso spent Friday morning in meetings and confirmed he left as scheduled around one o'clock because of the late nights with the client from San Francisco.

Danner waltzed in at nine thirty—it's good to be the boss—and he quickly dashed our hope of establishing a link when he told us Paragon did not have Smithfield, Royce, and Foley on retainer.

"Mr. Caruso received a hefty bonus," Payton said. "What did he have to do to earn it?"

"Our executives are paid incentives based on the company's performance," Danner said.

"Your company must have had one hell of a year," I said. Danner nodded, and though he didn't smile, he had the content look of someone who never lost any sleep over work. "Did anyone whose claim was denied ever threaten Mr. Caruso?"

"Threaten is a bit harsh," Danner said.

"We'll need the names and anything else you have," Payton said.

Danner shook his head. "That's confiden—" I held up the subpoena. He snatched it from my hand and expelled air loudly through his nose as he scanned it. "I'll see what I can do." He checked his watch. "I'm late for a staff meeting. Is there anything else?"

There wasn't, so we thanked him for his time and left his office. We were silent as we walked to the elevator, and when it arrived, I punched the "G" button and started to gnaw my cheek.

"I know that look," Payton said.

"Danner squelched our theory that Caruso and Ortiz were connected through her old firm, but where do you suppose someone would turn if the insurance company denied all their health care claims and medical bills exhausted their savings?"

"You're thinking a policyholder went to Legal Aid looking for help."

"Yes, I am."

We drove over to Legal Aid, and when we walked into Elizabeth Bauer's office, she was gathering some papers and shoving them into a briefcase. She looked up and frowned. "I'm sorry but I'm due in court at eleven."

"We'll make it quick," Payton said. "Was Adriana representing anyone in a lawsuit against Scott Caruso or Paragon Insurance?"

"Just because a lot of our work is pro bono doesn't mean attorney-client privilege goes out the window," Bauer said. "We still abide."

"We're not asking you to disclose your strategy," I said. "All we need to know is whether Adriana was connected. Now we can run a list of pending court cases, but it'll take time and there's a killer out there. Please, Counselor, give us a hand."

Bauer drummed her fingertips on the side of her briefcase as she considered our request. She sighed and said, "We're not involved in any legal action against Paragon or Caruso."

"Do you recall seeing a guy in a baseball cap hanging around the past few weeks?" I asked.

She looked at me as if I'd asked if she'd seen a monkey riding a unicycle. "You're kidding, right? Did you happen to look around the waiting area or even the street?" She picked up her briefcase. "I'm late."

We said "thank you" to her back as she disappeared through the door.

When we returned to the station, I walked straight to the whiteboard, picked up a red marker, and wrote, "Who is Baseball Cap Guy?" under Caruso's column. "So what do we know?"

"They grew up in different neighborhoods and attended different schools," Payton said as he pulled a chair from one of the empty desks and sat down. "They lived and worked in different neighbor-hoods. And there's no credit or debit card activity to indicate they frequented the same places."

"Ortiz left a big job and Caruso would've too if the job market didn't suck." I added "Problems at work" to the board.

"Ortiz had a drug problem but Caruso didn't," Payton said. "And they both got hate mail at work."

I added all the bullet points and then reviewed them. "A law-yer and an insurance executive. Maybe they had some sort of scam going. Medicare fraud or something."

"Or maybe Rivera is involved after all," Payton said. "They could all have some prescription drug slash insurance fraud going with a pharmacy or clinic and the deal went south."

We studied the board some more.

"Why an ice pick?" I said. "Why not a knife."

"It may be symbolic," Payton said. "He's chipping away at the coldness of mankind."

"He tortured two people. How can he even recognize coldness?" I rubbed my chin. "Ortiz was single and currently unattached, so it was a pretty safe bet her loft would be empty, but Caruso had a wife and child. How did the killer know Caruso would be home alone?"

Payton shrugged. "Maybe he was watching them."

My stomach knotted. Watching indicated patience. Deliberation.

The killer held Adriana Ortiz and Scott Caruso prisoner in their homes. He tortured them and then teased them by allowing them to call 911, giving them a glimmer of hope they'd survive. And he stayed after the murders to clean up after himself.

A chill flowed through my body, as if someone had injected ice water into my veins.

— CHAPTER 20 —

When I arrived at the station Tuesday morning, I had to navigate a minefield of TV news vans clogging Tyler Street. I parked in the garage, but instead of going up to the squad room, I walked through the lobby and out the main entrance onto Columbus Avenue. I found Officer Tommy Nolan standing with his arms crossed as he watched the spectacle, and I jerked my head toward the throng. "What's going on?"

"Ridley Wellington is holding a press conference," Nolan said.

How could it possibly bode well for us that the heir apparent of Bedford's founding family—and Rachel Caruso's boss—was talking to the press outside our office? "Press conference regarding…" I motioned for Nolan to fill in the blank but he shrugged. "Why did you let them set up here?"

"Wellington plays golf with the commissioner," Nolan said. "I'm eight months from my pension. Do the math."

I fought my way through the mob of reporters as they jockeyed for position to jam their microphones in Wellington's face. I spotted Payton on the sidelines and joined him.

"Just when you think it can't get any worse," he said.

Wellington was in a navy blue silk suit and his short brown hair was freshly trimmed for his close-up. He asked the reporters to quiet down, and after they did, he looked directly at the cameras and said, "Scott Caruso was a loving husband and father and he was viciously murdered last Friday. Given the pace of this investigation, the police need all the help they can get, so I'm offering a reward of fifty thousand dollars for any information leading to the apprehension of Mr. Caruso's killer."

Shutters clicked wildly and the reporters drowned each other out as they shouted questions at Wellington.

"This is going to turn our investigation into a three-ring circus," I muttered.

Nolan and another uni ran interference with the press as Wellington disengaged himself from the fracas. With reporters nipping at his heels, begging for one last sound byte, Wellington started to leave, but our eyes met and he detoured in our direction.

You'll wish you'd have kept going by the time I'm finished with you, I thought, and when he was within five feet of us I said, "What the hell do you think you're doing?"

Wellington extended his hand to me. "Mrs. Lukas."

The sound of my married name sliced through me like a knife and completely derailed my train of thought. I forced a smile and shook his hand.

"I was very sorry to hear about your husband," he said. "I didn't know him well, but he seemed like a good man."

I nodded. "The best." I motioned to Payton. "This is my partner, Greg Payton." I looked at Payton and motioned to Wellington. "Ridley Wellington."

"Lee, please," Wellington said as they exchanged handshakes. "My family is nothing if not pretentious."

I pointed toward the reporters. "Why did you do this? A reward is going to—"

"I'm sorry," Wellington said, "but I have a meeting in ten minutes." He turned and walked away.

I took a step to follow but Payton caught my arm. "Not worth it." We watched Wellington crawl into a silver Prius and drive off, and then Payton stuck his nose in the air and said, "Hobnobbing with Bedford's rich and famous."

I felt my cheeks flush. "Wellington is on Lakeview Bank's board of directors and we chatted *briefly* at a few holiday parties."

"You obviously made quite an impression."

I scoffed. "Shut up."

He chuckled but then grew serious. "It was strange to hear someone call you by your married name."

"Heh. For me too." Payton started to say something but stopped, so I answered the question he didn't ask. "A couple of weeks before my wedding, a cop in Narcotics started to receive harassing phone calls at home from a guy he was scheduled to testify against. I admitted to Dave that I was afraid of the job spilling over into my personal life the same way. He told me the HR director at the bank used her maiden name at work and he suggested I do the same. He said it might help mislead anyone with malicious intentions and it would sort of keep work separate." I shook my head a little at the absurdity of the idea. "It's surreal knowing the violence that took Dave's life came from his world and not mine…Maybe I *should* change my name, huh? As a way to honor him."

"Eh, I don't know," Payton said. "It was his idea, so you're already honoring him. And if you change your name, you'll have to get new credentials, which means a new picture." I grimaced. "Besides," he said, "I think Payton and Benchik has a nice ring to it."

"Mm, I don't know. I kind of like Benchik and Payton."

He shook his head. "Age before beauty."

"Oh, please." I rolled my eyes and yanked the door open and we entered the building.

Payton detoured to the break room for some tea but I went straight to the squad room. The moment I sat at my desk, Donovan parked his butt on the corner of it and said, "I've got a pool going on the sergeant's exam."

In June, Donovan, Payton, and I had taken the test to rank officers for future promotions. I'd done it mainly to have career options in the event Dave and I had a baby and I decided being a homicide cop and a mother were incompatible. At this point, I didn't even care about the damned results. I looked up at him. "Is there anything you won't bet on, Shawn?"

He stroked his chin as he considered it. "Nah."

"So what are the odds you're going to find Noonan?" I saw his body stiffen and I held up my hand. "I'm sorry. That was out of line."

"Not really," Garcia said. "You've got every right to be frustrated like any other relative."

"Is that why you've been hanging out in Tombstone?" Donovan asked.

Busted. "How did—?"

"Ran into Alex Raynor," Garcia said. "He told us he's been seeing you around."

"Kept an eye on you too," Donovan added.

I shifted my eyes between them, trying to get a sense of what they'd do next, but like me, they were skilled at masking their emotions. "Are you going to tell Morgan?"

Donovan shrugged his brows. "That depends on you."

I couldn't decide what made me feel worse. Disobeying Morgan's order or making these guys feel as if I thought they were incompetent. "Look," I said, "I trust you guys. I do. It's just…" I let out a frustrated sigh as I searched for a way to say what was on my mind without sounding too emotional or crazy.

"It's hard when you feel like your hands are tied and there's nothing you can do," Garcia said.

Talk about hitting the nail on the head. I looked him in the eyes. "Yeah. It sure is."

"We're talking to everyone who ever crossed paths with this guy," Donovan said. "Sooner or later he's going to pop his head out of whatever hole he's hiding in, and when he does, we're going to nail his ass. And you'll be the first to know when we do."

I nodded and hoped I looked more optimistic than I felt.

Payton walked up with his mug. "So who's the favorite to make sergeant?"

"Well, they said they'd announce the results by September first," Donovan said, "so the odds could change, but right now, the two of you are running neck and neck."

Payton winked at me.

"So you in or what?" Donovan asked. I waved him off and he shrugged and hauled his butt off my desk to go sit at his own.

"Val." Payton tipped his head toward the doorway.

Rachel Caruso was standing in the hall and I tossed Payton a *What is she doing here?* look.

"I think you should take this solo," Payton said.

From the level of anxiety I felt, you'd think he told me to go jump in a snake pit and I hoped my uneasiness wasn't evident as I greeted Rachel and led her to the visitor's room. I waited for her to settle in one of the chairs before I offered to get her a cup of coffee or tea. She declined and apologized for bothering us but I assured her it wasn't an imposition.

"I couldn't stop thinking about how terribly I treated you and your partner," she said.

I sat in the other chair. "You just had the worst shock of your life, Mrs. Caruso and—"

"Rachel, please," she said, "and I appreciate you trying to let me off the hook but I was horrible to you. You were trying to do your job and…" She was spinning her wedding band, though she probably didn't realize she was doing it. "I couldn't sleep last night," she continued, "so I ended up watching some recordings from Beth's matches and I found something I thought could be important." She reached into her purse and pulled out a DVD. "It's from the match last Saturday where Scott had the run-in with that man."

I took the disc. "I appreciate you bringing this in. I'm sure it'll be very helpful." An awkward silence hung in the room before I asked, "How are you holding up?"

She shrugged. "My sister is staying for another week."

"It's good you have someone with you."

A smile flashed briefly on her face and she nodded. She opened her mouth to say something but then sucked in her bottom lip. Her eyes darted around a little as she waged some internal debate before she softly said, "You know, when you told me you were sorry for my loss, I thought you were just spouting some empty words they tell you to use during your training, but Lee told me he knew your husband from the bank. He also told me why there isn't a better person to be working the case."

I held my breath, dreading what I sensed came next.

"I'm sorry for your loss," she said.

And there it was. I felt my bottom lip quiver. I wanted to thank her, but if I opened my mouth, I'd probably start to cry, which would be unprofessional, so I simply nodded my appreciation.

"You know, the night Scott—" Her voice caught and her face contorted as she struggled to maintain her composure.

I clenched my jaw and shifted my eyes over her shoulder. If she lost it, I'd lose it too, so I took a few slow, steady breaths.

"I can't stop seeing him," she said softly. "I close my eyes and… all I see are the holes on his body. I didn't know what to do. I stood there…staring at him."

"You couldn't believe you were seeing what you were seeing," I said. "It had to be a nightmare. You felt so numb you couldn't comprehend how you were even standing. It was like someone had reached in and ripped your heart from your chest."

She dabbed at her nose with a tissue and nodded.

I hesitated to say more because I wasn't sure I could keep it together. But if hearing about my experience could help her, I knew I had to go on. "The branch where my husband…It's a couple of blocks from the expressway and I remember how the sound of the cars whizzing by was distorted—like they were actually in my head." I tried to wet my lips but my mouth was too dry. "As I looked at him, I screamed and I punched and I threw things…but then I realized it was all in my imagination because, in fact, I was just kneeling on the pavement, holding Dave's hand." I sniffled. "I closed my eyes and wished for it to be last week…or even yesterday, but when I opened my eyes, he was still lying on the pavement and…I barely made it over to the Dumpster behind the building before I got sick."

Her eyes widened a little and then she let out a small sigh, relieved to hear even a homicide cop could be sickened by such sights.

I almost smiled now as I recalled the look on Pritchard's face when I asked if he or Payton had any gum. All I wanted was to rid my mouth of the sour taste, but Pritchard looked as if I'd asked him for a kidney.

"I've gotten so many phone calls," she said. "I've let them all go to voicemail."

I nodded. "I was ready to yank our phone out of the wall. People mean well but…"

She fingered her ring some more and then whispered, "How do I get these images out of my head?"

I shook my head a little. "I'm not going to lie to you, Rachel. I still carry the images of victims I didn't even know from my first days on the force."

"Victim," she said. "That word always described someone else. I still can't comprehend it applies to my husband."

Me either, I thought. "It's very different when you're the one to find the body," I said. "It's not all neat and tidy, like when you see your loved one for the first time at the funeral home. I regret going to the scene because it's impossible to erase those images, but you…We need to concentrate on good memories. That may seem impossible right now, but even the worst storm eventually passes, the sky clears, and the sun comes out again."

She sniffled and nodded.

I thanked her again for bringing in the video and walked her out, and when I sat down at my desk, I glared at Payton. "Thanks a lot, partner!"

He held up his hand. "The two of you needed to speak alone. You okay?"

"Uh-huh." I waved the DVD and loaded it into my computer. "Let's see what we have." I opened the file and fast-scanned through the video until I spotted Scott Caruso pacing the sidelines. I hit PLAY just as he threw a water bottle and screamed obscenities at the referee. "He's like Mike Ditka on speed," I said as I fast-forwarded and stopped in a segment where Caruso ripped into the players, telling them they were worthless.

"I don't believe this guy!" Payton said. "If someone went off on one of my kids like that, I'd be pissed."

"But if his murder has something to do with the soccer match, then what's the link to Ortiz?"

Payton shrugged.

We continued to watch Caruso pace the sidelines, pointing and throwing his arms in the air like a robotic mime while little girls scurried around the field. No one in a black cap seemed to be watching Caruso, but something about the video seemed important. I just couldn't put my finger on it until…I pressed PAUSE and pointed at the screen. "Those uniforms look familiar to you?"

Payton studied the screen for a moment. "Looks like we need to pay an encore visit to Smithfield, Royce, and Foley."

— CHAPTER 21 —

Edward Royce folded his hands on top of his desk and leaned forward expectantly. "Has there been some new development?"

"There has," Payton said. "But before we get to that, I forgot to ask the other day. Where does your daughter attend school?"

A puzzled look flashed on Royce's face. "Why is it you want to know?"

Payton shrugged. "I was just curious. My daughter's school may play your daughter's school sometime and—"

"St. Francis Academy," Royce said.

Payton nodded. "Does your schedule allow you to make it to all of her soccer matches?"

"Not nearly as many as I'd like," Royce said.

"I hear you," Payton said, one doting father to another. He pointed at the photo of Royce's daughter in her uniform. "Did you make it to the match against Lakeview Academy?"

Royce thought about it. "I'm not sure. I think so."

"It was the Saturday before last," I said. "Can you check? It's important."

He picked up his phone and scrolled. "It's in my calendar, and I don't see any other appointments, so I must've been there. Why?"

Payton reached across and laid the photo of Caruso on the desk in front of Royce. "Ever see him?"

Royce picked it up and frowned. "He's the coach of the Lakeview team. A total ass. Stomped up and down the sidelines throwing tantrums like a five-year-old. Talk about setting a bad example for a bunch of impressionable young children. The only thing he taught his team was that it's acceptable to be a bully if it means getting what you want."

I shook my head. "Whatever happened to playing for fun?"

"Don't get me wrong," Royce said. "I think a little competition is healthy, but this guy was out of control."

"So we've heard," Payton said. "Seems he was verbally abusive."

"It was sickening the way he behaved," Royce said. "His goalie failed to block a shot and he went ballistic. The girl's father stormed out of the bleachers and they really got into it. Took a couple of the other fathers to break it up."

"I'll tell you, if someone treated my daughter like that"—Payton waved his finger and shook his head—"I'd have gone after the bastard myself. Did he ever go after your daughter?"

Royce unfolded his hands and sat up straight in his chair. "What is this about?"

"His name was Scott Caruso and he was murdered last Friday," Payton said.

"And you think I had something to do with it," Royce said. The kindness I'd seen in his eyes and face when he spoke of his daughter had vanished as he shifted into lawyer mode.

"You're the only link we have between the victims at this time," I said. "And we know Adriana was having an affair with a partner."

"I *told* Carter he was making a mistake from day one," Royce said.

"Yet you didn't bother to tell us when we first spoke," I said. "Why? Maybe because he wasn't the only partner sleeping with her?"

"I've never cheated on my wife," he said. "And to my knowledge, Tim was never involved with her either."

"Where were you the past two Friday afternoons?" Payton asked.

"I had court last week. Judge Garrity." Royce checked his calendar. "The week before, we were taking a deposition. My assistant can give you the court reporter's contact information."

I nodded. "Mrs. Caruso told us that after the match with your daughter's school, her husband got into an altercation with a man wearing a baseball cap. Did you see anything?"

Royce thought for a moment and his eyes widened. "Actually I did. We were walking to the car and passed them in the parking lot."

"Do you know what it was about?" I asked.

"The other guy told Caruso he should be ashamed of himself," Royce said. "I assumed it was over his behavior as coach. He also said someday Caruso would get what he deserved."

"Did you get a look at the guy's face?" Payton asked.

Royce nodded. "Caruso had his back to me so I looked right at the guy as we passed. He was white and smaller than Caruso—maybe six feet and one sixty. With the hat, I couldn't see his hair, but the hat was black and had a red logo. And I think he was wearing glasses."

"That's very good," Payton said.

Royce shrugged it off. "You spend years asking clients and witnesses to give a detailed description in court, you pick up a few things."

I asked if he'd be willing to sit with a sketch artist and he agreed to come in later that morning. On the way out, Royce's assistant provided the name and number of the court reporter, and I called her and Judge Garrity's court services officer to verify both of Royce's alibis as we drove back to the station.

We entered through the side door but heard a commotion down the hall, so we kept walking to the lobby and found it crammed with people. Some sat muttering to themselves. Others milled around, unable to sit still as they fought to keep it together until their next fix.

"Wellington's reward must've kicked in," Payton said.

"No shit!" Sergeant Porter said. "Half of these people are nuts and the other half belong in rehab. County is sending over a van, but I've got to admit some of them have been damned entertaining. One guy claimed he's a hit man hired to take out your vics. Of course he also swore he whacked Hoffa. Claims he dumped Jimmy off the back of a speed boat into Lake Wellington with cinder blocks tied to his ankles."

Someone sniffled behind us and we turned to face a scrawny guy in his twenties with sunken eyes and track marks up his arm. "I uh...I have information about that Caruso guy," he said. "He was killed because he was part of a plot to blow up the Bermuda Triangle."

I looked at Porter. He shook his head once, warning me not to encourage the guy, but I asked anyway. "How...why would someone blow up the Bermuda Triangle?"

The addict looked at me as if I were the one with mental health issues. "Not that Bermuda Triangle. Our Bermuda Triangle."

A half mile south of our location at the corner of Columbus and Madison Street, City Hall, the County Building, and Liberty Center, housing the federal offices, all converged to earn the nickname.

He smiled and winked. "I thought that would get your attention." He scratched his arm and sniffled some more. "So do I get the reward?"

Porter pointed to a uniform standing outside the conference room off the lobby. "See that officer over there? He'll help you out." He watched the addict shuffle over to the uni and then he looked at me. "Why the hell did you ask?"

I shrugged. "Curiosity comes with the job."

Payton patted the counter. "Have fun, Sarge."

"Right," Porter growled.

Payton and I wove our way back through the confessors but before we reached the elevators, someone grabbed my arm. As a reflex, my hand shot to my gun as I spun around. Judging by the sleek black suit and briefcase, I pegged the guy as a lawyer, tired of waiting for assistance. I let my hand drop to my side and asked how we could help.

"Actually, I'm here to help you, Detectives," he said. "I know you're trying to find the individual responsible for these horrible stabbings."

"You have some information about the Ortiz and Caruso murders," Payton said.

"I do, and I was going to call but decided it was probably safer to talk in person." He pushed his rimless glasses back up his nose. "You need to check with the CIA."

So maybe the guy was a lawyer who'd suffered a psychotic break. I looked at my partner and he dropped his head to hide his smile from the man. I looked back at the man. "You think the CIA is involved in these murders?"

He nodded once. "Absolutely. And if you don't believe me, check the chips."

Payton turned his head like he was looking over his shoulder and whispered, "Probably found a potato chip with our killer's face."

I cleared my throat to mask my laugh. "Chips?" I said.

The man pointed to a mole on the back of his neck. "See this? It's a microchip. Big Brother is always watching."

"Uh-huh." I motioned to the chairs. "Why don't you have a seat and someone will be with you shortly." He thanked me and walked away. "As if we don't have enough real work," I said to Payton.

"We should get Wellington down here to deal with these fruit loops," Payton said.

"You're right." I walked right past the stairway door.

"Where are you going?' Payton asked.

"Pay a visit to Wellington International."

"Why?"

I paused and turned. "Because I want to rip him a new one for offering a reward."

Payton shook his head. "Bad idea."

I shrugged. "I'll go myself."

"Even worse." He trotted to catch up with me. "You know sometimes you can be a real pain in the ass."

"Sticks and stones," I said as I pushed through the door.

—— CHAPTER 22 ——

Riverview Tower is Bedford's newest high-rise, with thirty-one floors of sparkling steel and blue-green glass. Shops and restaurants circle the ground-level atrium, offices occupy floors two through twenty-one, and luxury apartments and condos fill the top ten floors. The doors on our glass elevator parted on the twenty-first floor, and we stepped into a dimly lit hall accented with rich, dark wood. "Wellington International" was scrolled in gold across double-glass doors.

The name and logo were repeated on the wall behind an efficient-looking brunette, who smiled warmly and asked how she could help.

"We're here to see Mr. Wellington," I said.

"Of course," she said with another smile. "May I have your names please?" I held up my shield and she pointed toward the northeast corner of the building without saying a word.

We moved through a sea of gray cubicles filled with earnest young professionals talking on phones and clicking away on computers. More glass doors opened into a waiting area designed to serve as a buffer between the peons and Wellington's inner sanctum. Another young woman—this one with auburn hair and small oval glasses with green frames—occupied the desk outside the executive suite. She must have gotten a heads-up from the receptionist because she sprang to her feet the moment we appeared in the doorway.

"You can't just barge in there!" She scrambled to block the door, but she was wearing leather pumps with an excessively high heel—not very appropriate for the workplace. I won the race and flung the door open.

Lee Wellington rose from one of two black leather chairs facing the door.

"I'm sorry, Mr. Wellington," she gushed.

"Don't hold it against her," I said. "She tried to stop us."

"It's all right, Barbara," Wellington assured her. He turned to the two younger men seated on the black leather couch. "We have to reschedule."

They nodded in unison and started gathering their papers and portfolios. While they wrapped up, Payton and I walked over to admire the view through the floor-to-ceiling windows.

I'd been fortunate to travel to twenty-three states so far in my life, but I still hadn't found a place I liked better than Bedford. It offers the hustle and bustle of city life yet we can escape to Paradise Mountain on the west side of Lake Wellington in thirty minutes or less.

"About fifteen years ago," I said, "this area was a wasteland of dilapidated factories left behind when the manufacturers filed bankruptcy or relocated for cheaper labor. Then some developer bought all the land along the Chestnut River, and a few years later, the Riverview district was born. I remember seeing an ad when they started taking bids for the condos in this building. Studio units started at half a million."

"And they don't even have a yard," Payton said with a shake of his head. "Guess that's the price you pay to be within walking distance of all those restaurants, clubs, and shopping."

"Don't forget the ice rink or the twelve-screen movie theater."

"How could I?" He laughed and moved on to survey the bookshelves along the length of the east wall while I continued to admire the view. "Why does Phoenix sound familiar?" he asked. "And I know it's not because it's the capital of Arizona."

I walked over to check out the photo of Wellington and several other men standing at the stern of a yacht. "The mythical bird that rose from the ashes," I said.

Wellington and his underlings talked in hushed tones for a moment longer before the men cast wary glances our way and left. Wellington closed the door and walked over to join us. Apparently the suit he'd worn at the press conference was only for the cameras because today he wore navy Dockers and a pale yellow oxford shirt with the sleeves rolled up and no tie.

"What were you thinking, offering a reward?" I asked.

Wellington smiled as if he were surprised we had to ask. "There's a cold-blooded killer poking holes in the good citizens of Bedford and I want him off the streets."

"Then stay the hell out of our case! Thanks to your grandstanding, officers are wasting valuable time talking to people who have nothing to contribute to the investigation. You could've at least given us a heads-up."

"I know the Patriot Act blasted civil liberties back to the Stone Age," he said, "but I'm not aware of a clause requiring private citizens to clear their decisions through the police."

"Monetary offers drive every nut job from miles around to confess," I said more calmly.

Wellington eased his head slightly in my direction, as if he hadn't quite heard me. "By nut job, would you be referring to the mentally challenged?"

I groaned in exasperation. "Like every other cop in this city, my partner and I are overworked and underpaid. We don't have time to be politically correct."

Wellington scoffed. "That's a convenient excuse."

"Look," I said, "we—"

"You raced in the Mackinac," Payton cut in.

My jaw dropped. What the hell was he thinking, derailing the conversation with something so stupid? I swung my head toward him and found him admiring a small gold trophy.

"You're quite a sailor," he added.

Wellington laughed. "Not really." He walked over and stood next to Payton. "A friend owns the sailboat and I'm afraid I was more of a hindrance than a help. The weather really kicked up and it got pretty dicey for a few hours."

"Bet that got the adrenaline flowing."

"Excuse me!" I said and they both looked at me. "I know you're accustomed to getting everything you want, Mr. Wellington, and you may think we're sitting around with our thumbs up our asses, but just because we didn't notify you doesn't mean we don't have leads."

"Really?" Wellington crossed his arms. "That's not what I heard."

"Heard from whom?" Payton asked.

"His honor." I pointed at the credenza behind Wellington's desk where he displayed a photo of himself with Mayor Foley. They were both wearing hard hats and holding shovels at some groundbreaking ceremony.

"I did what I felt needed to be done," Wellington said, "and I won't apologize."

"For the record, where were you Friday afternoon?" I asked.

"In a meeting," he said. "The metro editor for the *Bedford Tribune* is a friend, so when a reporter called in the story, the editor called my assistant and she texted me." He motioned to the door. "Now if you'll excuse me, I'm due at the airport."

Payton started for the door, but I walked over and stopped about a foot away from Wellington. He didn't step back but he lowered his arms to his sides and narrowed his eyes slightly. "You're excused, Mr. Wellington. This time. Stick your nose in our case again, and we're going to have a problem." I held his gaze for a moment before I turned and followed my partner out.

We silently waited for one of the four glass elevators. They may look pretty, but they move like they're being raised and lowered by hand, and I punched the DOWN button again.

"You do know pressing it multiple times won't make it move any faster," Payton said.

I glared at him and he cut his eyes to the door and started to whistle under his breath. I looked up at the floor indicator as 17 lit up.

"Erin's got a soccer match and we're going out for pizza after," Payton said. "Why don't you come?"

"I'd like to, but I'm having dinner with Dave's parents. We're going to work on the acknowledgments so..." The elevator chimed and we got on. "I'll take a rain check if that's okay."

"Anytime." He reached over, pressed the Lobby button and we rode down in silence.

I rang my in-laws' doorbell an hour later and Ken and Carol Lukas greeted me with big hugs. They could easily pass for early fifties, though they'd both turn sixty-two this year. Dave had inherited his eyes and wavy dark hair—minus the gray—from his dad. And I recognized Dave's dimple in Carol's right cheek whenever she smiled.

Though none of us acknowledged it, the empty chair across the table from me loomed over us like a thundercloud as we discussed current events, the weather, and every other benign topic we could think of while we ate.

I'd been the one to deliver the worst news they'd receive in their lives. I insisted Pritchard take me straight to their house from the bank because I couldn't allow them to hear about what happened to their only child on the news, and the devastated expressions on their faces would probably haunt me until the day I died. I needed to know they were coping, but I didn't want to spoil our appetites, so I waited until we'd cleared the dishes and settled in with our coffee and dessert before I asked how they were dealing with everything.

They exchanged uneasy glances and Ken drained what was left of his Scotch.

Carol refolded her napkin and brushed some crumbs from the table before she said, "Sometimes I get so angry that all I want to do is scream at the top of my lungs and hit something as hard as I can."

I nodded in empathy. Though it bucked the stereotype, I loved my mother-in-law and wished I could ease her pain. And then I realized maybe I could. Like I'd done with Rachel Caruso, I slipped a Victims' Services card out of my wallet and handed it to Carol. "These are very good people who do exceptional work. They can set you up with a group or private counselor if you prefer."

Carol fingered the card. "Have you gone to see anyone?"

"Not specifically to talk about what happened to Dave, but it came up during my trauma debriefing after I got shot." Shock flooded their faces and I gave myself a mental head slap for spilling the beans. Then I briefly explained what happened with Rivera and assured them I was fine.

"You look tired," Carol said.

I sighed. "Dealing with a big law firm and Paragon Insurance is enough to suck the energy from anyone."

"What does Paragon have to do with it?" Ken asked.

"Second victim worked there. His boss is a schmuck who's dragging his feet on turning over the complaints and any threats our victim received."

"I know a guy pretty high up at Paragon," Ken said. "We went to college together. His name's Ross Danner and I could—" He stopped when I pursed my lips. "Don't tell me. Ross is the schmuck."

I nodded.

"If it'll help you out, I can call him," Ken said.

Maybe a friendly request from an old buddy is just what Payton and I needed to grease Paragon's wheels and…what am I thinking? I shook my head. "Thanks, Ken, but it's not necessary."

"It's no trouble," he said. "It's just a phone call."

"Really, I appreciate the offer but you can't get involved." I wasn't convinced he'd listen, but the only way I could be sure he wouldn't call Danner would be to lock him up, and that wasn't an option, so I let it drop and drank some coffee.

"It's getting late," Carol said. "We should probably get started."

She got up to collect a stack of mail from the buffet and reluctantly, we started to go through the sympathy cards and letters. I recognized some of the names on the return addresses as people Dave worked with, including the CEO of the bank.

"Oh my." Carol put her hand to her chest as she gazed at the letter in her hand. "This is a hand-written letter from Ridley Wellington."

My stomach twisted with a twinge of guilt over my earlier behavior in his office.

"I'm not surprised he'd take time to write," Ken said. "He was on the bank's board."

"Still," Carol said. "He's one of the wealthiest men in Bedford, and for him to take the time to write a personal note." Her forehead pinched as she fought back tears. She folded the letter, slipped it into the envelope, and set it aside. She thumbed through several other envelopes but set them aside too. She put her left hand to her mouth and shook her head. I reached across the table and put my hand over hers. She sniffled and asked, "Do you think they'll ever catch him?"

Ken looked at me too.

I desperately wanted to respond with an enthusiastic *Absolutely!* yet I knew many suspects managed to elude authorities by disappearing to parts unknown. I couldn't lie, but I had to give them hope, so I looked them in the eyes and said, "Someone attacks a cop's family and it's like attacking the cop. As far as Detectives Donovan and Garcia are concerned, Dave was family and...ahem...they won't stop until they get him."

Carol reached out and took both of my hands in hers. "We don't want you to put yourself in any danger trying to find him. Do you understand?"

"My captain ordered me to steer clear so..." I caught their exchange of doubtful glances. "What?"

"We've known you for eight years, Val," Ken said. "We've seen the passion you have for your job when you don't even know the victim."

I shifted my eyes from Ken to Carol and wondered who'd have a bigger meltdown over my trips to Tombstone. My in-laws or Morgan? I decided it would be better for everyone—especially me—to never find out. I crossed my fingers under the table and said, "I don't want to do anything to jeopardize the case." Then I dug my fork into my dessert, but even Carol's decadent chocolate cake lacked the power to force visions of bullet holes and puncture wounds from my head.

— CHAPTER 23 —

I was at my desk Wednesday morning, studying the sketch of the guy Edward Royce saw at the soccer field, when my freakishly calm partner blew into the squad room like a tropical storm. "Everything okay?" I asked.

"The day you're running late is the day your kids will decide to have a food fight," he said. He sat down and took his frustration out on his keyboard. "How was dinner?"

"A little intense. A little awkward. Hardest thing was discussing the fact Noonan is still out there."

"I'm sure."

"Royce came in like he said he would." I held up the sketch. "Guy looks like a young Jim Carrey."

Payton studied it for a moment, angling his head left and then right as he tried to see the resemblance. "No, he doesn't."

"Sure, he does." I pointed at my eyes with my index and middle fingers. "It's the wigged out eyes."

Porter walked in and handed me a legal-size envelope. "Came by courier," he said before continuing on his rounds.

Payton asked who sent it. I glanced at the return label and saw Paragon Insurance, and I couldn't help wondering if Ken had listened to me.

"What was that?" Payton asked.

"What was what?"

"You got a weird look on your face when you read the label."

"No, I didn't."

"Yeah, you did."

I unzipped the seal. "It's no big deal, okay. At dinner, Ken mentioned he knew Ross Danner from college and he offered to call him to move things along."

Payton edged his head forward a bit. "You told him not to, right?"

"Of course I did."

"And yet the package arrives by courier this morning."

"Coincidence. I was at their house last night so he didn't have time to make the call. Besides, what difference would it make if he did? We've got a killer to catch and these files could hold a major lead." I removed a two-inch stack of photocopies and tossed the envelope in the garbage can under my desk. I looked over and saw the astonishment on Payton's face. "What?"

"It's just that after what you told me about using your maiden name to keep work separate, I can't believe you'd condone your family's involvement in a case."

"Making a phone call would hardly count as involvement," I said.

Payton flashed a *Whatever* look.

"Fine." I raised my hands in concession. "I'm corrupt. Report me because I considered taking advantage of a personal relationship. I don't care because I want this guy, Greg!"

"Clearly." He looked at me the same way I'd seen him look at suspects while he considered the validity of their stories.

"Now what?"

He studied me a bit longer. "I'm just wondering what else you're willing to do."

"Don't worry, okay? My first day on the street, the second thing my training officer told me was—and I quote—'leave your personal shit in your locker' so…"

Payton frowned. "Easier said than done."

Don't I know it?

"You trained with Frank Shannon, right?"

"Uh-huh."

"What was the first thing he told you?"

In the gruffest voice I could muster I said, "I take my coffee black."

"Not even a hello?"

"Not even eye contact. I walked up and extended my hand as I introduced myself, and he ignored my hand, put on his hat, and said, 'I take my coffee black.'"

"You do a pretty good Shannon," Payton said.

"Don't tell *him* that. What was the first nugget of wisdom your training officer gave you?"

Payton thought for a moment. "Whatever you do, rookie, just don't shoot me."

"That's terrible!"

"Yeah, well, I sort of had it coming." He rubbed his finger across his chin. "I accidentally discharged my weapon in the locker room when I was getting dressed." I winced and he smiled sheepishly.

Morgan arrived, and as she passed by our desks, she said, "My office."

Now what?

We followed her and stood before her desk. She dropped her purse in her bottom drawer and settled in her chair. "The commissioner got a call from Carter Smithfield, who was calling on behalf of his client, Edward Royce."

"The lawyer's lawyer," I said. "How redundant."

"First it was Smithfield and now it's Royce." Morgan looked at Payton and then at me. "When are you planning to harass partner number three?"

Payton cleared his throat.

"You do know who partner number three is, don't you?" Morgan asked.

"Timothy Foley," I said.

"And you know who Timothy Foley is."

"Partner number three," I said. Payton cleared his throat again and I looked at him. "I've got some cough drops in my desk that'll clear that right up." He shook his head slightly, warning me to be quiet, and I looked back at the captain.

"You're stepping on some pretty big toes," Morgan said.

I shrugged. "I can't speak for my partner, but I've never been much of a dancer. And it might interest the commissioner to know our pursuit of all leads is what gave us this." I held up the sketch of Baseball Cap Guy.

"He looks like Jim Carrey," Morgan said.

I stifled a laugh when Payton dropped his head in defeat.

"Edward Royce was the only one who paid enough attention to be able to provide this description," I said. "And not for nothing, but if the commissioner has nothing better to do than chat with the mayor about this case, we can always use more feet on the street."

Morgan's left eye twitched slightly. I looked at Payton. He was looking at me with his eyes all scrunched and his mouth twisted up as if he were examining an abstract work of art.

I shrugged my hands. "What? I'm just saying. And what is it with the mayor and this case anyway? No disrespect to a victim, but why does Ortiz matter to Foley? It's not like she was a major contributor to his war chest, so why does he care?" Another thought occurred to me and I held up my index finger. "Or maybe the better question is, why is Smithfield calling the mayor to lean on the commissioner when Ortiz didn't even work at the firm anymore?"

"Maybe they never ended their affair," Morgan said. "Or maybe the relationship meant a lot more to him than he let on."

"Unless it's not about Ortiz," I said. "Maybe it's the firm he's worried about. Maybe he's hoping we close the case before something comes out to damage the firm's reputation."

"Or the mayor's," Payton said.

"Sounds like you have some new avenues to pursue," Morgan said. "Get me copies of the sketch and we'll give them to some unis to do another canvass."

"Yes, ma'am," I said.

We provided Morgan with the copies and settled at our desks and spent the next two hours reading Caruso's mail.

"I don't know how much longer I can sit here and read this." I rolled my neck to try to loosen a kink. "I need a gallon of eye drops."

"There can't be many more," Payton said. He put another letter aside and started to read the next. He sat up a little straighter. "Hey."

"You got one?"

"Dated two months ago from a guy named Mark Filipiak," Payton said. "He wrote, 'Dear Mr. Caruso. How can you sleep at night? Paragon Insurance claims to provide the very best in health care coverage, but the only thing you give a damn about is your bottom line. You never had a problem taking our premiums, but when we needed help, you left us hanging. I'd be careful, Mr. Caruso, because life has a way of throwing you curves and karma can be a bitch.'" He looked at me. "Is it possible we finally have a suspect?"

"Perish the thought." I typed the name into our database. "If we solve the case, the mayor, the commissioner and Moraz won't have anything to do." The search results popped up. "Filipiak is thirty-nine and his only prior contact with law enforcement has come in the form of a few speeding tickets."

"You know what they say about the quiet ones," Payton said.

We clipped our guns on our hips and rushed out of the squad room.

— CHAPTER 24 —

Mark Filipiak's graying temples and the worry lines carved in his face made him look more like fifty than thirty-nine. He shuffled across the floor of his apartment on Thirty-Third Avenue and settled heavily into a threadbare recliner before he motioned for us to sit on the equally worn couch.

Payton sat and then hunched over to examine a picture on the end table. "Is this you outside Bedford Ice?"

Filipiak looked at him. "Yeah. My great-grandfather worked there for thirty years when he came to America. My grandpa took me there once."

Payton nodded. "What do you do for a living, Mr. Filipiak?"

"I'm a network engineer at Arvel Foods." He shifted his eyes between us. "Somebody hack our system or something?"

"Probably," I said, "but we're here regarding the letter you sent to Paragon Insurance."

"Bedford PD in the habit of reading other people's mail?" Filipiak removed a pack of cigarettes from the torn pocket of his washed-out T-shirt. "I had Paragon insurance for ten years when Anna, my wife, was diagnosed with a rare blood disorder. The only treatment was considered experimental so Paragon refused to pay a dime." He tapped a cigarette out of the pack.

"Did you know Scott Caruso?" I asked.

His eyes flared. "He's the bastard who signed the form letter denying our appeal. We were forced to take out a second mortgage, and we drained our savings trying to cover the treatments. Eventually, we lost our home. Then I lost Anna." He sighed deeply, resigned to his fate. "But, hey. We certainly weren't the only ones victimized by Paragon or any of the other carriers." He struck a match and his hand trembled slightly as he held it to the cigarette. He shook out the match and tossed it into an ashtray on the table next to his chair. "I've been quitting since my wife died." He smiled wryly.

"We're very sorry, Mr. Filipiak," I said.

He took a long drag and held the smoke in for a moment before blowing it out through his nose. "God help you if you have the misfortune to be stricken by a serious illness but I guess I should've been grateful to have coverage at all. A buddy of mine lost his job and he couldn't even get new coverage because he was unemployed." He snickered. "What the hell difference should it make if someone has a job or not as long as they pay their premium? They're going to cancel the policy if you miss one payment anyway, so they've got nothing to lose." He took another drag and shrugged his brows. "In the end, none of it matters because even if you have insurance, someone like Caruso is going to look for every possible loophole to avoid paying your benefits."

"You're right." I nodded in agreement. "It's all about the bottom line."

Filipiak spun his wedding band with his left thumb. "Look, I admit I've been having a difficult time dealing with my grief. I wrote that letter when I got home from Anna's funeral. If I would've put it aside for a day or two, I probably wouldn't have sent it."

I brought Ortiz's photo up on my phone and held it up to Filipiak. "Do you recognize her?"

He looked at the screen. "Yeah. She's a lawyer at Legal Aid. I met with her to see if I had grounds to sue Paragon, but she said the policy clearly indicated experimental treatment was not covered so we didn't have a case."

Bingo. We could tie him to both victims. I slipped the photo into my pocket and asked, "Where were you the past two Fridays between 3:00 and 5:00 PM?"

He took a long drag. "Look, I saw the news stories about both of them. Am I a suspect?"

"We're pursuing all possible leads," I said. "Did you ever confront Caruso personally?"

Filipiak shook his head.

"Would you mind if we have a look around?"

"Be my guest," he said. "I've got nothing to hide."

We searched the apartment but didn't find an ice pick or a stun gun, which didn't mean he was innocent because he may have disposed of them or hidden them somewhere else. When we finished, we found Filipiak sitting in his chair, smoking yet another cigarette.

"You have a storage locker?" Payton asked.

"What you see here is all I've got left," Filipiak said.

"I'm sorry," I said, "but where did you say you were between three and five the past two Fridays?"

He exhaled a mouthful of smoke. "I didn't say, but I was at work." He snuffed out the cigarette and we thanked him for his cooperation and left.

The high temperatures and low winds we'd been having had created a cap of smog over the city, yet the air outside Filipiak's place still smelled cleaner than the air inside. "I think his second-hand smoke took ten years off our lives," I said.

"How about it," Payton said. He unlocked the car and we crawled in. He cranked the engine and immediately lowered the windows.

I sipped from a warm bottle of water. "In Filipiak's eyes, Caruso and Paragon were responsible for his wife's death. Then Ortiz comes along and disappoints him again when he wanted to sue and she told him he didn't have a case, so we've got motive for both. And even though we didn't find it, I'll bet he kept an ice pick from his great-grandfather, which gives us means. Now all we need is for none of his coworkers to corroborate his alibi and we'll have opportunity too."

Payton twisted the cap on his bottle. "Forensics or witnesses would be good."

"One step at a time, partner." It seemed to be the tagline for my life these days. I held my arm out with my index finger extended. "Onward to Arvel Foods."

Payton glanced at me sideways. "Onward?"

I waved a dismissive hand. "Just go."

He chuckled as he eased the cruiser into traffic.

I felt more energized than I had in days as we drove to Arvel Foods, which has its corporate headquarters by Lincoln International

Airport. Unfortunately, what goes up must come down, and my good spirits dropped like a rock after we talked to six of Filipiak's coworkers and his supervisor. They all recalled seeing Filipiak at various times throughout the afternoon and early evening on the days Ortiz and Caruso were killed.

We got stopped for a train on Mason Street on the way back to the station, and I noticed Payton massaging his temples and doing neck exercises. "Your energy level seems to be lacking today, partner. Is everything okay?"

He finished a stretch and said, "We had a bit of an issue with Matthew last night. He told us he was going to his buddy's house and he'd be home by eight. When he didn't come home, Pam called and the buddy's mother tells Pam she hadn't seen Matthew at all yesterday. Turned out he was at the park by his school. I swear, the older he's getting, the more I think we should just implant a GPS chip in his butt."

"I think that's only allowed for pets," I said.

"I don't mind setting a precedence."

"The ACLU might."

"Matthew can't afford a lawyer," Payton said.

I thought about the guy in the lobby of the station who I mistook for a lawyer the day Wellington announced his reward. The one who rambled on about microchips. "Big Brother is always watching," I said.

Payton frowned. "Are you getting paranoid on me?"

"No," I said. "That asylum escapee who accosted us about Wellington's reward. Remember he said something about how Big Brother is implanting microchips in people."

Payton shook his head. "Pam would never let—"

I waved him off. "Not your kids. The killer. Maybe that's how he knew our vics were home."

Payton snorted. "You think he implanted microchips into our vics?"

"No! Not chips, but GPS. What is it?" I snapped my fingers as I searched my non-techie brain for the term. "Umm…tagging! Geotagging or whatever. Maybe the killer tracked our vics through their tweets or calls."

Payton fished his phone out of his pocket. "I'll get Cassidy to check it out."

I watched the box and tank cars roll by until my phone vibrated and I stupidly answered without looking at the caller ID.

"You coming here or am I coming there?" Connie asked.

Wednesday night pizza and DVDs.

"Let me guess. You can't make it."

I could hear the disappointment in her voice. "I'm sorry, Connie, but we finally got a decent lead on this case and—"

She sighed into the phone. "Fine. But next week for sure. I'll talk to you later."

A twinge of guilt rippled below my diaphragm as I stuffed the phone into my pocket.

"Avoiding your best friend," Payton said.

I kept my eyes on the train. He was right, but our weekly get-together would be a live-action reminder of the worst day of my life, and I hated the idea of admitting that to Connie even more than I hated lying to her because I didn't want to talk about it and that's *all* she'd want to do.

— CHAPTER 25 —

Payton and I were at our desks with large cups of our favorite beverages, mulling our small number of leads. We had no link between the victims and we were running out of people to talk to and places to look. We needed something to jumpstart the investigation, and I nearly drooled coffee and had to gulp it down when Colin Cassidy walked into the squad room Thursday morning to deliver the shot of momentum we needed.

"Cassidy?" I said. "I thought the force field in TRU was so strong you couldn't pull away from your computer."

"There's something you need to see." He pointed at Payton's monitor. "May I?"

Payton stood up and motioned *Be my guest* to him.

"I might have a name for Baseball Cap Guy," Cassidy said as he typed. "I was researching your victims like you asked—social media pages and such to see what's out there. I haven't found evidence yet that the killer tracked your victims' movements, and I didn't find anything on Ortiz, but Scott Caruso's name came up on a blog called Anticorp dot com." He pointed at the screen. "Check it out."

Fragments of a graphic gelled to form a cartoon sketch of white men—wearing suits with "Big Business" lapel pins and holding clubs—towering over a diverse group of people collectively labeled as "The Little Guys." The caption beneath the cartoon read, "This blog is dedicated to the fight against the tyranny of Corporate America. We must prevail."

"You've got to be kidding," Payton said.

"Under worst offenders, there are links to articles about a bunch of companies," Cassidy told us. "The articles detail everything from failing to recall defective products to toxic dumping."

"Are they legit?" Payton asked.

"A lot of the articles are reprints from mainstream newspapers and magazines," Cassidy said. "Someone named Allister does the posts, and from what I've read so far, he publicizes misdeeds he uncovers through his own unofficial investigations. There are anonymous interviews with whistleblowers. That sort of thing."

"So this Allister is some sort of watchdog," I said.

Cassidy nodded as he scrolled through the page. "There was a post the day after Caruso's murder. Listen to this. 'Did you hear about Scott Caruso, that insurance exec who was murdered? The papers are making it out to be a tragedy, but Caruso got a nice fat bonus every time he hit a claim denial quota, while the people who depended on Paragon got a death sentence. Seems as though Caruso finally got what he deserved.'"

"That's what Edward Royce overheard Baseball Cap Guy tell Caruso," Payton said.

I studied the screen. A black banner ran along the top of the page. Centered in the banner was a skyscraper emblazoned with "INC." inside a circle with a red line through it. I pointed at the logo. "A black hat with a red logo."

"You're right," Payton said. "You have an address for this guy, Cassidy?"

"Not yet. His profile is hidden but I'm working on it. I did run the name through the database and found three people in Bedford with Allister as a first or last name."

"Allister sounds British," Garcia called out from his desk.

"Maybe the butler really did it this time," Donovan added.

They laughed and reached across their desks to exchange high-fives.

Cassidy flashed more of a grimace than a smile as he handed the list to me. "In case Allister is not the blogger's real name, I also searched an origin of names website. Allister is a form of Alastair and it means avenger."

"Uma Thurman," Garcia said.

"Diana Rigg," I countered.

Payton gave me a nod of approval. "A traditionalist. I like it."

Donovan snapped his fingers. "The babe with the leather jumpsuits."

I squinted at him. "Why am I not surprised you remember *that*?"

He chuckled. "I'd wear a bowler hat any day to hang out with her."

I had the urge to count to ten. "Ignore him," I told Cassidy. "We certainly try to."

"So someone wronged this guy and now he's getting even," Payton said.

"The name is probably an alias," Cassidy said, "but I'll let you know the second I crack the profile."

"Fantastic job!" I called after him as he disappeared into the hallway.

We couldn't do anything more with the blogger angle until Cassidy got an ID, so we requested background on the Allisters living in the area and then headed out to talk to more of the Paragon policyholders who were angry enough to file complaints. The names changed but the stories didn't, and every one broke my heart.

We were silent as I waited for a break in traffic to exit from the Wellington University parking garage. We'd just spoken to a fifty-eight-year-old cafeteria worker who'd recently lost her husband of thirty-eight years after a yearlong battle with lymphoma. The husband had been laid off from a company where he'd worked for thirty-four years, and Paragon cancelled their policy because of one missed premium payment. She emptied their savings and eventually sold their home to pay for his treatment, forcing her to move in with their daughter.

"Some golden years," Payton said, as if he'd read my mind.

"The next time someone says 'how do you put a price on a human life?' I'm going to tell them to call an insurance company," I said.

Payton reached into his pocket, pulled out his phone, and answered it. He listened for a moment before telling the caller, "That's great! Good work!" He ended the call and reached over and flipped on the lights and siren.

My pulse quickened. "What's up?"

"That was Cassidy," he said. "Allister is online and the signal is coming from a Mugga Java near the convention center."

I burned a little rubber as I swung out of the driveway and sped down Garfield Street, but I had to jam on the brakes for a delivery truck double-parked to unload in front of a campus bar called Spring Break. I jockeyed around the truck and picked up speed, weaving and dodging through the eastbound traffic. We caught a red light at Lexington but I slowed before the intersection, hit the horn, and hung a left.

Payton swayed in his seat and braced his hand against the dashboard. "Take it easy, huh."

I sped north and Payton turned off the siren after we passed the convention center so we wouldn't alert Allister to our arrival at the strip mall on Kennedy Boulevard.

All Mugga Java locations offer free wireless, and this shop was sandwiched between an investment firm and a one-hour dry cleaner. We entered the building and looked around. Five caffeine cravers waited in line for their afternoon fix, with seven others scattered among the tables. None wore a baseball cap. I turned and headed for the counter.

"Line starts back there, bitch!" a woman called out.

I did an about-face.

Deep purple highlights streaked through the young woman's jet-black hair, a stud pierced her left eyebrow, and her lipstick matched her hair. She jerked her thumb over her shoulder.

I stepped into her personal space and stuck my shield in front of her face. "How about I use the pin on this to pierce your right brow, *honey!*"

Her eyes darted around a bit before she pretended to examine her black nail polish.

I turned, walked up to the counter, and held up the sketch. "Do you know this guy?" I asked the barista of the day, a kid named "Rob" according to his nametag. "He was just here. He was probably wearing a black baseball cap and would've been on a laptop or tablet."

Rob looked at me like he thought I was an idiot. "You're kidding, right? I was too busy mopping up the mess some...*customer* made because we got her order wrong."

"Do you have security cameras?"

"You gotta talk to the manager." He looked past me to the guy at the front of the line.

"Are you going to get him or should I just go on back there?" I asked.

"Sean!" Rob yelled.

Another kid came through the swinging door and shuffled up to the counter. "Can I help you?" His tone implied he didn't care if he could or not. I identified myself and asked for the security video. He told me he had to call the regional office but he didn't move.

I flung my open hand toward the phone on the wall. "You need us to look up that number for you?"

He sighed deeply before he shuffled over to the phone.

I bobbed my head and looked at Payton. "And they say customer service is dead."

"You might want to switch to herbal tea," he said.

"Why?"

His forehead twitched and he let out a little laugh, as if he couldn't believe I had to ask. "For starters, how about your Nascar drive over here? And now you're offering to poke holes in potential witnesses." He shook his head. "Not the way to foster a sense of cooperation."

"Excuse me for trying to solve the case," I said, "but Rachel Caruso is going through hell and we deserve to know what happened."

Payton cocked his head. "We?"

"She," I corrected myself.

"Freudian slip," he said flatly. He moved closer so he could talk even softer than usual. "I can't imagine what it's like for you on the job right now, but you're wound a little tight. I saw it happen in Iraq—especially after an IED attack."

I let out a slow breath, hoping to keep my voice even. "Why did you become a cop, Greg?"

He shrugged. "I figured I could use what Uncle Sam taught me to help people stateside."

I nodded. "Serve and protect, right? I wanted to try to keep bad things from happening to good people too, but right now I'm not feeling particularly competent so—"

"You don't need to prove anything," he said.

"Maybe not to you."

"You know this is going to take time," he said. "You need to cut yourself some slack."

"You think this killer is going to cut *us* some slack?"

He sighed and said, "Yeah," but it sounded less like agreement and more like a married man experienced at conceding an argument he couldn't win.

Sean, the underage manager, returned to the counter. "Corporate said you can look at the video here, but if you need to take it, you'll need a subpoena."

I motioned toward the back. "Lead the way."

I reviewed the security footage for the hour before we arrived. The cameras covered the door and counter, and while I didn't see anyone resembling the guy in our sketch, I did get to watch a reenactment of Brad Paisley's music video for "Celebrity" with a woman playing Jason Alexander's cameo role. She sipped from her cup, puckered her face, and poured the contents of the cup onto the counter in front of the barista who'd failed to meet her standards. What a bitch. I stopped watching when I spotted the two of us entering the store, and I rejoined Payton out front.

"Talked to everyone here," he said. "No one noticed our suspect." He glanced toward the window. "He could've tapped into the wireless from his car."

"Let's check with the other businesses," I said. "Maybe there's a camera on the lot."

We checked with every other tenant in the strip mall but none recorded the lot, and our adrenaline rush quickly dissipated. What managed to get our blood pumping again—and force Morgan to abandon her mountain of paperwork—was a visit from Cassidy shortly after we returned to the station.

"I've got a name for your blogger," Cassidy said as he snapped the slip of paper in his hand. "Rosaria Maltese."

My jaw dropped. "Allister is a woman?"

Payton snatched the paper from Cassidy and keyed the information into the database. "Nothing in Bedford," he said. He retyped the name and address into the Internet search box and his eyes scanned the results on his screen. His shoulders sagged. "Damn it."

"What?" I tensed at the possibility we'd hit another dead end.

"I found a Rosaria Maltese who died on March 25, 1911," he read from the screen. "At fourteen, she was the youngest of one hundred and forty-six victims killed in the fire at the Triangle Shirtwaist Factory in New York."

"Mostly female immigrants," Morgan said. "I remember reading that a survivor on the sidewalk was killed when she was struck by the body of someone who'd jumped." We all looked at her and she spread her hands. "We studied the case in a class I took once. There were rumors of locked doors and fire code violations, and some survivors claimed the owners offered them a thousand dollars to change their stories before the trial."

"A thousand bucks was a lot of money back then," Payton said.

"Maybe Allister is a relative of Ms. Maltese," Cassidy said.

"More likely, it's symbolic," I said. "Her story is a public and horribly tragic example of what can happen to people in the pursuit of profit."

"Like Anna Filipiak with Paragon Insurance," Payton said. "This guy could be some sort of radical trying to inspire action against corporate greed."

"We've got too much could and maybe," I said. "We need a solid lead."

"Well, we're not going to find it tonight," Payton said.

"I agree," Morgan said. "Good work accessing the profile, Cassidy."

Cassidy beamed like a kid who'd won a trophy as he walked out.

"You too," Morgan said. She pointed at the door. "Go. Get a fresh start in the morning."

"Yes, ma'am," Payton said.

We left a few minutes later, and by the time I backed into the garage I felt spent—both physically and mentally. I also understood how it felt to be a mouse in a maze, darting this way and that, running into one dead end after another and having no clue where to turn next.

For two consecutive weeks we received word of a dead body in a bathtub, and the start of another Friday loomed five hours away. Would 3:29 PM tomorrow bring horrible news from the Bunker of yet another frantic 911 call from a desperate victim?

I could swear I heard the seconds ticking away in my head.

—— CHAPTER 26 ——

Payton beat me to work Friday, and when I sat down, he craned his neck across his desk to get a closer look at me. "You didn't get much sleep…again."

I ignored him and logged on my computer.

"Background came in on the Allisters of Bedford," he said. "We've got a ninety-four-year-old in assisted living and a sixty-nine-year-old retired nanny."

"I think we can rule out Father Time and Mary Poppins. What about number three?"

Payton shook his head. "He had heart surgery last month and he's been in rehab."

"Great. More dead ends, and if the killer follows his pattern we have"—I checked my watch—"seven and a half hours to figure out who he is and find him."

Morgan walked in carrying a cardboard holder with three large cups. She crooked her finger at us and headed toward the whiteboard. Payton and I exchanged *What's going on?* looks and joined her. She motioned to the two empty chairs and waited until we sat before she said, "There's talk of a task force."

I felt as if blood would spurt through the top of my head like Old Faithful and I popped up out of my chair. "Stupidity must be a required skill on the deputy commissioner job description because we're on this, Captain!"

"I know you are," she said.

"What does Moraz think a task force will do that we aren't already doing? Does he want us to invent a suspect just to take the heat off, or would he prefer we catch the guy who is actually guilty?"

"Benchik," Morgan said.

"I hate this. Politics mucks up the case, and pressure to make an arrest lands innocent people in prison." I tossed my hand in the air. "Where does he get off anyway? The only time he's left his office since this whole thing started has been to come here to bust our chops and—"

"Benchik!" Morgan snapped.

"What?" I snapped back. I added "ma'am" when I saw the displeasure on her face.

"I'm not worried about Moraz," she said. "If he thinks for one minute he's going to run my team's cases, he's sadly mistaken."

At that moment, my admiration for Morgan doubled.

She motioned for me to sit and I did. She distributed the cups to Payton and me and then she calmly said, "Let's review what we've got."

"Jack shit," I muttered.

Morgan cocked an admonishing brow at me before she turned to face the board. "It's possible these people were simply in the wrong place at the wrong time and landed on the whack job's radar." She turned to us. "But I doubt it because they did have something in common. Both victims earned a considerable amount of money in professions that are not always highly regarded. And their activities could've directly or indirectly caused harm—or at least great financial loss—to others."

"It's like *Serial Mom*," I said and their eyes locked on me. "It was a black comedy. Kathleen Turner played this perfect wife and mother who went around killing people for lapses in judgment...like wearing white after Labor Day."

They both chuckled and it broke the tension all around.

Morgan sipped some coffee and asked if we were able to link Allister to Ortiz.

Payton shook his head. "There's no mention of her on the blog, but they could've crossed paths if the firm represented one of the companies he targeted."

Morgan studied the board. "He allows the victims to call for help. Why? To increase his own sense of power? Or is it about how it makes *them* feel?"

"Hopeful one moment and desperate the next," I said.

"Coupled with the torture, he's one sadistic SOB," Payton said.

"Or else he's trying to make them feel what he feels," I said.

"You've been operating on the theory he kills them in the bathtub to destroy physical evidence," Morgan said, "but there could be more to it. The cleansing could be symbolic."

"Baptism is purification," Payton said. "He could be washing away their sins."

"Considering what Cassidy found yesterday," Morgan said, "I think you should look into recent criminal negligence cases and—"

Payton's phone rang and he listened to the caller for a moment. "That's great!" He pulled his notepad from his jacket pocket and said, "Okay. Give it to me." He scribbled something down. "Good job, man." He hung up. "Cassidy traced Allister's signal again. This time it's a house."

I sprang up from my chair. "We'll need a warrant and backup."

"I'll take care of it," Morgan said. "Go!"

Ten minutes later, we were parked in the lot of the public library branch across the street from the address Cassidy provided. I'd just checked my watch for probably the tenth time when a brown cruiser parked in the street and Donovan and Garcia got out and walked over.

"Uniforms are on their way with the warrant," Donovan said.

As if on cue, a squad pulled in behind the cruiser, and Officers Willard and Malecki got out and joined us.

"You've seen the sketch?" I asked and both officers nodded. "Okay. You and Donovan cover the back. Let us know when you're in position."

They nodded in unison and trotted along the side of the Cape Cod, with blue trim and shutters, listed to Arthur and Mildred Crenshaw. Payton, Garcia, and I drew our weapons and started for the front. Payton stood to the left of the door, I stood to the right, and Garcia fell in behind my partner. Payton had the radio, and in a few seconds, Donovan's voice crackled "in position" over the air.

"Let's do it," I said and my heart nearly thumped out of my chest as I rang the bell.

"Who is it?" a soft female voice asked through the door.

I responded "Police" and held my shield in the small diamond-shaped window near the top of the door. The deadbolt slid back, the door opened, and a woman in her seventies with bluish gray hair peered out. "Mrs. Crenshaw?" I asked. She stood open-mouthed and nodded. "Step back, ma'am," I said as I entered the house. I gently steered the frail woman into the living room as the guys flooded in behind me and moved quickly across the room.

Mr. Crenshaw rose slowly from a recliner in the corner. He had no hair and only slightly more meat on his bones than his wife. "What's going on?" he demanded.

I held up my hand. "Please stay where you are, sir."

"Don't tell me what to do in my own house!" he shouted. "What the hell is going on?"

I asked if anyone else was in the home and they both said, "No." I heard the guys shout "Clear!" in turn as they moved from room to room. I held up the sketch. "Do you recognize this man?"

Mrs. Crenshaw lifted the glasses dangling from the chain around her neck and she studied the photo. "No," she said. "I don't know him."

I looked at Mr. Crenshaw.

The muscles in his jaw bunched as he shook his head. "I don't know what this is about, but you'd better get the hell out of here!" He raised a bony finger toward the door. "Now!" He started toward the door but his face contorted and he clutched his chest.

"Arthur!" Mildred Crenshaw shrieked as her husband crumpled to the floor. "He has a bad heart!" She hobbled toward him.

"Call a bus!" I shouted, and I gently directed Mrs. Crenshaw out of the way. I kneeled at his side and pressed my fingers to his neck but couldn't feel a pulse. I positioned his head to open his airway, but I didn't see, hear, or feel him breathing, so I blew two rescue breaths into his mouth. When he didn't respond, I began chest compressions. Payton rushed in, dropped to his knees, and took over the breathing.

We'd probably been at it for only five minutes, but we were both sweating and out of breath when the paramedics arrived. We traded places, and they hooked Crenshaw up to the monitors. He was flat-line and they zapped him with the defibrillator. He didn't convert so they zapped him again. This time the line started to pulse on the monitor.

I exhaled and felt a little lightheaded, probably because I'd been holding my breath as I watched the medics work. I rushed out of the house and sucked in some fresh air as I ripped open the straps on my vest. I pulled it off and flung it on the ground.

"What'd it ever do to you except save your life?" Payton said behind me.

I spun to face him, my chest heaving. I stooped over to pick up my vest. "You think there's some connection between Allister and the Crenshaws or did the son of a bitch set us up?"

"Not sure what to think on this case," Payton said.

I walked around in a circle on the grass until I realized my action was a metaphor for the direction of the case and I stopped.

The front door opened, and we watched silently as the medics wheeled Crenshaw out and loaded the stretcher into the ambulance. One medic hopped in back, and the other slammed the door and then helped Mrs. Crenshaw climb into the passenger seat up front before she trotted around and jumped in behind the wheel.

"We set out to apprehend a psychotic killer and all we manage to do is to scare a senior citizen half to death," I shouted over the screech of the siren as the ambulance sped away. I looked at my partner. "Are we good or what?"

— CHAPTER 27 —

We searched the Crenshaws' house but failed to find anything incriminating, so we were fuming by the time we returned to the station and stormed into the Technical Response Unit.

Cassidy threw his palms up to hold back our impending tirade. "I am so sorry you guys." The look on his face reminded me of a puppy that just peed on the floor.

"How the hell could this happen?" I asked.

"Allister must've been pirating the wireless connection," he said. "All he had to do was drive around until he found a signal that wasn't security-protected."

"And it looked like the Crenshaws were online," Payton said.

"You need to keep at this, Colin," I said. "Find out who's behind the screen name."

Cassidy nodded vigorously. "I'm on it."

We left him to mine his megabytes and returned to our own workspace, where I walked straight to the whiteboard.

I crossed my arms, stared at the photos of Ortiz and Caruso, and softly said, "How did he choose you?"

Payton appeared at my side and mimicked my pose. "Detecting by osmosis?"

"Heh. I wish."

"Morgan just heard from the hospital. Mr. Crenshaw is stable."

I sighed with relief. "That's good news."

We studied the board in silence for a bit and I started to get a sick feeling in the pit of my stomach. "He's out there stalking his next victim and we've got nothing."

"Maybe not," Payton said. "Maybe we can find Allister *through* his next victim."

"You have some psychic superpower you never told me about?"

He chuckled. "Matthew would love that but no. What we have is Anticorp dot com."

I tried to figure out how that could possibly help unless Cassidy broke the profile, and then I realized what he was thinking. "Find the ones Allister seems particularly angry with and…"

"We may ID our next vic," he finished my sentence. "It may be tricky to do without alarming them, but we can call and ask if they've seen Baseball Cap Guy—"

"Who we're calling Allister until we know different," I said.

"Right," Payton said. "We ask if they saw him or got the sense they were being followed."

"Let's do it."

We sat down and logged on.

"There must be twenty pages of postings here," Payton said.

"I've got eye drops," I said. My cell buzzed in my pocket and I pulled it out as Connie's number flashed on the screen. "Hey," I said and she asked how I was doing. "I'd be better with a suspect but what's up?"

"I was calling to make sure you're still going to be able to sit for Emily tomorrow."

I closed my eyes. Kevin's cousin's wedding. Connie had asked us to baby-sit a month ago. Dave and I had been looking forward to it as a test-drive for parenthood.

"Val," she said apprehensively.

I kneaded my forehead with my fingers. *I do not want to do this. But Connie and Kevin have been so supportive.* "I'll be there."

She sighed into the phone. "We *really* appreciate this. We have to be in church at three o'clock so we should probably leave by two."

"Okay."

"Thanks again," she gushed. "And if I were you, I'd get a really good night's sleep."

I wish. She ended the call and I stared at my phone. *I'm in deep trouble. Or maybe Emily is the one who's in for it.*

"Be where?" Payton asked.

"Connie's. At the Warrens' Fourth of July cookout, Dave and I agreed to baby-sit."

"It'll be good for you. Emily will be a great diversion."

I forced a smile and we dug in to review page after page of rants. We'd been at it an hour when Payton said, "I don't believe it!"

I perked up. "Got something?"

"Did you know companies are shrinking the package size but charging the same price?"

I smiled. "Pam obviously does the shopping."

He seemed genuinely shocked. "You knew that?"

"You name it, they've shrunk it. Coffee. Ice cream. Chips. They should be required to label the package, 'New smaller size. Same price. To boost our bottom line.'"

"Incredible." Payton checked his watch. "All this talk of food, I'm hungry. What do you want? I'll run out and grab something."

It didn't matter because I'd lost my appetite when I lost Dave and eating had become a necessity rather than a pleasure. "Wherever you go is fine."

"That could be dangerous." He aimed a cautionary finger at me. "I'll be back in fifteen."

We continued to review the website over lunch. Payton polished off a foot-long veggie sub and bag of chips while half of my turkey sub lay on the paper next to my computer.

"This sounds promising," Payton said, eyes riveted to his screen. "'Everyone is so up-in-arms about the homicide rate, but why worry about all those killers running loose on the street when we have so many murderers sitting in boardrooms across America? Those fat cats with their obscene golden parachutes cut corners to reduce expenses and they put profits above all else. Screw Corporate America and screw ThoriChem for killing us one drum at a time.'"

"Toxic dumping," I said.

Payton nodded and punched a number into his phone. After a lengthy runaround, he finally reached someone in a position of authority and they talked for several minutes. He hung up and said, "I guess we can scratch Richard Thorndike off our list. His shady ways caught up with him and he's one month into a fifteen-year sentence."

"Good." I paged down. "Listen to this one. 'Congress passed Sarbannes-Oxley. What a farce! If ethics are so lacking in society that it requires congressional legislation to correct the problem, what makes the politicians believe people are ethical enough to obey the law? Hell! Our legislators are some of the most unethical individuals in the country because they've written loopholes in the laws to protect big business. Someone has to stop this and they should start with Mayer Consulting. They conspire with the corporate elite to uncover ways to pad the bottom line, which usually means hard-working, dedicated people get the boot while the top guys get rich.'" I typed the company name into the search box. "These guys are efficiency experts."

"How could anyone hold a grudge against them?" Payton said with feigned indignation.

"You know, I'm beginning to question my sanity," I said.

"Why? Because a guy we think is a nut actually makes some valid points?"

"You too, huh?" I reached for my phone but it rang before I could start dialing Mayer Consulting's corporate number. My heart skipped a beat when I saw 3:31 PM on the screen. "It's the Bunker," I told Payton and I answered.

"We just got another untraceable call, Detective," Bevin said. "A woman."

I closed my eyes and muttered, "Son of a bitch."

We followed the same drill we'd followed after Scott Caruso called 911. We checked with TRU but learned the call had been placed on another disposable phone. And Missing Persons had not received any new reports.

All we could do is wait until someone found the body.

—— CHAPTER 28 ——

I had ample time on my hands now that I'd finally obeyed Morgan's order and stopped cruising the streets of Tombstone, but the 911 call set my nerves on edge.

I'd spent Saturday morning dusting, vacuuming, and doing laundry like a maid on steroids to try to avoid thinking about the woman who'd placed the call. Payton's theory about my godchild being a great diversion was spot-on because Emily kept me so busy Saturday afternoon and evening that I didn't have time to dwell on the case. But on the drive home, images of bloody punctures filled my mind and continued to plague me throughout another restless night. Each time I woke with a start, I told myself if a body had turned up, I'd have gotten a call.

And at 9:23 AM Sunday morning, I did.

I met Payton at the station to pick up our cruiser, and fifteen minutes later we drove through the brick archway of Canterbury Estates, a development of three-story mansions on the north shore of Lake Wellington. We meandered along the winding streets and I pulled in behind the squad parked in front of the ivory-brick, Tudor-style home owned by Donald and Lucy Hollander.

Payton stopped in the entryway to chat with the uniforms, but I climbed the circular stairs to the third floor and found my way to the bathroom. The cinnamon toast I'd eaten while perusing the Sunday paper started talking back to me when I looked into the claw-foot bathtub.

I drew a long, slow breath through my mouth to stem the wave of nausea as I stared at the punctures covering Lucy Hollander's nude body. I didn't need to count the wounds to know there were twenty-seven. I studied her face, feeling as if I should know her, but I couldn't figure out where I'd seen her before.

Payton walked in and gazed at the body for a beat before he said, "Her phone was in her purse. No burner numbers on the incoming log. And the service door to the garage was jimmied."

"So this time he broke in."

Payton nodded.

I heard footsteps in the hall, and when I turned toward the door, I caught a glimpse of myself in the large mirror over the double-basin black marble vanity. With my pale face and the dark circles beneath my bloodshot eyes, I looked like the main character in a zombie movie. Come to think of it, I'd been acting like one too. Clomping along with outstretched arms, reaching for that one lead to crack the case, only to wind up with another dead body.

Leilani Norris entered the bathroom and her shoulder drooped. "Not another one." She sighed as she set her bag on the floor and kneeled next to the tub to examine her patient.

Payton tapped my arm. "We should talk to the husband."

Husbands. Wives. Widowers and widows. How many more would there be before we caught this guy? And how long would I feel this ache in the pit of my stomach at the thought of interviewing another spouse who'd suffered such a devastating loss?

We found Donald Hollander sitting on the love seat in the den. When he looked up at us, his eyes looked a lot like mine.

"Who would do this?" he asked. "Who could…?" He glanced toward the stairs. "I tried calling from the airport but she didn't answer and I figured she was out in the garden." He ran his hand through his hair. "If only I'd have been home I…"

"There's nothing you could have done to prevent this, Mr. Hollander," I assured him. His eyes begged me to make it true though I knew from personal experience he didn't believe it. "You said you called from the airport?"

He sniffled and nodded. "I was in Beijing since the first."

"Was Lucy employed?"

He nodded again. "She's a vice president at Mayer Consulting."

The name struck like an uppercut to my stomach. *If only I'd made that call before Bevin called from the Bunker. We may have been able to piece things together Friday.* I took a breath before I asked, "What did she do at Mayer?"

"She worked with their largest clients. Helped them improve operations."

"Any problems you're aware of?"

He shook his head.

"Did you happen to notice any strange cars or unfamiliar people around?" Payton asked.

Hollander tensed and gaped at Payton. "You think whoever did this was watching her?"

"It's possible," Payton said. "Did she have any routines?"

Hollander thought about it. "She stopped at a Mugga Java near work for coffee every morning. And…uh…she jogged around the neighborhood three days a week when the weather was good."

"When was the last time you spoke?" I asked.

He squinted. "Uh…Thursday. I tried calling yesterday morning but her phone wasn't in service. She's terrible about keeping the battery charged and…" He caught the look that passed between Payton and me. "Was she already—oh, God!" He put his face in his hands. After a moment, he sniffled and rubbed the back of his neck. He took a deep breath and raised his head. "Lucy was so strong." He wrung his hands. "She suffered two miscarriages, but in spite of the pain of loss, she wanted to try again because she said having a family was worth the risk and—" His voice cracked and he put his hand over his eyes.

I dropped my head and scrunched my eyes shut, trying to push back the memory.

"Are you fighting with something in there?" I called out as Dave rummaged around in the hall closet.

"No!" He slammed the door. "My loafers got trashed when I was at the site before they poured the parking lot. I was looking for my rubbers but I can't find them. I guess I'll need to get new ones before winter."

"Not if we're going to make a baby, you won't."

He spun around. "Why wouldn't I need rubbers?" he asked as if he hadn't heard me.

"Didn't you and your dad ever have the talk?"

He smiled. "It sounds like you've made a decision."

My heart thumped and my mouth felt like I'd eaten a box of saltines. "I…uh…I'd be willing to cease all attempts to the contrary and let nature take its course."

"You're sure?"

"No. I'm still terrified because I've seen how easily it can all be taken away, but if family isn't worth the risk, then what is?" I shrugged. "Why should I bother going to work every day to try to clean it up if there's no hope?"

Dave lifted my chin. "I love you." We kissed and—

"Detective Benchik?"

I snapped my head in Payton's direction.

"Do you have any other questions for Mr. Hollander?" he asked. I shook my head. "Not at this time."

We left Hollander sitting numbly in his empty living room and stepped out into the bright sun.

I looked up at the cloudless blue sky. "I was about to call Mayer Consulting when Bevin called. We were so close."

Payton slipped his sunglasses on. "It was already too late by then."

I knew he was right. "What did I miss?"

"Not much," he said. "I showed him pictures of Ortiz, Caruso, and the sketch of Allister but he didn't recognize any of them. And neither he nor his wife ever dealt with the law firm, Legal Aid, or Paragon Insurance."

"So we're still without a link. Great."

"Maybe not," he said. "Mr. Hollander gave me Mayer's cell number so…" He punched it into his phone and told Robert Mayer we needed to speak with him immediately. He listened for a moment and ended the call. "Ever been to the clubhouse at North Lake Country Club?"

"I'm not even sure they let women in," I said.

He tucked his phone into his pocket. "Assuming they admit African-American males, I'll take a picture for you."

— CHAPTER 29 —

We arrived at North Lake Country Club a little after noon, and as we wound our way along the cobblestone path to the clubhouse, we passed an African-American couple and two Hispanic women all dressed in golf attire.

"Apparently it would be our paltry paychecks rather than our race or gender that would keep us out of here," I said, and Payton laughed without humor.

We reached the clubhouse and found the bar, but older white men lounged around half the tables in the room, so we asked the bartender and he pointed Mayer out.

As we got closer to the corner table, Payton said, "I don't believe it. He's with Mayor Foley."

We identified ourselves and apologized for the interruption. Mayer motioned to the bar, picked up his drink, and we put some space between his foursome and us.

When we broke the news, Mayer's face turned ashen. "Dear God." He drained his on-the-rocks glass and set it on the bar. The bartender promptly refilled it.

"When was the last time you had contact with Lucy?" I asked.

"Before she left on Thursday."

"Where was she Friday?"

"Took a sick day," he said. "I'm not sure what was wrong. She left me a message a little after 6:00 AM, saying she wouldn't be in. She apologized for not waiting until I arrived to speak in person, but she said she'd been up half the night and felt lousy. Said she happened to wake up and figured she'd better call before she went back to bed. She told me she'd see me Monday, and of course I didn't want to bother her. Maybe if I had…"

I wondered if the killer was already in the house and forced her to place that call.

"What exactly was her job?" Payton asked.

"She identified opportunities for our clients to improve operations."

"Opportunities like job elimination?" Payton asked.

Mayer stiffened defensively. "Sometimes it's necessary for a client to right-size staff."

"Corporate-speak for lay off," I said.

He glared at me. "Right-sizing is sometimes a matter of not replacing an employee who leaves voluntarily. Like it or not, my company provides a valuable service."

"We have reason to believe the killer may have held a grudge against Lucy," Payton said. "Did she ever receive any threats?"

Mayer scoffed. "You two been living in a cave?" He drained half of his drink. "Couple years back, those anti-Wall Street protestors vilified corporate executives. Burned us in effigy. Haven't you heard? We're Satan."

"If you say so," I said, "but you didn't answer my partner's question."

He set his jaw. Maybe he was counting to ten. "Yes. Lucy received her share of menacing phone calls and e-mails. People venting."

"Any of them seem capable of going beyond venting?" Payton asked.

"There was one guy on a recent project," Mayer said. "Bank foreclosed on his house and he keyed Lucy's car. But it can't be him."

"Why not?" Payton asked.

"He committed suicide a few weeks ago," Mayer said as if it were the most natural thing in the world.

"We're going to need his name," I said, "as well as any other complaints she received."

"I'll have someone forward it to you tomorrow. Is that all?"

"No," I said. "Did your firm work with Smithfield, Royce, and Foley or Paragon Insurance?"

Mayer shook his head once.

Payton held up the photos of Ortiz and Caruso and the sketch. "You recognize any of these people?"

Mayer studied each one and shook "no" again. We thanked him for his time and he carried his drink back to the table.

"Appreciate the interruption!" Mayor Foley called out and he hoisted his glass in our direction.

"Just trying to solve these murders like you've been demanding, sir," I said with a crisp salute.

I'm surprised his glare didn't scorch the fine wood finish of the wall behind me.

I fumed all the way home, and when I got there I went straight to the shower to wash off the day's grime, but the case wouldn't let go. I pictured the whiteboard—covered with bits and pieces of our victims' lives—while I lingered under the hot, pulsing spray of our massaging showerhead. It was as if the clues were written in invisible ink, and if I stared long enough, something would magically reveal itself. The water started to feel cool, so I turned off the faucet, toweled off, and pulled on a T-shirt and shorts. I shuffled down to the living room, slumped onto the couch, and closed my eyes.

I turned to leave but Dave pounced in front of me and blocked my way. He slipped his arms around my waist and began walking us back toward the couch. As a trained police officer, I should've been able to avoid such a confrontation, but the offender was much too studly to resist. He threw his leg over the back of the couch and pulled me over on top of his very fit, six-foot-two, one-hundred-eighty-five-pound body. We both giggled like a couple of teenagers.

"You hungry?" he murmured in my ear.

"What's on the menu?" I asked. He kissed my neck and I giggled. "Guess that would be me."

"Uh-huh." He ran his hand up my thigh. "Shut up and kiss me."

"That's the title of a Mary Chapin Carpenter song. I really like it."

"Are we going to do this, or are you going to recite the country music countdown?" He slipped his hands under my T-shirt.

"Are you still playing basketball tomorrow?" My voice sounded a little husky.

"Yeah," he mumbled against my neck.

"Don't the pros refrain from sex before a game?"

The kissing stopped and he looked at me. "You've seen us play. Do we look like pros?"

I chuckled. "True." I peeled off his T-shirt and he peeled off mine and—

I bolted up and ran my hands through my hair, and then I moved over to the recliner, as if switching seats would stop the memories. "'That which does not kill us makes us stronger'," I softly reminded myself. If that's true, I should be able to go out to the garage and lift Dave's Mustang by its bumper. Like Jaime Sommers—minus the bionics. So why did it take so much energy to simply get out of bed every morning?

My stomach growled, and though I didn't feel like eating, obviously my body had a different opinion, so I plodded into the kitchen and made a peanut butter-and-cherry preserve sandwich. I decided to wash it down with some milk, but my hand trembled a little as I poured and I missed the glass. "Damn it!"

I reached for a dishtowel and knocked a mug off the counter and it shattered when it struck the tile. I wiped up the spill first, and then I grabbed the brush and dustpan from under the sink. "Once a klutz." I swept the shards into a pile and onto the dustpan and I dumped them into the garbage. About half the mug had remained intact and skittered over by the cabinet. I squatted again to pick it up and icy fingers gripped my heart when I saw the picture of the Manhattan skyline on the side. Dave bought the mug on the same trip I bought the tiny replica of Lady Liberty I keep on my desk. Now, like our life together, the mug was shattered.

The sense of loss pressed down like a barbell with too much weight and my knees buckled. "I can't do this!" I wailed to the empty room. *I need to go somewhere...anywhere that every sight, sound, and smell doesn't remind me of him. But where? A hotel would be too expensive. And though the Warrens would welcome me with open arms, Connie would hover to the point of smothering me.*

I thought of Camp Cadaver, the storage room at the station that was converted into a makeshift dorm and named by a homicide cop after a thirty-six–hour shift. I got myself upright, set the broken mug on the counter, and ran up the stairs to our bedroom. I grabbed a nylon duffle bag from the closet shelf and stuffed in pants, tees, underwear, and socks. I dressed, snatched my gun and ID from the nightstand drawer, and bounded back downstairs and out the back door.

A bolt of lightning zigzagged through the black sky as I headed south on Kennedy Boulevard, and thunder rolled a few seconds later. I drove with no particular destination in mind until I crossed the river. Then I knew exactly where my subconscious wanted to go. A few minutes later, I turned into the branch parking lot, drove around back, and switched off the engine. *This is so not healthy*, I thought as I sat in the darkness, staring out the windshield at the rear door. *I should start the car and leave.*

I crawled out and walked over to the first parking space outside the back door. My stomach tightened at the prospect of seeing Dave's bloodstain, but when I looked down, the pavement was clean. They must have power-washed the lot in preparation for the grand opening. Wouldn't want the specter of a murder hanging over their shiny new branch.

I noticed something shoved into the dirt by the shrubs outside the door and squatted for a closer look at a small wooden cross bearing Dave's name and date of death. One of Dave's coworkers must have felt compelled to mark the spot.

A thunderclap rocked the air and a huge drop of rain plopped on my nose. Several more drops peppered my arm, and within seconds, rain pasted my hair to my forehead and neck, and my shirt clung to every curve.

The last time it rained was for Dave's funeral. After nearly a month of dry weather, large drops had started falling the moment we passed through the cemetery gate, and we all huddled at the graveside beneath green canopies erected by the caretakers. I took the downpour as a sign even Mother Nature mourned his loss.

I leaned my head back, closed my eyes, and took a deep breath as the rain slapped the pavement and thunder drowned out all other sounds. A hand grasped my shoulder and I drew my gun as I spun around and aimed upward.

"Whoa!" Donovan recoiled and held out his hand like a traffic cop.

"Benchik?" Garcia squinted at me through the rain. "Didn't your mother ever tell you to get in out of the rain?"

I holstered my gun as I stood.

"Is this you staying out of the case?" Donovan shouted over the rain and thunder.

"I just…I uh…" I shook my head and a drop trickled into my eye. I swiped my hands over my cheeks to dry away the rain, but I tasted salt and realized it wasn't all rain.

"Go home, Val!" Garcia shouted before he and Donovan trotted to their cruiser.

I slid behind the wheel of my SUV and slammed the door. I cranked the ignition, flicked on the wipers, and sat watching the blades sluice water from my windshield.

— CHAPTER 30 —

My clothes still felt damp when I got to the station, so I took a hot shower and changed into jeans and a T-shirt from my duffle. I bought a bag of multi-grain chips and a can of root beer from the machine and settled at my desk to try to figure out what we were missing.

My head bobbed and woke me up at 2:10 AM and I decided to try to get a few hours sleep in Camp Cadaver.

I tossed and turned because the cot was as comfortable as a sleeping bag full of twigs, but when I woke up a little after six, I realized it was the first time in three weeks I'd been able to measure my sleep in hours rather than minutes. I got up and walked to the conference room to peek out the window for a check of the weather. Gray sky but no rain, at least for the time being, so I decided to walk to Mugga Java for some good coffee. I should have brewed a pot at the station because I ran into Dr. Konrad and he asked if I had a few minutes to chat. I reluctantly agreed and Konrad motioned toward a booth.

I sat facing the door like I always do when given a choice, and I glanced up at the TV mounted in the corner, tuned to the Channel 6 news. Claudia Campbell, the morning anchor, said, "It appears a murderer dubbed the Friday Afternoon Killer may have struck again."

"You're the ones who dubbed him, you moron," I muttered and Konrad glanced over his shoulder at the TV. "No one remembers the names of the victims," I said, "but thanks to the press and their little nicknames, everyone can name the psychopaths. Instead of being repulsed, people are fascinated by the whole thing."

"Human nature," Konrad said. "It's why we can't help looking at a car wreck on the highway."

"My friend, Connie, works Emergency at Wellington, and she told me they average a dozen gapers a year who get into their own accident because they're gawking at someone else's."

He bobbed his head little, acknowledging the stupid yet inevitable. "I heard the second and third victims left spouses behind," he said. I nodded and he frowned. "Those interviews must have been very difficult."

And yet I got through them. Cool and professional as always. Why is that? I sipped some coffee and stared at the cup. Part of me wanted to ask if my behavior was normal, but if I told him I'm an armadillo, he'd have me committed. Of course I could tell him Connie thinks I'm an armadillo and he'd have her committed. Which would solve my problem of her pressuring me to talk.

"What's on your mind, Val?"

I looked up. "Why don't you just read it and save us both some time?"

He smiled. "It means more when you come to the realization yourself."

"Of course it does." I slid the cardboard ring up and down the cup while I tried to frame my response. "I guess…I've become so skilled at controlling my emotions on the job that…" I exhaled forcefully, as if I were about to jump into an ice-cold pool. "What if ten years on the job have hardened me to the point where I can't cry? Or even care?"

His face crinkled at the absurdity of my comment. "You care, but you're required to control your emotions to do your job well. It can't be personal."

"But this is!" I tensed and flattened my palms on the table. "As personal as it could ever be." I slouched against the back of the booth.

He waited until my breathing evened out and said, "You can't turn off being a cop just because it's personal, so you've put Dave's murder in the same place in your mind where you put other murders to allow yourself to function." He arched his brows, seeking my confirmation he could be on the right track. I nodded and he continued. "Everyone deals with grief in their own way, Val…in their own time. You will too when you are emotionally ready."

So I'm not a cold-hearted bitch. I'm simply very adept at dealing with horror. Good for me. "I should go." I thanked him for the chat and left him in the booth, and I got back in line to buy a cup of tea for my partner and two coffees to serve as olive branches with Donovan and Garcia.

Payton's eyes lit up when I set the tea on the desk in front of him. "What's the occasion?"

I shrugged. "It's Monday."

Donovan and Garcia offered a blanket "Morning" as they entered and I walked over and handed a cup to each of them.

Donovan took his with a smirk. "It's going to take at least a beer."

"Maybe two," Garcia said.

"Maybe a steak to go with it," Donovan added.

I nodded. "Whatever. But you need to know I did not go there with the intention of interfering. I was just driving and..." Rather than risk babbling, I paused to collect my thoughts. "You're good cops and I know you're going to get Noonan."

They looked at each other. Donovan raised his brows and Garcia nodded and then they both looked at me.

Garcia said, "We want this guy too, you know."

"Yeah," Donovan said. "Thanks to that bastard, we're short a man on the court."

Leave it to Donovan to nip sentimentality in the bud. I smiled and nodded and returned to my desk. I started to log on to my computer but stopped typing when I felt Payton's eyes glued to the side of my head. "Something wrong?"

"Damn straight."

I looked at him. "It's not like I planned it or anything. I was in the neighborhood and—"

"In the neighborhood for what?" Payton snapped. "Since when do you hang around Tombstone?" He rubbed his fingers across his forehead for a moment as he tried to rein in his frustration. "What would you have done if you actually encountered Noonan?"

Putting a bullet between his eyes would have been good. "I would have called for backup," I said.

"Bullshit."

I put my palm on my chest. "It pains me to know you have so little faith in me."

Payton rolled his eyes. "Give me a break."

"All right, fine." I tossed my hands up. "I don't know what I would have done." I stared at him for a moment, my chest heaving. "That night, as I stood watching Leilani wheel Dave's body to her van, Pritchard whispered in my ear that he was going to find the guy and take care of him. And I had to make him promise he wouldn't do anything stupid because Dave wouldn't want it and neither did I but…" I sniffled and shook my head. "I want the bastard to go down. I want it so badly it hurts!" I clutched at the knit top over my heart. "It physically hurts, Greg!" I had to wait for my breathing to even out before I could go on. "Part of me wants to see him rot in prison, but part of me hopes he makes the wrong move and someone takes him out. And part of me wishes it could be me."

Payton sighed deeply. "Finally. That's the most honest you've been since he died." His brows pinched slightly and his eyes filled with empathy for my pain.

"Those lines we use with victims' families…they're bullshit," I said. He nodded and I sighed and jerked my head toward the door. "Let's get over to the Mugga Java where Lucy Hollander stopped on her way to work. Maybe one of the regulars noticed something that will help us solve this case."

— CHAPTER 31 —

When Donald Hollander told us his wife stopped at the Mugga Java near her office, we didn't know Mayer Consulting's address, so it shocked us when her coffee shop turned out to be the same strip mall location where Cassidy had traced Allister's WiFi signal on Thursday.

We talked to customers first so we'd catch them before they left, but none of the regulars recognized Lucy Hollander or our sketch of Allister because they'd been too busy reading the paper, texting, or talking on their phones to notice anything short of an explosion.

Rob was at the register again today, and when he saw Hollander's photo he said, "Ms. Fat-Free-Decaf Latte. Man, you wouldn't want to get on her wrong side."

"Why?" Payton asked.

"Remember when you were here last week and I told you I didn't see anything because I was cleaning up?" He pointed at my phone. "She's the reason why."

I wanted to kick myself. Lucy Hollander looked familiar when I saw her in her bathtub because she'd been the one to reenact the Brad Paisley video. A twinge of remorse twisted my stomach when I recalled thinking she was a bitch. I asked Rob if Hollander ever got into it with any customers.

"Uh, yeah," Rob said. "She had no problem giving people grief if they got in line before they knew what they wanted or if they took too long to order. And one day last week, she got into it with some guy by her car. They talked for a minute and then things heated up. I couldn't hear what they were saying but it looked like she was yelling. When she finally left, she screeched out of the lot, waving the bird out the window."

"Can you recall if the guy was wearing a black baseball cap?" Payton asked.

Rob's face scrunched up as he thought about it. "Come to think of it, yeah."

"Do you remember what kind of car he drove?" Payton asked.

Rob's eyes grew wide. "Dude, was she being stalked?"

"Dude," Payton said with wide eyes and an extra-mellow tone. "Do you remember what kind of car he drove?"

Rob stared at Payton for a moment. He was probably trying to decide if he should be offended. Then he scratched his chin and said, "Gray, I think."

"Gray is not a kind," I said. "What about make or model? Coupe or sedan?"

Rob shrugged and glanced at the growing line. "I've really got to get back."

We moved aside. The next customer directed an exasperated sigh at us as she stepped up.

"Allister could've been parked in the lot when we were here Thursday," I said.

"Probably was," Payton said, "but beating ourselves up about it isn't going to solve the case." He checked his watch. "Dr. Norris probably started the autopsy. Maybe he left something behind this time."

When we took our places across the table from our deputy ME, she glanced up through her face shield and said, "The wounds are consistent but she was petite so he didn't need the stun gun." She lifted Hollander's left wrist and pointed to the abrasion encircling it. "I found some navy fibers in the skin. Sent them to the lab." She lowered Hollander's wrist. "Time of death is consistent with the other cases. Full tox is pending, but there's no evidence of drugs or alcohol."

"She and her husband were trying to start a family," Payton said.

Leilani frowned. "They succeeded."

My breath caught. "She was pregnant?"

"About five weeks," Leilani said. "It's possible she didn't even know."

"Could be why she called in sick the day of the murder," Payton said.

Another future destroyed, I thought, and I knew if I stayed in that autopsy suite for a second longer, I'd lose it. "I...uh...I've got to make a call," I said and I felt their eyes on me as I made a beeline for the door.

I walked briskly down the corridor, and as I ran up the stairs, I wondered what thoughts had gone through Lucy Hollander's mind when she got up on the last morning of her life. Did she know she was pregnant? Did she daydream about how she would break the news to her husband?

My gait quickened as I crossed the lobby and burst through the glass doors onto Vermont Street. I propped my foot and back against the wall and closed my eyes as I sucked in some air to try to cleanse my mind of the horrible crime scene images. I felt a hand on my arm and I flinched and opened my eyes to find Payton beside me.

"The world is spiraling out of control," I said. "Wars on terror. Global warming. Serial killers poking holes in lives and dreams."

Payton's faced brimmed with empathy. "Those things were here yesterday."

"And they'll still be here tomorrow, right?" I said. He nodded and I did too. "Well, I'm sick of it!" I pushed away from the wall. "I get why people disapprove of our vics' decisions or even their occupational choices." I started to pace in front of my partner. "It would've been refreshing if the Paragon board had directed Caruso to approve a few more claims instead of dangling a denial bonus in front of him. And watching Hollander get drenched by a latte—courtesy of a right-sized employee—could have been damned entertaining. But none of them deserved to be slaughtered like some..." I stopped pacing, crossed my arms, and stared at my feet. "I was so arrogant." I raised my head to look at him. "I cruised through life believing we had all the time in the world even though the job showed me the broken and mutilated bodies of other people who thought the same thing. If anyone should know life can turn on a dime, it's a cop."

Payton removed his sunglasses and rubbed his thumb and forefinger over his nose. "Look, Val, under the circumstances, Morgan would not hold it against you if you wanted off the case."

"I know. But I would. Besides, I can't let you have all the fun."

A smile tugged the corners of his mouth. "You're so damned stubborn."

"I prefer to think of it as persevering." I squinted at him in the blazing sun. "Meltdown over." I backhanded his upper arm. "Let's get back to work."

We tracked down five people from Lucy Hollander's Contacts list, and except for her husband, people who knew Lucy didn't get a warm and fuzzy feeling from the experience. Her hair stylist told us she was looking through the dictionary one day and saw Hollander's picture next to the definition of *bitch*. And Hollander's mechanic agreed with the stylist.

To cover our bases, we also stopped by Legal Aid but Elizabeth Bauer had never heard of Hollander and knew of no cases related to Mayer Consulting. The only encouraging sign at all came as we were leaving Bauer's office, when Argus texted to say he had something to show us.

We reported to the lab as requested and Payton said, "Hey, Todd!" at his normal volume as we entered but Argus winced and I asked if he was okay.

"Beer garden at the Bedford Birthday Bash yesterday," he said softly. "Where were you?" He pointed an accusatory finger at me. "You've lived here for over twenty years yet you didn't bother to show up. I'll bet you don't even know anything about our city."

"I know Bedford incorporated on August 13, 1948, which was the year after the wide release of *It's a Wonderful Life*," I said. "Local historians claim the founders chose the name because they envisioned our city would offer the same sense of family, community, and hope depicted in the Frank Capra classic. And I know we're close enough to the Wisconsin border that with a stiff northern wind, we can almost smell the cheese. What else is there?"

Argus scoffed. "Mere trivia. If it were up to Nigel Wellington, of the Boston Wellingtons, you'd be living in Wellington. Nigel's younger brother Ridley— grandfather of our very own Ridley the Third—had traveled the country after returning from France in World War II. He was camping near Paradise Mountain when ol' Nigel caught up with him and—"

"Your history lesson is very informative, Todd," I said, "but—"

"Ah!" He held his finger to his lips, signaling me to be quiet. "Ridley the first saw only beauty and tranquility, but money-grubbing Nigel saw dollar signs. He bought the land along the western shore of the lake, built a resort, and marketed rustic getaways, primarily to the wealthy residents of Chicago, Milwaukee, and other midwestern cities. Those who stayed all summer began to long for the fine dining and cultural distractions of home. The entrepreneurs among them acquired land on the east side of the lake, and voila—Bedford was born. So where were you?" Argus demanded. "Your partner and his family came out to bask in the beauty of Veterans Memorial Park and celebrate our great city. Where were you?"

"Lakeview Bank is a sponsor," I said. "Dave was supposed to work the dunk tank so I decided to skip it this year."

Argus closed his eyes and mumbled, "Insert foot as usual."

"No worries, Todd, but you're into trivia so riddle me this. By any chance, was August thirteenth a Friday the year Bedford was incorporated?"

Argus snorted. "How the hell would I know?"

"You seem to know everything else."

"Since when are you superstitious?" Payton asked.

"I'm not, but even a supernatural explanation of being incorporated under a bad sign is better than the big ol' nothing we've got." I looked at Argus. "What's the big discovery?"

"I identified the navy fibers found on your victim's wrists," he said. "They're nylon. Double-braid dock line to be specific."

"Like from a boat?" I asked.

"Yep," Argus said with a nod.

We thanked him and headed to the squad room to ponder our new information.

"Leilani figured Ortiz was bound with electrical cord," I said. "He used what he could find at her place, but he brought rope with him for Hollander, and probably Caruso too. We just didn't find any trace of it. He put a lot more time into planning the second and third murders."

Payton nodded and began to shuffle through his messages. "Uniforms finished the canvass of Hollander's neighbors. No one saw anything."

"Is this guy a ghost or what?" I took my frustration out on my keyboard as I logged on. "And how much hate mail did Hollander get that we still don't have copies?"

"It's probably Mayer's way of getting even with you for bothering his mayoral foursome. He's showing you who's got the power."

My lip curled at the thought but he was probably right. "Ortiz is the square peg. Her murder wasn't as well planned. She wasn't a corporate type but she's the one who had to die and he keeps killing because…" I motioned for Payton to take it away.

"He likes it?"

I frowned.

Payton opened the folder that someone had left on his desk. "We got Hollander's financials." He scanned the report. "They were well-off. Combined accounts total just under two million bucks." He flipped the page. "Neither of them had any scrapes with the law, so I doubt there's a professional link through Ortiz. And there's no record of any insurance policies with Paragon." He stood and walked over to the whiteboard. "How did the killer get them home on a Friday afternoon? And how did he know they'd be alone? Ortiz wasn't too risky. She lived alone so the chance of anyone barging in while he tortured her was slim, but Rachel Caruso or Donald Hollander could have come home unexpectedly."

I walked over and stood next to Payton. "Marine varnish at Ortiz's and now marine rope with Hollander." I shook my head. "I know Smithfield has an alibi but what if the good old boys are covering for each other? Smithfield, the mayor, and the congressman are lawyers, so lying is second nature to them. Maybe our vics saw something they shouldn't have seen or heard something they shouldn't have heard and they were killed to cover it up"

"Such as?"

I shrugged. "I don't know, but that's a lot of power and influence."

Payton squinted at me and I figured he was trying to decide how long it would be before I hurled around the bend completely. "To be killed because of something they heard or saw means they would've had to have been in the same place at the same time," he said, "and we haven't found any evidence of that. And a conspiracy theory might work except you're forgetting Commissioner Malloy was with them." I shook my head once and he smirked and said, "So he's part of your mental conspiracy?"

"Are you using 'mental' because I formulated the theory in my mind?" I asked. "Or are you insinuating my theory seems insane?" He grinned as my cell started to vibrate. "You're lucky," I said before I answered my phone with, "Give me good news, Cassidy."

"Allister is online right now," Cassidy said, sounding as if he'd just run a hundred-yard dash. "And he must like coffee even more than you do because I'm picking up a signal from the Mugga Java across from the museum campus."

"Stay on with me so you can tell me if he logs off," I told him and I headed for the door.

With the lunch rush over, traffic on Columbus moved fairly well, and Payton even found a parking spot on Jefferson down the street from the coffee shop. When the weather cooperates, this location hosts a sidewalk café in an area bordered by wrought-iron fencing. I counted nine people with laptops, tablets, or phones scattered among twelve tables. Seven were men, and of the five wearing baseball hats, three hats were black.

"So many caps, so little time," Payton said. "We have no clue how old Allister is. Any thoughts on how we narrow our options?"

My forearm brushed against the gun on my hip and it gave me an idea. "Maybe we can spook him." I tossed my blazer onto the seat.

Payton smiled and followed my lead. We walked over and loitered along the wrought iron fence. No one who bothered to look up seemed to be the least bit rattled.

"Hmm," I said. "I guess they're accustomed to seeing guns and shields given our close proximity to coffee and donuts."

We scanned the tables. The guy with the laptop at the table just ahead of us scrolled through his responses on an online dating site. *Here's a tip. Log off your computer and talk to actual people.*

"Tablet guy, street-side," Payton said.

I shifted my gaze. "Nah. He's either on a porn site or chatting with his mistress." I scanned the tables. "Baseball cap and Jim Carrey eyes. Far side along the fence."

"Got him," Payton replied.

Baseball Cap Guy closed his laptop. A few seconds later, Cassidy's voice came over the line. "Allister just logged off."

"That's our guy," I told Payton. I thanked Cassidy and stuffed my phone into my pocket. Allister cast a nervous glance our way as he jammed his laptop into a sleeve. By habit, I brushed my palm against the butt of my gun. "Game's over, jackass!" I said to myself and I started toward him along the walkway between the fencing and street.

Payton fell in behind me to block the walkway. Allister scanned the street in both directions, and then he tucked the laptop under his arm and vaulted over the wrought-iron fence.

I shouted, "Stop! Police!" and ran after him.

Allister dodged two women pushing strollers, but the movement threw him off balance and he knocked over the Daily Specials easel outside a sandwich shop. I dodged around the strollers and leapt over the easel. Allister ran into Jefferson Street, I followed, and horns blared as we darted through traffic. Allister ran toward the parking lot on the corner and cleared the gate as it came down behind a minivan. I had to duck under the gate and I stopped to scan the rows of vehicles. I spotted Allister fumbling with his key by a Smart car.

I ran up as he opened the door and I clutched a handful of his T-shirt, swung him around, and shoved him against the car. "I told you to stop, jackass! Guess who's going to get what he deserves this time, huh?"

— CHAPTER 32 —

Allister's real name was Raymond Krupinski, and he was cuffed to the table in an interview room while we ran background.

"Can you believe this guy attended MIT for two years?" Payton said as he scanned his screen. "Imagine what he could have accomplished in medicine or research."

"Why get a real job when we live in a society where you can start out as a hacker and end up a billionaire?" I stood. "Shall we?"

Deputy Commissioner Moraz stormed through the squad room doorway and barked, "Both of you! Now!" as he headed for Morgan's office. He blew by our desks so quickly that several sheets of paper caught in his wake and drifted to the floor.

I pointed toward the hall. "Sir, we have a sus—"

"Now, Benchik!"

We grudgingly followed him.

Moraz slammed Morgan's door. "I wanted to come by and personally commend you on your outstanding police work, Detectives."

I wondered how he heard about the arrest so quickly.

Moraz flung Saturday's newspaper onto Morgan's desk, exposing photos of Adriana Ortiz, Scott Caruso, and Lucy Hollander—below the headline FRIDAY AFTERNOON KILLER CLAIMS THIRD VICTIM. He snatched the paper up, flipped it over, and slapped it back down on the desk. A smaller headline below the fold read SENIOR STRICKEN AFTER POLICE RAID.

"The Crenshaws are a real threat with all of those suspicious e-mails to their grandchildren in Ohio," Moraz said. "I just spent half my day with the commissioner, the mayor, and the city attorney, strategizing on damage control. How the hell did you screw this up?"

"Allister hacked into the Crenshaws' connection," Payton said. "Made it appear as if—"

"I don't give a shit how he did it! He made us look like a bunch of fools!"

It was insulting for Moraz to include himself as a member of the team and I tossed an indignant glance at Payton. His expression warned me to keep my mouth shut so I did.

Moraz fixed his dark, close-set eyes on me. They looked like the plastic eyes in stuffed animals—except the eyes in stuffed animals convey more humanity. "If you do not make an arrest soon, I'm giving the case to a task force."

"Sir—"

Moraz ignored me and shifted his glare to Morgan. "If that happens, Captain, you're going to have the shortest command in the history of the department." He tossed one last glower at each of us and slammed the door on his way out.

Morgan puffed her cheeks and blew out some air. "Do you have anything to go on?"

"Yes, ma'am, we do," Payton said. "We were on our way to interrogate Allister when the deputy commissioner arrived."

She spread her arms. "Why didn't you say so?"

"He cut me off, Cap!" I said. "Besides, why should we give him something to take credit for with the mayor?"

She pursed her lips to disguise a smile. "So why are you standing here?"

Payton held the door for me and we left Morgan's office and went straight to Interview Room One. I sat across from Allister, who slouched in his chair. Behind his tortoise-framed glasses, his eyelids drooped like he needed a nap or a caffeine transfusion.

Payton sat to my right and opened the file. "Raymond Krupinski. What's with Allister?"

"It means 'avenger,'" Krupinski said in a voice that sounded as droopy as his eyelids.

"Yeah, we know," Payton said. "Why use a false name?"

Krupinski snorted. "You think people would have read my blog if I'd used my real name?"

"Why did you pirate the Crenshaws' WiFi?" Payton asked.

"Uh." Krupinski scratched the stubble on his cheek. "I don't know who that is. I thought I was picking up the library connection."

"Rosaria Maltese was a nice touch," I said.

He smiled smugly. "It seemed fitting."

"Is there a reason you have only a burner phone?" Payton asked.

Krupinski's eyes darted between us and then swept the room suspiciously, as if someone else could overhear. "You really need to ask given the stories I bring to light?"

"Let me guess," I said. "You need to stay off-grid because Big Brother is watching."

He clicked his tongue and shot his finger at me.

Payton dealt head shots of the victims onto the table. "You know these people?"

Krupinski glanced at the photos and grimaced but didn't respond.

I held up our sketch. "How about him?" Krupinski's eyes grew wide and I slapped the paper onto the table in front of him and jabbed it with my finger. "That's you!"

"Have you ever been to Garfield Park?" Payton asked.

"Maybe. At some point in my life." His chin jutted out defiantly. "Why?"

I figured he had no way of knowing if someone had recorded the argument on a cell phone so I said, "Because we have video of you harassing Scott Caruso."

His eyes bounced between us. "Okay. I'll cop to being in Garfield Park. Caruso was stonewalling me when I tried to talk to him about how the ratio of denied claims related to executive bonuses. I found out his kid played soccer and figured I'd take a different approach."

"We also have a witness who will testify you got into a heated confrontation with Lucy Hollander at the Mugga Java on Kennedy Boulevard," I said.

"Damn right we got into it!" He sat up straighter. "She and her company were responsible for three hundred layoffs in the past year alone. Hard-working people who were just trying to earn a living for themselves and their families."

"So you hated their guts," I said. "They were part of the corporate elite and well on their way to joining the 1 percent. Tell me why we shouldn't just lock you up right now."

"Uh, because I'm innocent." He slumped back in his chair. "Not that you'd give a crap. You're goose-stepping cogs in the establishment."

I looked at Payton. "Did he just liken us to Nazis?"

Payton looked at me. "I believe he did."

We both looked at Krupinski.

"You know what I think?" I folded my hands on the table. "I think you're one of those guys who's addicted to video games, but it reached a point where simulated victories weren't enough for you. So you created your own live-action game that's a cross between Occupy Wall Street and *Grand Theft Auto*."

Krupinski held up his hands. "Just slow down, okay?" He took a deep breath and blew it out. "I talked to Caruso and Hollander to give them the opportunity to comment on their actions before I posted my blog, but I do not know that other woman. And did you ever hear the phrase, 'The pen is mightier than the sword'? I may be passionate about exposing corporate misdeeds but I am not a murderer!" For the first time, he didn't sound like he'd just crawled out of bed. "My goal was to bring about change peacefully."

"Nothing peaceful about stabbing someone to death," I said.

"It wasn't me!" He closed his eyes for a minute, like he needed to collect his thoughts. He opened his eyes and pushed his glasses back into place on the bridge of his nose. "You know, these people bring it on themselves. We make choices every day to do the right thing or not. They chose wrongly, and they paid the price. Greed is like a flesh-eating disease, and if it isn't excised, it spreads. We wouldn't even need unions today if owners could be trusted to treat people fairly, but greed leads to unsafe conditions and worker exploitation so—"

"Spare us the civics lesson," Payton said.

Krupinski spread his hands. "I'm just saying if someone *is* killing people because of corporate greed, then the bodies are going to keep piling up."

"Why is that?" Payton asked.

"Because Paragon Insurance and Mayer Consulting were minor league compared to some of the bullshit going on in Bedford," Krupinski said. "If I were the killer, I'd have targeted Ronald Thorndike from ThoriChem."

"He's in jail," Payton said.

Krupinski slapped the table. "About damn time too. Ronald Hyatt would have made another great example except he crashed his car before they nailed him for all of Reseda Pharmaceutical's problems. And don't get me started on bankers. They deserve to go down a notch!"

The comment landed like a gut-punch. Dave played absolutely no role in the lending decisions yet he died because of them.

"They made billions in interest on all the sub-prime mortgages they approved," Krupinski continued. "After the collapse, they gobbled up the taxpayers' bailout money and then refused to funnel it back into the economy to help homeowners and small businesses. And then they paid back all the TARP funds and proceeded to dole out bonuses to their executives."

I slammed my fist on the table. "Not all bankers were greedy bastards! Some of them were just as upset by what happened as the rest of us but they lacked the power to do anything!"

Krupinski pressed back against his chair and held up his hands. "Whoa! Hey! You got a thing for bankers, fine. I just—"

Payton stooped over next to Krupinski's ear and calmly said, "Not another word about bankers."

Krupinski looked up at Payton and then at me. He was breathing a little fast.

So was I. "Where were you at three thirty on the past three Friday afternoons?"

"On air," he said. "I do a live radio show from Wellington University from three to seven."

If he was telling the truth, we were screwed again. I stared at him.

Payton cleared his throat to get my attention and then he tossed a glance toward the door. "We need to verify a few things," he told Krupinski. He opened the door but paused. "There is one more question you can answer for me as a corporate watchdog. How is it my taxes keep going up while a company the size of GE ends up with zero tax liability?"

Krupinski flashed a wry smile. "Because unlike the top 1 percent, you can't afford to buy a member of Congress to write loopholes into the tax code."

We nodded and Payton closed the door behind us. We spent the next half hour on the phone, and when we finished, we'd verified Raymond Krupinski's alibi for all three murders.

"Even if the radio station lied and the show was taped," Payton said, "the calls to Ortiz or the Bunker didn't come from his burner. Either he had another phone or he isn't our guy."

The euphoria I felt when I cuffed Krupinski had been overtaken by the sense he was merely a passionate young man trying to expose corporate wrongdoing. Exhausted, I put my face in my hands.

"You were right, you know," Payton said.

I lowered my hands. "About what?"

"He does look like Jim Carrey."

I chuckled.

"You know," he said, "it's possible whoever we're looking for is a frequent visitor to Allister's—Krupinski's site."

I wagged my finger at him. "You're thinking the killer drank Allister's Kool-Aid." I punched the speed dial for the Technical Response Unit and told Cassidy we needed him to start running the usernames of anyone who posted comments on the site. I heard him gulp. He probably had a dozen other high-priority requests but he told me he'd get right on it. I hung up and said, "Rachel Caruso said her husband had become disillusioned with his job. Maybe he found out something and threatened to go public. Same could be true for Lucy Hollander. She could have come across incriminating information during one of her consulting gigs. They both could have gone to Ortiz to discuss their legal exposure if they came forward, and in the meantime, the companies found out and hired someone to do a little risk management."

"So now companies are bumping off whistleblowers?"

I shrugged my brows. "It's a theory."

"Maybe for a Tom Clancy novel. Besides, with their money, our vics wouldn't have gone to Legal Aid."

"They would if they were concerned the top lawyers in Bedford were acquainted with their bosses."

Payton couldn't help but laugh. "Your lack of sleeping is starting to catch up with you, partner." He stood and walked around my desk. "Go home, take a hot bath, have a stiff drink, and come back clear-headed in the morning. That's what I'm going to do. Minus the hot bath of course." He switched my lamp off and walked out.

Payton is a smart guy and I would've taken his advice—if I'd gone home.

— CHAPTER 33 —

I tossed and turned all night on the Camp Cadaver cot and woke up for good a little before six o'clock. I cleared my head with a workout, and by the time I showered it was time for my shift. When I exited the locker room, I heard excited voices coming from the squad room, but the moment I walked in, the lively conversations stopped mid-sentence and all eyes locked on me.

I did a quick check to be sure I'd zipped all my zippers and buttoned all my buttons. I even checked the soles of my shoes in case I stepped in something I shouldn't have. Nothing seemed out of place. I walked up to my desk and said, "Morning," and I sat down.

"Morning," Payton said.

"Do I have bird shit in my hair or something?"

"There's been a development," Morgan said.

I looked at Payton, thinking there'd been a break in our case, but his somber face told me which case Morgan was referring to.

"We got a call last night," Garcia said. "A guy was walking along the expressway near Nineteenth, looking for cans to recycle, and he came across a black Ford pickup. The driver was inside with a single gunshot wound in his right temple. When the unis got there, they found a wallet. It was Noonan."

My head spun a little and I blinked to clear the stars from my eyes.

"They also found a .38 automatic in his hand," Donovan said. "Ballistics confirmed it was the gun that killed Dave."

It was over. The bastard who killed my husband was dead.

"There was an empty bottle of tequila on the seat," Donovan said. "Based on the level of decomposition, Doc Norris estimates the body was there for approximately three weeks."

I felt so parched I was barely able to pry my tongue away from the roof of my mouth to speak. "He drove there from the bank."

"Probably," Donovan said.

My breath came in and out in choppy little waves. I took a deep, steadying breath and slowly exhaled. "Well, you closed the case even without my help," I said, hoping cop humor would dissipate some of the tension.

Donovan spread his hands. "We can't all be crack detectives like you and Payton."

"Gives you something to aspire to though," Payton shot back.

Donovan glanced toward his desk drawers and then looked at Morgan and gave a little shrug of his brow toward me. Morgan nodded once.

I jerked my chin toward him. "You got a porn stash in there or something?"

"You busted me." He reached down and slid his bottom drawer open and plastic crinkled as he removed an evidence bag. He closed the drawer, got up, and came around to my desk.

I stopped mid-breath and my shoulders sagged when I recognized Dave's watch through the plastic.

"The case is closed except to write up the final report," Morgan said, "so—"

"I hope Garcia does the paperwork," I said, "or you'll be waiting awhile." I felt my bottom lip quiver when I forced a smile.

"I see no reason why you shouldn't have that," Morgan said.

I took the bag from Donovan and gripped Dave's ring through the plastic. I turned the bag over so I could read the inscription on his watch. *Forever.* "I gave this to Dave on our first anniversary," I said. If I allowed my thoughts to go where they wanted I'd have a meltdown in the middle of the squad room and that wasn't going to happen, so I opened the top box drawer of my desk, tucked the bag inside, and closed the drawer.

"Detective." Morgan arched her brows, silently seeking confirmation I'd be able to keep it together.

"I'm good, Cap," I said, though I felt as if my body were slowly crumbling into a million pieces...like a building when it's imploded.

She nodded and returned to her office.

I positioned my fingers over my keyboard, but they trembled too much for me to type. I flexed them a few times, but I squeezed my left hand so tightly my wedding band dug into my flesh. I stopped flexing and started to spin my ring.

The mere touch of Payton's hand on my shoulder sent cracks rippling through the emotional dam I'd constructed when Pritchard told me about Dave.

"I'm…uh…ahem…I'm going to need a minute." I sprang from my chair and rushed out of the squad room, feeling as if I were careening over rapids in a leaky raft.

My feet struck every other step as I ran the two flights to the roof. I pounded the push-bar, rushed through the door and ran to the north side of the building. I spread my arms like an eagle, flattened my palms on the ledge, and looked out at the city below.

No million-dollar vista like Lee Wellington's here. Just other roofs, a sea of treetops, and a glimpse of the Planetarium dome in Veterans Memorial Park, two blocks away.

Dave loved the park. At Christmas, sipping hot chocolate while we watched the ice sculptors chain saw their way through blocks to reveal sleighs or reindeer or elves. How many times did we drink coffee by the fountain? Or walk hand-in-hand along one of a dozen paths? How many more times would we have done all of those things if…

"You stole my life!" I screamed at the top of my lungs.

I should go to the morgue and spit on the bastard! How dare he shoot himself in the head and rob me of the chance to put a bullet in HIS chest!

Heh. Right. Like I would have been able to shoot him in cold blood.

My entire body quivered with rage. "Son of a bitch!" I did a one-eighty and slid down along the half wall. I pulled my knees to my chest and plunged over the falls, submerged in a raging river of tears fed by my soul.

I don't know how long I cried before the shuddering sobs finally transitioned to hiccups of breath. I sat there, sniffling and trying to get my bearings, until Payton called my name. I squeegeed my cheeks with my palms as I scrambled to my feet. "I'm—"

"Don't even," Payton said with a small shake of his head. He spread his arms.

I didn't move. Cops don't do public displays of emotion or affection and I'd already shown more than my share in his presence.

"Would you just—" He stepped closer.

I hesitated but then I stepped forward and rested my head against his shoulder. He wrapped his arms around me and I allowed myself to wallow in the security of his embrace for a moment before I pulled back and rested the small of my back against the wall.

"Maybe you should take a picture and send it to Connie. She's been very concerned about the way I've buried my feelings so she'd be relieved to see this." I licked my lips. They felt puffy and tasted salty. "I guess some people would consider this closure."

"Or as close as anything comes," Payton said softly.

I sighed heavily and sniffled again. "I think I'd better hit the restroom."

We went back down to the sixth floor and I detoured to the locker room. I snatched a couple tri-fold paper towels from the dispenser, soaked them with cold water, and pressed them to my face. I peeled the towels away and looked in the mirror. My eyes were still red and my skin was still a little blotchy, so I rewet the towels and pressed them back into place. I heard the door swing open and I peeled back the towels again to see Morgan in the mirror.

"Hey, Cap," I said to her reflection.

"How are you?"

"I'm better than I was when I got here this morning." I balled up my paper towels and tossed them into the trash bin in the corner. "I...uh...I know it's short notice but I need a little personal time this morning."

"They should hear it from you," she said.

I gave a nod of appreciation and left. An hour later I was back at my desk.

Payton gave me a moment to get settled before he asked, "How are Dave's parents?"

"Pissed, relieved, and a dozen other things," I said.

When I told my in-laws their son's killer was dead, Carol gasped and Ken simply closed his eyes.

"I called my parents too," I said, "but I got their machine. I hated to leave a message but some of their friends still live here and..." The pen I'd picked up wouldn't write and I threw it down and plucked another out of the holder Matthew had made for Payton.

"You tell Connie?"

"I swung by the hospital but she was tied up with a multi-vehicle accident." I drew in a deep breath and slowly exhaled, trying to calm my nerves.

"To answer your question," he said, "it was."

I looked at him, confused. "What was?"

"Friday," he said. "I did a little research, and in 1948, the thirteenth of August fell on a Friday. But you're not superstitious, remember?"

"Right."

He held up a folder. "We finally got the information from Mayer."

Thank God. Something productive to do. "Let's get to it."

We spent most of Tuesday morning talking to the people who'd been the casualties of Lucy Hollander's recommendations. Except for one woman, who seized the opportunity to make some changes in her life, all of the workers expressed anger and frustration over Hollander's actions.

We were on our way to talk to a guy with four kids who'd been laid off in May when my cell vibrated. I groaned when I saw the caller ID but answered anyway. "What now, Pritchard?"

"Huh! Is that any way to greet the guy who got a lead on your shooter?"

"You found Rivera?" The news hit me like a triple shot of espresso. Payton's brows arched and I held up my finger.

"I got a location," Pritchard said. "You can take it from there."

I thanked him and ended the call. "Maybe we can arrest at least one felon today after all," I told Payton.

— CHAPTER 34 —

Pritchard's tip took us to a pool hall on Mission Street. Rivera wasn't there, but the owner recognized his mug shot and told us he'd been coming in almost every afternoon. Payton parked on McClellan within view of the front door and we settled in to wait.

My phone vibrated but I let it go to voicemail when I saw Connie's number. I watched the screen until the message icon popped up and then played it back.

"I just wanted to touch base," Connie said. "I know you're immersed in the case but all the more reason for you to take a break. I can't wait for pizza and a DVD tomorrow. Take care. Love you."

I slid the phone into my pocket.

"Are things okay between you and Connie?" Payton asked.

I looked at him and wondered if he saw her name on my display or if he was just that good. "Yeah, it's just…as much as I enjoy the movies and TV shows in my collection, not one has the power to make me forget the last time I watched a DVD and ate pizza with Connie. I don't want to hurt her feelings but—"

"You're best friends," he said. "Telling her what you just told me is not going to hurt her feelings, but blowing her off will."

"Wow!" I gazed at him, amazed. "That's pretty insightful for a guy."

"Watch it with the generalizations." He checked his watch. "I wonder if Rivera is even going to show today."

"Speaking of Rivera," I said, "there's something you need to know about him…about me, actually. In that alley, when Rivera shot me…" I kneaded my thumb into my palm for a moment as I worked up the courage to confess. "I froze. I allowed myself to think about what it must've been like for Dave to stare at the gun in that bastard's hand. And I wondered what his last thought—" I decided to stop talking before emotion got the best of me.

"I figured it was something like that," Payton said.

My jaw dropped. "Why didn't you say something?"

He swung his head toward me. "Why didn't you?"

I nodded. "You're right. I'm sorry."

"You should be." He checked the rearview mirror. "Heads up."

I hunched down a little to look in my side mirror. I saw Rivera shuffling toward us, wearing a black T-shirt and jeans. We got out of the car. When we slammed the doors, Rivera looked up and stopped.

"He's going to run again," I said.

Payton jumped back in the car and started it up.

"Police, Rivera!" I shouted. "Stop where you are!"

Rivera spun around and ran south on McClellan.

Here we go again!

I yanked my gun from my holster and took off after him. I heard tires squeal behind me when Payton hung a U-turn. Rivera's arms flapped like a windmill as he rounded the corner toward Meade. Payton sped past us and Rivera glanced over his shoulder to get a fix on me. I kicked it up a notch and Payton rounded the corner into the alley. Rivera stopped cold and his right hand disappeared from my sight.

I felt an overwhelming sense of déjà vu as I stopped, raised my Glock, and aimed at center mass. Rivera spun to face me with his automatic raised and I shouted, "Drop the weapon!"

My hands remained steady as I held him in my sight. Payton stood with his gun trained on Rivera over the roof of the car. After a few seconds of internal debate, Rivera opened his hand and the automatic clattered onto the concrete.

I ran up, shoved Rivera against the wall of the corner house, and kicked his feet apart. "You got him?" I called to Payton without taking my eyes off Rivera.

"Got him."

I clicked on the safety and holstered my gun.

"I ain't done nothin'!" Rivera shouted.

"Shut up!" I twisted Rivera's right arm behind his back, snapped the cuff on, and then did the same with his left. I told him his rights as I patted him down for other weapons, and then I spun him around.

"What's the charge?" Rivera whined.

"I guess he missed the part about remaining silent," I said to my partner.

Payton dropped Rivera's gun into an evidence bag. "You shot a police officer."

Rivera smirked. "Way I heard it, that cop ain't dead."

I imagined how it would feel to punch him in the mouth. It would hurt like hell but it would be very satisfying. Then again, it would probably draw blood, and with Rivera's history, that could be dangerous. I got right in his face. "You're right. I'm not."

Rivera's eyes flared and his head recoiled slightly.

I smiled. "Can't wait to get your gun to Ballistics, Cesar. You should've stayed beneath whatever rock you crawled under after you shot me." I led him to the cruiser, stuffed him into the back seat, and slammed the door.

"Damn, girl!" Payton said. "No hesitation there."

I laughed and crawled into the car.

Ten minutes later, we hauled Rivera into an interview room. Payton sat across from him and I stood against the wall behind Payton.

"Why'd you kill Adriana Ortiz?" Payton asked.

"What?" Rivera snickered.

Payton tossed the evidence bag containing Rivera's phone onto the table. "Guess what? There were several calls to Adriana Ortiz's phone from that burner phone. *Your* burner phone."

Rivera's right leg bounced a mile a minute under the table as he stared at the phone in the bag. "I wanna deal."

Payton smiled. "You're a funny guy, Cesar. We've got you for attempted murder of a police officer. There won't be a deal."

Rivera shrugged and folded his arms. "That the way you wanna play it, fine, but maybe you better listen to what I gotta say first 'cuz what I got could be real big. Could be I got information on this Friday Afternoon Killer."

I stepped forward and braced my palms on the tabletop to get in his face. "That's funny because we think we're looking at him right now. You killed Adriana in a jealous rage and then you killed the others to throw us off."

"No way!" Rivera said. "I didn't kill Ari! She's my drug, ya know? No matter what I did, I couldn't get her outta my brain. I'll cop to callin' her, but she wasn't takin' my calls so I went to see her. But that was it!" He jutted his chin out. "So what do I get?"

"A warm, fuzzy feeling from knowing you did the right thing for once in your miserable life," I said.

Rivera's eyes rolled toward the ceiling. "I think I better get me some Ginko Gelatto or whatever. My memory ain't what it used to be."

I slapped my palms on the table. "What do you know about the murders?"

Rivera shook his head. "A deal in ink."

I pulled out the chair to Rivera's right and eased down onto it. "You shot a cop, Cesar. You *will* do time, but if you tell us what you know..." I swallowed hard so I wouldn't choke on the next words. "I will personally talk to the ASA assigned to your case and ask him or her to go for the minimum."

Rivera's eye twitched a little as he studied me. "Aw right. Aw right, Look, I ain't sayin' I was stalkin' her or nothin' but I mighta followed Ari home from work the day she died. And I mighta seen a guy go up to her on the street and then go in with her."

"What did this guy look like?" Payton asked.

"White guy."

"That narrows it down," Payton said.

Rivera smiled. "They all look alike to me." He flinched when I slammed my fist on the table, but then he slowly looked up at me. "You should switch to decaf, sweet meat."

Payton sprang up, knocking his chair back.

"He was an older white guy!" Rivera blurted out.

I wondered if he'd seen Carter Smithfield and asked, "How old?"

Rivera shrugged. "Forty maybe."

Too young for the adulterous senior partner and too old for Krupinski. I wanted to be Goldilocks and have a suspect who was just right. Payton rolled his finger, signaling Rivera to keep talking.

"He was about your size," Rivera said, flicking a finger toward Payton. "Maybe a little taller. Brown hair. He's one of them go green types."

"How do you know?" Payton asked.

"Saw his car. A silver Prius."

I asked if he noticed the license plate.

Rivera shrugged again. "Sorry."

I slid the chair back from the table. "Thanks for nothing."

"You still gonna talk to the ASA?" Rivera asked anxiously.

"I said I would," I told him, and as we walked out of the room, my stomach churned at the thought of asking the prosecutor to go easy on the garbage that shot me.

We finished up with Rivera's booking a little after six, and I called Porter and left a voice mail, asking him to assign some unis to re-canvass Caruso's and Hollander's neighbors to see if anyone noticed a silver Prius. Payton invited me to Matt's baseball game and I crossed my fingers behind my back when I declined on the grounds I had to get home to deal with a pile of laundry. Once he left, I changed into shorts and a tank top and headed downstairs to the gym for thirty minutes on the wind bike and some stretches.

I showered and dressed and I stopped in the break room for dinner. To mix it up and add some dairy to my diet, I opted for cheese curls to go with my root beer. I settled at my desk and pinched each side of the bag, but Morgan appeared in the doorway and I flinched. The bag ripped and curls scattered across my desk. "Hey, Cap." I reached for my trash can, raked the curls into a pile, and brushed them into the can. "You working late tonight?"

"No," she said. "I had dinner with friends at McNamara's and I figured you must be getting tired of soda and chips." She reached over and set a white paper bag in front of me. "Hope you eat beef."

"Yes, I do, but—"

"The commissioner is going to start charging you room and board."

"No, I just…"

She cocked her head.

I realized a lame excuse at this point would be plain stupid. "It's a little hard to be in the house right now."

She nodded. "I remember." She drew in a deep breath. "Every night, I drove past the corner where Roger died until they caught the punks who shot him."

"So did I until Donovan and Garcia busted me." I winced at how easily I'd taken the bait.

Her eyes brimmed with empathy. "As your CO, I had to issue that order, but as a fellow officer and widow who's been there, I didn't expect you to be able to obey it." She rubbed her hand across the back of her neck, like she was trying to calm a tension headache—which I probably caused. "The job will only fill part of the void, Val. You need to find a way to live in your home. Or maybe you need to find a new home because hiding out here is not an option."

Maybe not long-term, but for now, it works for me. "I know and I will...Just not tonight."

"You're beginning to look like an ad for sleeping pills. Get some rest." She tapped her knuckles on my desk and gave me a stern look. "That's an order I expect you to obey."

If only it were so easy.

"Thank you for dinner," I called after her.

She tossed a wave over her shoulder and walked out.

I initiated a search of registered Prius owners and stared at the bag as I waited for the results. I wasn't hungry, but my mother's voice echoed in my head. *You need to eat, Val.* Morgan had gone out of her way to bring me dinner, so I guess the least I could do was eat a few bites. I carried the bag to the desk by the whiteboard and picked at the butter-soft sirloin tips, roasted red potatoes, and grilled vegetables as I studied the bullet points of our case.

Corporate misdeeds still seemed like our best motive yet there was no link between Smithfield, Royce, and Foley and Paragon Insurance or Mayer Consulting.

Unless there was and we'd simply failed to find it. Maybe Mayer and Ross Danner at Paragon lied about having Smithfield, Royce, and Foley on retainer. But if they did, how would we prove it given the partners would never admit it?

I carried the empty takeout tray back to my desk and tossed it in the trash. I sat back in my chair and watched the Bedford PD emblem drift aimlessly across my computer screen.

Raymond Krupinski told us he suspected Hollander wouldn't be the last victim because there was plenty of corporate mayhem in

Bedford. We already knew the executive from ThoriChem had gone to jail, but what was the other company he'd mentioned?

I drummed my fingers on the desk and then snapped them. "Reseda Pharmaceuticals." I tapped the mouse, reentered my password, and typed the name into the search box. I skipped the first link to the company's website but clicked the second and scanned a *Bedford Tribune* article about a drug recall.

Over a two-week period in June, five people died from bacterial infections in different hospitals on the East Coast. The victims included an eight-year-old girl in Boston and a ten-year-old boy from Bedford, who was vacationing on Martha's Vineyard with his family. A joint investigation by the CDC and local health departments revealed only one common denominator—all five had been treated with an antibiotic manufactured by Reseda. When tested, the serum was found to be 90 percent saline, rendering it ineffective. A quality control inspection at the company's plant revealed a problem with the equipment used to produce the serum. Reseda issued a recall in early July and no further problems were reported, but several wrongful death lawsuits were filed. In a press release, the company stated it had complied with FDA guidelines and was conducting a full review of quality-control procedures. All inquiries regarding the recall were referred to Reseda's legal counsel—Smithfield, Royce, and Foley.

"Shut the front door!"

I returned to the search results and scanned the links. Several were additional stories about the recall or Russell Hyatt's death, but another *Bedford Tribune* article from the Lifestyle section titled, "Are Bedford Philanthropists Cruising to Divorce Court?" seemed so out of place I clicked on it out of sheer curiosity and read:

A conspicuous no-show at a recent Aleron Foundation fundraiser was Nina Wellington, wife of Aleron's founder and chairman, Ridley Wellington III. Rumors of a floundering marriage have circulated for over a year, but now insiders place Nina at the couple's Hawaiian condo, where she has reportedly sequestered herself to mourn their ten-year-old son, Ethan, whose death has been linked to the recent recall of a tainted antibiotic manufactured by Bedford-based Reseda Pharmaceuticals.

I stared at the screen, barely able to breathe. I knew Wellington lost his son because Dave told me after he heard the news through Lakeview Bank's CEO, but at the time of the boy's death, they didn't know the infection had resulted from tainted antibiotics. "How awful," I whispered.

I clicked back to the search results and rolled the pointer over another article about the recall, but my finger froze over the left button when I recalled a detail from Wellington's press conference that I should have remembered when we had Rivera in the box. After he announced his reward out front, Wellington drove away in a silver Prius.

I typed "Ridley Wellington III" into the search box and proceeded to scour the results. After graduating from Harvard, he and a buddy did very well with an Internet start-up, which they sold for millions, and that success opened the door to other opportunities. His paternal ancestors made their fortune in the railroads. Then while the family empire was under his father's stewardship, they got into a nasty lawsuit involving child labor in Sri Lanka. In contrast, Wellington's maternal relatives came from modest means. His great-grandfather emigrated from Russia and supported his family by delivering—ice!

If Wellington kept any tools from his great-grandfather's trade, he'd have means and motive.

I started to call Payton until I read 4:47 AM on the display. My head pounded like a bass drum and my eyelids felt as if they were filled with sand. I folded my arms on the desk, put my head down, and closed my eyes for a minute, hoping to slow my pulse and clear my head.

CHAPTER 35

I smelled coffee and my eyes popped open. My mug was a few inches from my head, which was propped on my forearms. I moved to sit up but my stiff neck and shoulders screamed at me while my hands and forearms felt numb. I slowly sat up and dragged my arms off my desk and let them dangle at my sides. My fingers began to tingle as blood started flowing again, and I pushed my shoulders back and rolled my head around, eliciting a snap in my neck muscles. "Thanks for the coffee," I said to Payton.

He stopped typing long enough to glare at me.

I did another head roll and sipped some coffee and wondered if I'd been dreaming about a link between Wellington and Ortiz or if I'd actually found one. Like me, my monitor had gone into sleep mode, so I nudged the mouse and logged back on my computer. And there it was.

"I can't believe you spent the night at your desk," Payton said.

"It was worth a stiff neck to find a suspect with a motive to kill Adriana Ortiz."

"Uh-huh," he said as he listened to his voicemail.

I stared at him, mouth open, barely breathing. How could he be so nonchalant about a break in the case? "You don't even care."

"It's not..." He slammed the receiver down and rubbed his forehead. "How much longer do you think caffeine is going to be able to compensate for lack of sleep?"

"I'm fine!" *How many times had I'd uttered those two words in the past three weeks? A hundred?* "And like I said, it was worth it."

Payton stared at me for a moment. "Okay, I'll bite. Who and why?"

"Ridley Wellington," I said. Payton scoffed and dropped his head so I waited until he looked up to explain. "His ten-year-

213

old son, Ethan, died after treatment with a drug manufactured by Reseda Pharmaceuticals."

Payton's forehead crinkled. "Why does that name sound familiar?"

"Because Krupinski told us Reseda's CEO, Russell Hyatt, deserved to go to jail but died in a car wreck before it could happen. Care to guess which firm represents Reseda?"

"Smithfield, Royce, and Foley," Payton said.

"Yep. We have our link between Ortiz and corporate misdeeds."

"I'm sorry to hear about Wellington's son," Payton said, "but I guess I missed the motive and how all of this relates to our case."

"Maybe the bigwigs at Reseda discovered the problem before anyone died," I said. "They met with their legal team to discuss strategy and decided against a recall. It also explains Ortiz's bonus. She confided in Smithfield that she was uncomfortable with the cover-up, and he persuaded the partners to toss some money her way to soothe her guilty conscience."

Payton folded his hands on the desk and his skin blanched as he pressed his fingers into the backs of his hands, likely as he prayed for patience to deal with me.

"I know it's weak," I said defensively, "but it's a link we didn't have before."

He tapped his thumbs as he formulated one of his calm, rational responses. "If the drug company knew of the problem, why would they delay the recall?"

"Because their bean counters decided it would be cheaper to deal with the fallout," I said. "Like *Class Action*."

Payton angled his head a little. "Like what now?"

"It was a movie with Gene Hackman and Mary Elizabeth Mastrantonio. They played father and daughter lawyers on opposing sides of a lawsuit against an automaker. Hackman represented the plaintiff, and alleged the company knew about a defective circuit that could cause a particular model car to blow up. The company chose not to do anything because their actuarial figured paying out on a few lawsuits would be cheaper than retooling the assembly line."

Payton looked at me in amazement. "How do you—?"

"I was a couch potato in my youth."

He nodded a little and then his gaze dropped to his monitor, and with the way his eyes narrowed, I knew he was processing the new information. "Okay," he said and he looked up. "The Reseda angle is interesting, but I still don't get how you peg Wellington as a killer here. With his money and power, he could just ruin them."

"True, but he would have needed proof to do it." I got up, walked around, and sat in the chair next to his desk. "Hyatt was dead, and Wellington knew the other executives at Reseda and the senior law partners would never divulge anything, so he approached Ortiz. He figured he'd bully an associate into giving him a copy of a memo or something that would prove Reseda's negligence, but maybe she admitted everything—including how much she wanted to come forward but didn't. Emotion got the best of him and he lost it. Killing her in a fit of rage would also explain why he had to improvise with the lamp cord." I'd yet to drink any coffee but my nerves hummed as if I'd downed an entire pot. I arched my brows at him in a *What do you think?* look. He stared at me, and the pity I saw in his eyes forced me to look away. "You think I'm crazy."

"Not crazy. Just…" He sighed. "I think you're a grieving woman, in a tremendous amount of pain, who's looking for a positive way to channel some of her feelings. You finally have some closure on your husband's murder and you want the same thing for Rachel so—"

"No!" I held up my hand. "That has nothing to do with this." He kept his sympathetic eyes on me and I worked my jaw a few times as I tried to think of something to say to rebut his theory, but nothing came out.

"I'm sorry, Val. I shouldn't have said anything."

"Yes, you should. We're partners. We need open communication. And I admit I feel a connection to the next of kin that I probably never felt in the past, but it's not like we have any solid leads, so what do we have to lose?"

From the incredulous look on his face he wanted to say *How about everything?* but he kept calm and said, "For the sake of argument, let's pretend your exhaustion-induced theory holds water, and in some blind rage triggered by his son's death, Wellington killed Ortiz. What's his motive to kill the others?"

"Maybe something snapped when his son died," I said. "One murder gets you a needle the same as ten, so he makes it his mission to stop others who've acted in a similar way in order to avenge those who've died in the pursuit of profits."

He rubbed his fingers over his right cheek and then across his chin as he struggled to reconcile logic with having my back. "Is there a Mrs. Wellington we could speak to?"

"Sort of," I said. "Apparently, the marriage is in trouble. The strain of their son's death took its toll and they've separated." He sat up a little straighter, driving me to talk a little faster. "According to the articles I read last night—this morning—the Wellington fortune was built on dirty deals and unfair labor practices. And Wellington's hatred of his family's social irresponsibility is what drove him to establish the Aleron Foundation. It was his way to atone for his family's past."

"So he's the Bill Gates of Bedford. We can't arrest him for being too rich."

I held up my finger, begging patience. "When he came to America, Wellington's maternal great-grandfather delivered ice." Payton's eyes widened and I asked, "So what do you think?"

He held my eager gaze for a moment. "I think Morgan's going to laugh us right out of her office."

"Uh…" I popped my lips. "I was sort of hoping we wouldn't have to tell her just yet."

"Uh-huh." He sipped some tea and pondered what I'd told him. "You know we need something more than speculation."

I rubbed my tired eyes with my thumb and middle finger. "I know."

"If it's Wellington, why did he offer up a reward?"

"Misdirection."

"Because the killer wouldn't offer money for his own capture," Payton said.

"Uh-huh. Or maybe he was trying to ease his guilt over what he put Rachel through."

"Okay, we're getting a little ahead of ourselves here," Payton said. "We don't have any proof Ortiz was even connected to Reseda, and the partners aren't going to admit anything."

He was going to shut me down.

"But," he added. "Wellington told us he was in a meeting when he got a text about Scott Caruso, and at the time, we had no reason to doubt him. Now we do. In the interest of diligent police work, we should at least confirm his alibi."

I felt as if he'd lifted a bag of cement off my shoulders as we headed for Wellington's corporate office in Riverview Tower.

Wellington's assistant was at her desk, ear buds in her ears, typing furiously on her laptop. When we appeared before her, the typing ceased and she glanced at us over the top of her green frames.

"Hi!" I said. "Barbara, isn't it?"

She warily shifted her eyes between us as she tugged at the ear buds and nodded.

"We're doing some follow up," Payton said. "It's our understanding the metro editor at the *Bedford Tribune* is the one who called to tell Mr. Wellington about Scott Caruso."

"That's correct," she said.

"And where was Mr. Wellington?" Payton asked.

"Well, he was…" Her eyes dropped to her keyboard. "He was in a meeting."

A downward gaze often signaled lies. "With?" I prompted.

"I'd have to check his calendar," she said.

I wagged my finger toward her computer. "Could you do that, please?"

Her eyes jumped from me to Payton and back. "I don't see why that's relevant."

I smiled. "Like we said. Just routine."

She hesitated for a while longer before she accessed her boss's calendar. "Uh…I'm afraid the planner doesn't show who the meeting was with, which isn't unusual because sometimes Mr. Wellington instructs me to block out chunks of time for him to meet with potential donors for the foundation. They'll go sailing or play golf, and he's always reachable by phone if needed."

"Was the meeting here?" Payton asked.

She shook her head.

"What about the Friday before and Friday after?" I asked. She clicked around with her mouse, but with the way her eyes were bouncing around the screen, I sensed she already knew the answer.

"He had offsite meetings on those days too," she said.

"Do you know where he was or who he was with?" Payton asked.

She closed her eyes and nervously ran her fingers over her forehead as she mentally weighed her duty to her boss against her desire to be truthful.

"Loyalty is a wonderful thing, Barbara," I said. "You don't see much of it anymore, but if we find out you knew and didn't tell us, you can go to jail for withholding information and obstruction of justice."

She winced and said, "I don't know where he was. Honest." She sighed and looked up at us. "He comes in Friday mornings but always leaves around lunchtime. If anyone is looking for him, I simply say he's in meetings."

"How long has this been going on?" Payton asked.

Sadness filled her eyes. "Since Ethan died."

"This conversation should stay between us for now," Payton said.

She scoffed. "I'm sure not going to tell him I divulged anything."

"You did the right thing, Barbara," I said.

Her shoulders sagged and she looked away. Maybe someday after the feeling of betrayal faded, she'd believe me.

We left and as I punched the DOWN button to call the elevator I said, "We could put Wellington's photo in an array and re-canvass the victims' neighbors."

"We could," Payton said, "but Wellington is a public figure, and a lawyer would argue anyone who recognized him did so because they'd seen him on the news rather than at the scene."

I looked at my watch. "If this guy stays true to form, we have about fifty-two hours to find him."

"Wellington wasn't on our radar when we reviewed all the security video the first time around," Payton said. "Let's take another look. Maybe we can find something from Ortiz's neighborhood or Mayer Consulting."

We returned to the station and reloaded the security cam footage, but for the second time, we came up empty.

A little before six, Morgan turned off her light and walked over. "You two have been busy little bees today. What's up?"

Flat-out lying to Morgan would be stupid, but if we told her the truth with our flimsy evidence, she'd shut us down. "We... uh...we thought we'd go back over the security video to see if we could spot anyone resembling the guy Rivera claims he saw outside Ortiz's place."

Morgan's brows arched. "Chasing leads provided by a penny-ante drug dealer? Your investigation really has hit a brick wall, hasn't it?"

Payton cleared his throat and I tossed him a silent plea not to tell Morgan.

"Night," Morgan said.

I waited until I heard the elevator door before I told Payton I owed him one.

"And you can repay me by going home and getting a good night's sleep," he said. "Let's come at this with fresh eyes in the morning." His stern eyes bore through me as he waited for me to move.

"Is that the look you use on the kids when they misbehave?"

"Uh-huh."

"Pretty effective." I logged off my computer but I told him I had to make a pit stop so he left without me. I rationalized that it was only half a lie because I did stop working. I just didn't tell him I wasn't going home. And I really did have to pee.

As I washed my hands, I mulled our working theory that Wellington killed Ortiz because of her involvement with Reseda Pharmaceuticals. Unfortunately that theory had a gaping hole right now because we couldn't prove Ortiz knew about the drug company's problems.

Or could we?

— CHAPTER 36 —

Jeremy Konrad was sitting with one foot propped on the window-sill when I tapped on the door to his inner office. "Val," he said with a smile and he walked over to meet me.

"Sorry to just show up," I said.

He waved it off. "I told you my door was always open. No pun intended." He motioned to the chairs in front of his desk. "Can I get you some coffee?"

I involuntarily grimaced as I recalled the last cup I'd had here.

"I'll take that as a no." He poured himself a cup and sat. "It's obvious we're both using work to avoid grief, but if it's not my horrible coffee, what brings you here on this beautiful summer evening?"

"I need your help with this case."

He nodded once. "If I can."

"That's the catch. I know your oath prevents you from saying anything, but I'd like to tell you a story." He didn't tell me to stop so I continued. "Several weeks ago, Adriana Ortiz showed up at a meeting, very close to relapsing because she knew a big company in Bedford had covered up a problem that ultimately cost five people their lives."

Konrad sipped some coffee and set the mug on his desk. He folded his hands in his lap and looked at me.

"I'll take your lack of denial as confirmation I'm right." Though his expression remained neutral, I felt like I was on a roll. "Did she give any indication she had proof?"

His expression still didn't change but he tapped his index finger against his knuckle as he considered his response. "She regretted not going to the press because the deaths could've been prevented if this company had recalled their product when they first learned of the problem. Apparently they delayed the recall until after the quarterly earnings were released."

And there it was. Motive.

His brows pinched a little. "You think that's why she was killed?"

I nodded. "Did anyone in the group seem upset by what she said?"

"If something transpires that leads me to believe a person is a danger to himself or others, I am obligated to notify the police," he said. "In the sessions I facilitated, I did not observe any behavior that caused me concern."

"Okay. Thank you. I know how hard it was for you to do that—"

"And yet." He raised both thumbs as if to say *You did it anyway.*

If he was trying to make me feel guilty, he succeeded. "I guess I've been doing a lot of things that are out of character lately," I admitted.

"Such as?"

"Asking you to violate your oath as a mental health professional."

"You're not the first," he said. "What else?"

I shook him off. "Nothing."

"How about pushing yourself to the brink of exhaustion?"

I stared at him. He stared back. As good as I am at playing the silent game with suspects, I had a feeling he was better. I exhaled sharply and said, "It's like I'm someone else. I seriously considered allowing my father-in-law to use his connections to get information we needed. I've been shutting my best friend out of my life. I pursued a dangerous suspect without backup. I interfered in someone else's case."

"Your husband's?"

I nodded.

"Why do you think you're doing those things?"

"Pfft. Damned if I know."

"We both know that's not true." He raised his eyebrows, a signal he expected an answer.

It felt like algebra class all over again when the teacher called on me and I didn't know the answer, only this time, I did know. I tried to swallow but my mouth felt like I'd used super glue instead of toothpaste this morning.

Konrad got up and filled a glass of water from the pitcher on the credenza behind his desk. He handed the glass to me and settled quietly in his chair.

I sipped some water and then softly said, "Sometimes it feels like I'm in the ocean and…this wave crashes over me and I'm underwater and I'm struggling to get to the surface. I've pushed and pushed and put all my energy into this case because I believed getting justice for the relatives—especially Rachel Caruso—would make a difference for them."

"Why 'especially Rachel Caruso'?"

I knew he knew, but he expected me to say it. "Because she's a widow and I'm a widow, and I couldn't be involved in Dave's case, so catching her husband's killer is the next best thing."

He looked pleased with my assessment. "So how did it feel to learn the man who shot your husband was dead?"

I thought back to that moment in the squad room with Donovan and Garcia, and the only thing I could remember feeling was the same emptiness I felt before they broke the news. "I looked up 'closure' in the dictionary the other day," I said, "and one of the definitions was 'the bringing to an end. Conclusion.'" I shook my head. "The only thing my job brings to an end is the open case. There's a conclusion to the who, but in many cases, we never know the why."

"Cases like Dave's," Konrad said.

I nodded. "When I thought about Dave the day Rivera shot me, I was wondering if Noonan said anything, or if Dave tried to reason with him." I sniffled. "The killer's dead so I can't ask, but even if he were alive, there's no guarantee he'd talk to me." I sighed. "All these years in Homicide really built up my ego. I walked away from visits with the victims' next of kin feeling like I'd lightened their burden by telling them the offender was in jail or dead." I clucked my tongue at my own arrogance. "But now, having been on the receiving end, I realize hearing the person who blew your world apart is dead isn't nearly as satisfying as I'd imagined it was when I was the one saying it. It may bring some peace of mind to know that no one else will suffer, but the pain is still there. There's no conclusion to the loss. At least not yet." I swallowed the lump in my throat. "I think I'm a little afraid that from now on, solving a case isn't going to be the high it was because I know it doesn't have the impact I always thought it did."

Konrad frowned and his shoulders sagged a little, like a parent who has just watched his child fail in spite of giving her all. "I think you'd be surprised the impact it has," he said. "Getting murderers off the street is a big deal, and I know you're struggling to find your way, so try to hold on to that." He maintained eye contact as he considered what more he could say. "It's a hell of a thing, Val, but you have new insight into your job. A lot of cops have empathy, but thankfully, they never have personal knowledge of what it's like to lose someone to violence. The way I see it, this can go one of two ways. You can let the experience consume and eventually break you, or you can channel it into your work and allow it to make you a better cop."

I met his eyes.

He raised his brows in a *What's it going to be?* look. He sat back and smiled, quite satisfied with himself. "I have a pretty good idea how it'll turn out."

I hoped he was right as I shifted my gaze to the window. Florescent lights left on by workaholics, cleaning crews, or absent-minded occupants lit up the skyline like a game of Electronic Battleship.

"Every day is a challenge," he said, "whether you are dealing with loss or not. All you can do is take it one day at a time."

Hour by hour is more like it. "Right now I'd settle for closing this damn case."

"What's the consensus on your killer?" Konrad asked. "Do you think there is some connection between the victims or are you dealing with a serial killer?"

I shrugged my brows. "If they were involved in something that got them killed, we haven't been able to find it." I rubbed my forehead as if it would stimulate my brain cells. "We're thinking the first murder was personal because of some trauma, and he's gone on killing in a perverted attempt to find justice."

"What seems perverted to us," Konrad said, "would make perfect sense to him. In his distorted view of the world, he's setting it right."

I thought about the night Dave died. I'd stood staring at his body, with my fists clenched so tightly that the middle fingers of both hands broke skin. If Noonan had been standing in front of me, I probably would've shot him.

"Val?" Konrad's voice drew me back to the moment.

I shifted a little uneasily in the chair. "You know, at this point I really don't care why he did it. He's a murderer, and I just want to nail his ass to the wall."

"It must bring you some comfort to have such clarity of right and wrong," Konrad said. "Unfortunately, dealing with the human psyche isn't always so clearly defined."

"I'm sure." I sipped some water as I tried to decide how to solicit Konrad's opinion of Wellington. Mental health services in Bedford were a beneficiary of Aleron Foundation's fundraising efforts, so it was a good bet Konrad and Wellington had met at some point—hell, even I'd met Wellington before the case. But given how much I'd been coloring outside the lines, would it be appropriate to ask?

"How can I help?" he asked.

I laughed. "You can tell me how you read me like that."

He folded his hands and looked at me with an expression that said *It's what I do.*

"I hope I'm not so transparent when I've got a suspect in the box."

He smiled. "Takes a trained eye."

I nodded a little, still unsure how to ask, but I finally said, "You know Lee Wellington."

Konrad smiled. "Well, we're not golf buddies, but he and his foundation staunchly support mental health services in this city so it pays to play nice."

"So would that trained eye of yours have an opinion of him?" When Konrad's eyes narrowed, I held up my hand. "Wait. I don't want you to violate doctor-patient confidentiality. Again. It's just that he's been a pain in the ass with his reward and I don't have the best track record dealing with guys like him."

He shook it off. "No, it's okay. He's not a patient."

"So any advice on how to deal with him?"

Konrad sipped some coffee.

"Come on, Doc," I said. "You can't stop analyzing people any-more than I can stop scoping out my surroundings whenever I enter a room."

He tipped his head in concession then sighed. "Lee can be very impulsive at times, as you well know, and I'm afraid it has earned him a reputation. People see him as the proverbial golden boy, blessed with wealth, power, and rugged good looks. Star quarterback in college, Harvard Law graduate. Everyone thinks he's had it easy, but he's had his share of problems. I assume you know about Ethan."

I nodded.

"He puts up a good front," Konrad said, "but he's finding it more difficult to cope with his son's death and the failure of his marriage than he wants those around him to know."

"So a little empathy may go a long way," I said.

He nodded.

"I've taken enough of your time." I set the glass on the table and stood. "Thanks for listening, Doc."

"Anytime," he said.

The 911 calls played in my head like a broken record while I walked to the car. I crawled behind the wheel and turned the key, and when the dashboard clock flashed on, I couldn't help doing the math. We had forty-four hours until 3:29 PM Friday, when odds favored another frantic call to the Bunker.

I took Dickens north to Olympic and cruised along with the windows down. I cranked the country station when Kenny Chesney and Uncle Kracker began to sing the praises of a tropical paradise. Dave and I had talked about booking a winter trip to some all-inclusive Caribbean resort where we would've spent our days sipping colorful rum-based libations, and where our toughest decision would've been what to eat for dinner.

So much for clearing my head.

I caught the red light at Lexington and my mind drifted back to that day in Wellington's office when Payton admired Wellington's sailing trophy. The ETs found marine varnish in Ortiz's place and fibers from marine rope on Hollander's wrists.

The light turned green and I cut over to the left lane, turned into a gas station, and looped around back onto Olympic. I drove Olympic to where it runs into Lakeview Drive and I continued south to the marina.

A chatty dockhand told me the *Phoenix* was a beautiful forty-footer moored in slip number three on pier one, which allows prime access to both the yacht club and the water. A dozen slips lined each side of the pier, but only five boats were docked. The cabin lights were out on all of them, affording me some privacy as I squatted to get a closer look at the rope securing the *Phoenix* to the dock. Navy in color, it looked like nylon, which to the naked eye made it a match to the fibers Leilani found on Lucy Hollander's wrists. Too bad I didn't have a warrant. Then again, the dock is public property.

I scanned the marina for possible witnesses as I fished in my purse for my pocketknife. I wedged my nail in the groove to pry it open, but my phone vibrated. I flinched and the knife flew out of my hand and clattered onto the deck of Wellington's boat.

I snatched my phone from my pocket, and when I saw Connie's number, I almost let it go to voicemail—again—but she didn't deserve the silent treatment, so I answered.

"Hey," she said. "I was just calling to see if I should call for the pizza or hold off."

"I'm sorry I couldn't get back to you but I'm not—"

"Val!"

"I'm sorry but we got a lead and—"

"First you got shot by that drug dealer and now you're working overtime. If I were the insecure type, I'd think you were planning these things to avoid me."

I hesitated a moment before I said, "Not you."

"Aw, Val, I didn't…" She sighed into the phone. "I should've realized it's what we were doing when you got the news. I'm sorry."

"No. You didn't do anything that you need to apologize for." I stared up at the stars. "Just so you know, I miss it too. And it's irrational to think I'll never eat pizza, or watch a movie, or do them together again in my life because…well…it's me and we are talking pizza but…I'm going to need a little more time."

"I get it," Connie said, and if she were standing next to me, she'd have given me a big hug. "I hope it doesn't take another line-of-duty injury for me to see you again. And *please* be safe."

She ended the call and I slipped the phone into my pocket and scanned the deck of Wellington's boat for my knife. I spotted it about a foot from the side. I couldn't reach it from a squat, and I didn't want to step on deck, so I laid flat on the dock, held the docking rope, and reached over. I managed to catch the knife with my fingertips and flick it to the side to scoop it up. I pushed myself up onto my knees, and then I cut a two-inch length of rope from the tail looped around the cleat. I dropped my sample into a plastic bag, snapped my knife shut, and dropped both into my purse as I started toward the parking lot.

— CHAPTER 37 —

I'd called Argus on the way home and asked him to meet me in the lab early Thursday, before anyone else arrived. He confirmed the rope I cut from the dock matched the brand used to bind Lucy Hollander, but he also told me a lot of sailors used that brand, so it was inconclusive. I was preoccupied with our continued lack of evidence when I sat at my desk with my coffee.

"You look like something the cat dragged in," Payton said. "I hope that means you went over to Connie's and stayed up half the night catching up on girl talk."

"Nah. I skipped it."

"You decided to curl up on the couch for some quiet time at home, huh?"

"Mm-hmm." I reached for my coffee.

"I think your doorbell's broken," he said, "because we came by after Matt's baseball game to take you with us for ice cream."

The mug stopped halfway to my mouth.

"Where were you?"

"I had some stuff to do." I could be so articulate. I sipped some coffee.

"Stuff," he said. "As in following Lee Wellington?"

I choked a little as the coffee went down. "No! Of course not!"

Growing impatient, Payton crossed his arms on his desktop. "What did you do?"

I wiped the drip of coffee from my chin. "I *may* have taken a sample of rope from his boat but—" Payton threw his hands in the air and I shrugged my palms. "What?"

"If we're not careful, we're going to hand his lawyers their defense on a silver platter."

"Well, that's a chance I'll have to take because I refuse to sit around and do nothing on *another* case." I made a *Deal with it* face at Payton. "We can link him to Ortiz through the firm and he knew Caruso personally, so we need to figure out how Hollander landed on his radar. Given we've already ruled out restaurants, health clubs, and everything else through their financials, we need to—"

"Aleron," Payton blurted out. "Maybe Hollander was active with the foundation."

I think I was already in the hall by the time Payton stood up.

I hoped we'd find a competent volunteer to assist us at the Aleron office, and I was shocked when we walked in and found Rachel Caruso chatting with a young woman at the front desk. Like me, she probably figured work would keep her mind occupied. *Yeah right.*

Rachel invited us to her office and seemed disappointed when we told her why we were there. Understandably, she hoped we came to tell her we solved the case, but she jumped right onto her computer and pulled up the information we requested.

"I'm not showing Lucy Hollander in the system," she said, "but that doesn't mean she never attended an event. Sometimes people come as a plus one of a guest, or at the last minute, that sort of thing."

"Does anyone ever buy a table?" Payton asked.

"Sure," Rachel said, "and in those cases we don't always know who the guests are."

"Try Robert Mayer or Mayer Consulting," Payton said.

She typed it in. "Here it is. The company paid for a table at our summer kickoff." Payton and I looked at each other and Rachel asked if the information was important.

"Very," Payton said.

She put her hand to her chest. "You have no idea how good it feels to help." She bit her lip when she realized what she'd said. "How silly of me. I'm sorry. Of course you know how it feels." Her forehead crinkled a little and her eyes drifted down. She probably recalled some special time spent with her husband. She smiled to herself and seemed comforted.

"Seems like a good memory," I said.

Rachel looked up and nodded. "That event was the last one Scott and I attended together, and it actually turned out to be one of our more energized events. Scott and Lee and some of the other donors got into quite a discussion over health care reform, which turned into a debate over the bottom line versus ethics."

Goes to motive, I thought.

"There is one other thing," Payton said. "Did you ever notice a silver Prius hanging around your neighborhood? Maybe cruising by or parked up the street?"

"Uh…as a matter of fact I did," she said. "It was maybe a week before…" She sucked in some air to stifle her emotion. "It's funny because at the time, I thought it was Lee, but then I dismissed it because if it were him, he would have waved or something."

Not if he didn't want you to see him, I thought.

We thanked her for her help, and on the way back to the station, I called Donald Hollander. He confirmed he and Lucy attended the fundraiser and told me his wife had loved the event, mainly because they'd had the opportunity to chat with Lee Wellington.

The background report on Wellington was sitting on Payton's desk when we got back. He immediately opened the folder and scanned the contents and then he frowned and tossed it down.

"What?" I asked, though I wasn't sure I wanted to know.

"Wellington has never been arrested or even investigated for anything."

"So he never got caught," I said. "Probably stole a yacht in high school and his father managed to cover it up."

"Maybe Cassidy can dig something up," Payton said.

I thought about the mini-history lesson Argus gave us after Bedford's birthday bash. "Not Cassidy. Argus. He's a walking ency-clopedia." I jerked my head toward the door. "Come on."

When we walked up and stood behind Argus, he slowly raised his head and swiveled his stool. "What's going on?" he asked with a wary expression.

"What do you know about Wellington the Third?" I asked.

He crossed his arms. "Oh, so now you're interested."

I didn't have time for his indignation at my blowing him off the other day. "Don't push me, Todd," I said. "We ran his background but he's clean."

"Officially, maybe, but off the record, he's got skeletons like everyone else."

"Such as?"

"I can't authenticate the accuracy of my information," Argus said.

I signaled with all my fingertips for him to let us have it.

"Okay then," Argus said. "Rumor is Ridley the Third was kidnapped when he was fifteen by a former employee at one of the Wellington companies. The guy lost the use of his arm in some sort of industrial accident and blamed Lee's father because the company allegedly ignored safety regs. Lee was held captive for a week, during which time the guy repeatedly threatened to kill him. Things were never the same between Lee and his family afterward."

"Why didn't this come up in background?" Payton asked.

"Per the kidnapper's instructions, the family never called the police," Argus said. "And they own the *Tribune*, so if they wanted to quash a story, it was quashed."

I looked at Payton. "Puts a whole new spin on things, huh?"

"It could go to Wellington's state of mind," he said.

I thanked Argus and he smirked. "Maybe now you'll learn to appreciate me."

"We've always appreciated you, Todd,. We just don't always have time to listen as you share your wealth of knowledge." I waved bye on our way out.

We kicked around ways to use our new information as we rode the elevator up to the sixth floor, and we were walking past the break room when Payton said, "Everything we've got right now is circumstantial, so I don't know what options we have short of following Wellington every night."

"Why the hell would you do that?" Morgan said behind us.

She's a ninja captain!

Payton and I looked at each other and turned to face Morgan. She did not look pleased. And she didn't waste time ordering us into her office. She simply commandeered the break room and demanded full disclosure.

I filled her in on Reseda, Ethan Wellington, the fact we could link Wellington to all three victims, the rope from the *Phoenix*, and Argus's scoop on Wellington's kidnapping. I wrapped it up by saying, "Which supports the theory Wellington snapped." But I said it too enthusiastically and it came out sounding like a psychotic break was a good thing.

Morgan crossed her arms. Not a good sign as it often indicates a closed mind. "First you go after Carter Smithfield. Then Edward Royce. And now Ridley Wellington. What are you doing? Working your way down the list of the city's richest and most influential men?"

"If we were doing that, we would have started with Wellington," I said. She scowled at me and I held my breath as I waited for her to pull the plug.

"And you!" Morgan swung her head in Payton's direction. "I can almost forgive her poor judgment, but what the hell were you thinking, keeping this quiet?"

I mouthed sorry behind Morgan's back.

Morgan turned back to me. "Justice is an ideal, Benchik, and it's honorable if you are a police officer seeking justice for the victims. On the other hand, grief and guilt and retribution are emotions, and if you are being driven by a need to ease another widow's pain, then we've got a problem because it means you're allowing emotions to dictate your actions. Am I clear?"

"Crystal, ma'am."

She wagged her finger around. "That's what all the activity was yesterday."

"Yes, ma'am," I said. "We—I didn't tell you because I didn't want to waste your time in case—" I shut up when Morgan started to shake her head.

She glowered at us for a moment. "Tell me again how you obtained the rope sample."

"I cut a piece from the end of the line securing the *Phoenix* to the dock." She snorted and I spread my palms. "How is what I did any different than taking a coffee cup from the garbage? I never set foot on the boat and the rope was in plain sight on a public dock."

Morgan took a cleansing breath. "Let me be sure I understand. You believe Ridley Wellington buried the trauma of what he endured as a teen at the hands of the kidnapper but his son's death dredged it all up. Your theory is Ortiz was personal, but her murder gave him a sense of control over what he'd felt powerless over for his entire life and he started targeting others. And now, every time he kills, he strikes a blow to erase a small piece of his past." We nodded and she said, "You haven't been able to place him at any of the scenes."

"Our witness can place his car outside Ortiz's house the day of the murder," Payton said.

Morgan scoffed. "Without a license number, all you can do is place a car like Wellington's at the scene. And even if he was there, it could've been for a legitimate business reason." She studied us. "And yet, I sense you expect me to go to the state's attorney for a warrant to search Wellington's home and office for the weapon."

"And his boat," I added.

Morgan flashed an admonishing glare. "You basically want me to request a warrant without probable cause so you can look for evidence that would constitute probable cause."

"This is bullshit," I said under my breath.

"Tell me about it, Detective," Morgan said, "but it's what the defense would claim and you know it." She drew in some air and blew it out. "Even with a witness who isn't a felon, Wellington's attorneys will argue—"

"What about the weapon?" Payton blurted out.

"What about it?" Morgan snapped.

"We never released details about the weapon," he said. "The news reports and articles said the victims were stabbed, and when you say stabbed, don't most people assume a knife?"

"Probably," Morgan said.

He nodded. "But when we talked to Wellington, he said something about the killer poking holes in the citizens of Bedford. That's pretty descriptive and implies knowledge the weapon was something with a point versus a blade, so either Rachel said something to him or—"

"No," Morgan and I said in unison, two widows who knew how difficult it would be for Rachel to talk about.

Payton shifted his eyes between us.

"I don't think she could've talked about details," I said.

Morgan thought for a moment. "Just counting our squad, the ETs, the ME's office, and the commissioner, there are a dozen people who know about the weapon and could've told two friends and so on." She made a rolling motion with her hand.

"Don't forget Moraz," Payton added.

"I wish I could," she said. "We can't argue Wellington is a suspect simply because he happens to have privileged information. He's a personal friend of the mayor and our boss. Hell, Wellington could've run into the commissioner at some rubber-chicken dinner where Malloy had too much Scotch and let it slip."

"Or Wellington knows because he's the killer," I said.

"Or maybe you're both crazy!" Morgan said. The way she raised her brows and glanced out of the corner of her eye, she looked like Groucho Marx when he told people they'd said the craziest thing he'd ever heard.

I couldn't decide if we should be amused or offended.

"We've got to give the prosecutor something to work with," Morgan said. "DNA. A print. Or one *reliable* witness who can place your suspect at the crime scenes."

All things we didn't have. And in the meantime, Wellington was stalking his next victim.

Morgan was on her way out the door when my mind flashed to the stack of cards and letters on my desk at home. "If we match his DNA to the unidentified hair found at either the Ortiz or Hollander crime scenes, will you try for the warrant?"

She spun on her heel. "I thought you couldn't make the match. And we sure as hell can't trick a guy with Wellington's connections into providing a sample."

"We don't need to trick him. He volunteered it and I've had it all along."

The same bewildered expression flashed on both of their faces and Morgan asked, "If you had Wellington's DNA, why have we been going through this little dance?"

"Because I just realized it." I sighed. "He sent me a handwritten note of condolence and I kept the envelopes so I'd have the return addresses."

"Let's hope it wasn't self-stick," Morgan said.

"I'll be back in an hour," I said as I broke for the elevator.

I got back in eighty-nine minutes because thunderstorms snarled traffic.

Morgan, Payton, and I hovered over Argus as he worked his magic to extract a DNA sample from the envelope. When he finally finished, I held my breath waiting for his answer.

"The DNA from the saliva matches unidentified hair from the Caruso scene," Argus said.

I deflated like a popped balloon. "That's it? Nothing from the other scenes?"

He frowned. "I'm sorry, Val."

"Rachel works for Wellington," Payton said. "His attorneys would argue the hair was left on another occasion when he was at the house for dinner or something." His phone rang and he answered and listened. "Uh-huh. Yeah." His shoulders sagged. "Thanks, Sarge." He ended the call. "That was Porter. The unis finished the canvass of Hollander's neighbors and one of them recalled seeing a silver Prius about a week before the murder but—"

"That's three for three," I said.

"But the neighbor didn't get a license number or a look at the driver," Payton said.

"If you fold so easily, we should play poker sometime," Morgan said. Our heads pivoted toward her. "When Wellington clogged up our sidewalk out front with his little press conference, he said we needed all the help we could get. Given he's so civic-minded, perhaps we should give him the opportunity to put his mouth where his money is. Ask him to come in for a chat. If it is him and he's killing because he sees it as righting a wrong, you may be able to get him to admit it. Just be sure he understands he can have his lawyer present and he's free to leave at any time."

"Seriously?" I asked.

She looked at me with a blank expression. "I'm a captain, Benchik. We're always serious."

— CHAPTER 38 —

When I called Wellington's office, Barbara put me straight through. I told him his press conference paid off—which wasn't a lie because that's where I'd seen his car—and I asked if he could come down to discuss some new information. He told me he'd be happy to help and he'd see us in a half hour.

We settled in the Interview Room and told him his noncustodial rights, which are basically the same as the Miranda Warning except he was free to leave at any time and wasn't entitled to a lawyer on the public's dime.

"You're talking as if I'm a suspect," he said.

"High-profile case," I said. "The brass is hovering like vultures and it's to the point where we practically have to ask the ASA for permission to pick up the telephone." I opened the folder in front of me and dealt photos of Adriana Ortiz and Lucy Hollander onto the table. "Do you recognize these women?"

He studied the photos and pointed to Hollander's picture. "I think she was at a fundraiser a few weeks back."

"And the other woman?"

His face hardened. "She's a lawyer. Works for the firm that represented the drug company responsible for my son's death."

I could almost feel his pain. I pressed my lips and nodded once to acknowledge his loss before gathering the pictures and placing them back in the folder. "When we came to your office after your press conference, you told us you offered the reward because a cold-blooded killer was poking holes in the citizens of Bedford."

He smiled sheepishly. "I'm sorry about that. I was angry and worried about Rachel. I know you're doing all you can."

"Your comment was very descriptive," Payton said.

"How would you put it when someone is killing people with an ice pick," Wellington said.

"Good point." I held up my hand. "Sorry, that didn't come out right. How did you know the killer was using an ice pick?"

"Your commissioner and I play golf at the same club," he said. "After Scott was murdered, Jim and I had a drink after our round and we talked about the case."

Payton scoffed and looked at me. "Moraz threatens to yank us from the case, yet his boss divulges information that we deliberately withheld from the press."

"Uh-huh," I said. "And if that detail hit the news, they would've fingered us as the leak." I sighed in frustration. "Who even has an ice pick anymore?" I said as a rhetorical question, and then I looked at Wellington.

He held my eyes for a moment. "As a matter of fact, I keep several on my boat as a sort of homage to my maternal great-grandfather and a reminder to myself."

"How's that?" Payton asked.

"He didn't come from money," Wellington said. "He came to America with barely anything but the clothes on his back. He worked three jobs to support his family and he was the most honest and ethical person I've ever known."

"Who has access to your boat?" Payton asked.

"Depends on how you define access," Wellington said. "Nina and I are the only ones with keys to the bridge and cabin, but if you count guests at the parties and fundraisers we've hosted, you're talking hundreds of people who've been onboard." His brow furrowed. "Do you think this killer is someone I know?"

Intimately, I thought, but I didn't respond and neither did Payton.

Wellington sank back in his chair. "I can't believe it." He sat shaking his head for a moment and then looked up. "If you'd like, I'll have Barbara compile a list of contact information for the crew and guests for the past…What? Six months?"

"We'd like that," I said, "because it's not just the ice pick. The rope you use on the *Phoenix* is a perfect match to the fibers found on one of the victims, so we're trying to establish when someone may have been able to get onto your boat."

Wellington's eyes narrowed. "How do you know the rope—?"

"Public dock," I said, "and speaking of Barbara, where did you say you were when she texted you about Scott?"

Wellington smiled but suspicion had crept into his eyes. "It almost sounds like you're asking for an alibi."

"Covering our bases," I said.

"I'd have to check my calendar," Wellington said.

"How about the Friday before and the Friday after Scott's murder?" Payton asked.

Wellington's eyes slowly met mine and seemed to question how I could do this to him.

"Let me guess," I said. "You have to check your calendar."

He kept his eyes on mine, but after a few seconds, he seemed to be looking right through me, lost in his own world. He folded his hands on the table and lowered his gaze to stare at them.

"Barbara already checked for us," I said. "She's very loyal. She only cracked after I threatened her with an obstruction of justice charge. But she said telling people you're in meetings is her standard response whenever someone looks for you on Friday afternoons. So where were you the past three weeks? And remember you can talk to your lawyer first and you're free to go at any time."

Wellington hunched his shoulders, leaning a little closer to his folded hands, like he was trying to curl into a protective ball. Sort of like me if Connie's armadillo analogy held any truth.

"Fine," I said. "Here's our theory. We think you met with Ortiz, hoping to get proof Russell Hyatt and the other honchos at Reseda delayed the drug recall. She admitted they knew and you lost it. Now under normal circumstances, a jury might understand a father's rage, but the bad economy has stirred an anti-wealth sentiment. All we need is to get twelve people who've lost their jobs or their homes, and they just might convict a guy with a North Shore mansion, a condo in Hawaii, a yacht, and a net worth estimated at nearly a billion dollars. Our evidence may be circumstantial, but I think we've got a good shot at a win."

"You asked where I've spent the past three Fridays," he said in a monotone. He started wringing his hands, though I doubt he realized he was doing it. "The truth is I take Friday afternoons off to be alone. My son died on a Friday afternoon and working has become an exercise in futility because my mind insists on dwelling on the circumstances of his death." His hands grew still. "That's something I'm certain you can relate to, Detective." He raised his head and looked directly into my eyes.

If I hadn't been sitting, my knees would've buckled. Fractured concentration. Images that insinuate themselves into your thoughts at the worst possible moments—like now. I blinked but managed to reestablish eye contact.

He nodded, knowing he struck a nerve. "Rather than revisit unpleasant memories, I go to actual places Ethan and I visited together, or sometimes I just go to my boat." His gaze grew distant for a moment before he blinked and refocused on us. "I swear to you on my son's"—his voice cracked and he cleared his throat—"I swear on Ethan's memory I did not kill anyone."

I wanted to believe him and the thought of compounding his grief with murder charges made my heart ache. "Does anyone besides Barbara know your routine?" I was relieved my voice sounded strong because I felt like crying.

"Several close friends," Wellington said. "They know not to try to contact me because they know I won't respond."

Though we'd struck out when we ran crimes committed at 3:29 PM, I couldn't help feeling the time of the phone calls meant something to the killer. "I don't mean to be insensitive," I said, "but what time did Ethan die?"

"One forty-three PM," Wellington said.

"Does three twenty-nine mean anything to you?" Payton asked.

"I'm sorry," Wellington said with a shake of his head, "but no, it doesn't."

I pushed back from the table. "Thank you for coming in to speak with us, Mr. Wellington."

"Lee," he said, holding my gaze.

I had an overwhelming urge to apologize but knew it would've been inappropriate, so I stood up and walked out. Payton silently followed me to our desks.

"I think we should baby sit him," Payton said. "At least until tomorrow afternoon when we see if another call comes in."

I mumbled "sounds good" as I typed my password. Something felt off but I couldn't put my finger on it.

"You okay?" he asked.

"Uh-huh." I stopped typing and looked up. "No." I ran my hands through my hair. "I believe we're on track with the motive. It's the only thing we've come up with so far that explains the first vic being a lawyer and the others being corporate types but—"

Payton narrowed his eyes. "You believe him."

I nodded and defensively held up my hands. "I don't want to because it means we are once again without a suspect only twenty-some hours before there's likely to be another murder, but Wellington's son died almost two hours before our vics are calling nine-one-one."

"He could be lying about the time," Payton said.

"That's easy enough to find out." I punched in Leilani Norris's number and asked her to look up Ethan Wellington's time of death. She verified the time as 1:43 PM. I hung up and told Payton.

He studied me for a moment. "Do you really believe he's innocent or do you just want him to be innocent because he lost his son?"

"Both," I admitted.

His phone buzzed and he glanced at the display. "Pam" he mouthed before he answered with, "Hey, babe." He listened for a moment and his brows pinched. "Where are you? Okay." He exhaled sharply as he ended the call. "Matthew wiped out on a half-pipe. Pam had to take him to the ER."

"What are you still doing here?"

"I can't just go."

"The hell you can't! It's your kid." I shooed him toward the door. "Go!"

"Don't crack the case without me."

I scoffed. "Don't think you need to worry about that."

— CHAPTER 39 —

I was sitting on the desk across from the whiteboard, stewing over our clues.

We knew Ortiz hadn't even confided in her best friend about why she quit the firm, but she had discussed her dilemma at her group counseling session, which made the group a likely place for someone to target her. But Dr. Konrad told me he didn't observe any behavior in the sessions he facilitated to cause him concern. So maybe the killer was in the session and just never went back because he found another outlet for his anger or...I sat up straighter as I processed Konrad's words. "The sessions he facilitated," I said out loud.

That night at the church, Konrad told me he was covering the substance abuse meetings because the regular facilitator was on leave. So maybe something happened in a session facilitated by the regular doctor.

I dug through my purse for Konrad's business card and called his cell but got voicemail. I listened to his greeting until I realized I could probably get faster results from the Victims' Services Unit—four floors down—so I ended the call and hit the stairs.

I found the program coordinator, Mary Jo Gardner, in their conference room, assembling and stapling some packets together. We chatted for a bit about how much we hoped for a break from the heat, and then I told her the reason for my visit.

"I don't think I'd be breaching any confidentiality rules by providing that information," she said. "Come on." I followed her to her desk and waited as she clicked around the screen. The printer hummed and she walked over to retrieve the pages. "I think this will do it for you," she said as she handed me the printout. "And you may want to speak with Dr. Driscoll too. She was kind enough to cover the support groups during Dr. Konrad's bereavement leave. She's out of town right now but I can give you her cell number."

"I don't think we'll need it," I said. "What I'm looking for probably happened since June."

"Well, that's why I mentioned it," Mary Jo said. "Dr. Driscoll covered for him the last week of July when he went to Boston."

"Um…" I shook my head, trying to loosen the cobwebs formed by stress and lack of sleep. "I'm confused. His granddaughter died in June. Why did he take leave in July?"

She frowned. "It was so sad. His daughter, Colleen, committed suicide. As you can imagine, she had a very hard time dealing with her little girl's death. Her husband found her in the bathtub. She slit her wrists on what would have been their daughter's ninth birthday."

I felt a twinge in my chest for his suffering. "That poor man."

"I know." She put her palm over her heart. "It's just awful, isn't it?"

I stood shaking my head at the tragedy. First, he lost his granddaughter after what should have been a routine appendectomy and then…uneasiness started to creep over me.

The other child who died after treatment with Reseda's antibiotic was an eight-year-old girl from Boston. And Konrad's daughter killed herself in her bathtub—the week before Ortiz was murdered.

I gulped. "I'm sorry, Mary Jo, but with everything that's been going on, I'm afraid I've forgotten…What exactly happened to Dr. Konrad's granddaughter?"

"It was horrible," she said. "I'm sure you heard about that drug recall a few months back involving Reseda Pharmaceuticals? Well, little Caitlin was treated with the drug before the problem was discovered."

My stomach tightened. Konrad told me Ortiz unburdened herself in one of the counseling sessions without being specific, but he knew the details and could've easily put the pieces together about Reseda Pharmaceuticals. If he believed Ortiz was aware of the problem before the recall, he would've also believed her silence contributed to the deaths of his granddaughter and daughter.

Jeremy Konrad had a motive.

I thanked Mary Jo and rushed out. Fueled by nervous energy, I ran the stairs to the sixth floor. I swiped my key fob and the buzzer sounded as the lock released, but I stood there when it hit me how crazy it was to think Konrad was the killer. He was a respected psychiatrist—practically a member of our team through his work with Victims' Services. He'd been my sounding board throughout this nightmare and I confided things to him I'd been incapable of admitting even to Connie.

"No way," I told myself in the empty stairwell. Frustration, grief, and fatigue were driving me to try to create a connection where it didn't exist.

But what if it did?

I swiped my fob again, yanked the door open and strode down the hall to the squad room. Though I'd requested a search on Prius owners the day Rivera told us about the car, I never reviewed the results because I read about Wellington and locked onto him as a suspect, so I logged on the vehicle registration database and double-clicked the file. I sorted the results by last name and scanned the *K*s until I found Konrad.

My computer chimed, alerting me to new e-mail and I opened my inbox. Barbara, the epitome of efficiency, had already sent over Aleron's fundraiser guest lists and contact information for the *Phoenix* crew. I opened the fundraiser file and typed "Konrad" in the Find box. My heart sank when the cursor jumped to his name. He'd attended a fundraising cruise aboard Wellington's boat held to benefit mental health services, which meant he had access to the ice pick and rope. And flecks of varnish from the deck could've easily become embedded in the soles of his shoes.

I crossed my forearms on top of my head and rocked back in my chair as I tried to fit the pieces together. Konrad knew Ortiz was involved with Reseda from her revelations in the group meeting, but how had Caruso and Hollander become targets? It was possible Lucy sought counseling after her miscarriage, but it didn't track that she would discuss her work.

I tapped my fingers on the back of my head and it must've stimulated my brain cells because it finally hit me. Konrad didn't target Caruso and Hollander through personal contact. He chose them because of what he learned in his grief-counseling sessions from people he perceived as their victims—relatives of those lost because of Paragon's and Mayer Consulting's work. People like Mark Filipiak, or someone related to the man who committed suicide after losing his job courtesy of Hollander's recommendations.

I let the chair snap back and I propped my elbows on my desk and pressed the heels of my hands to my eyes. How had I missed this? I knew Konrad's granddaughter was eight and died in Boston after surgical complications. Why hadn't it clicked? Had my grief blinded me that much? Or had our horrible losses painted him as a kindred spirit in my mind to the point I'd simply been unwilling to see it?

I lowered my hands. *What difference does it make? I know it now and that's all that matters.* I took a deep breath and blew it out. Payton needed to know, but he also needed to be with his family. Tomorrow was Friday, and our case against Konrad would be airtight if we caught him in the act, so the best thing to do now would be to follow him.

My phone rang with an unknown number and I answered.

"Detective," the male voice said. "It's Lee Wellington. I need your help."

What the hell? I suspected him of murder and he's calling me for help? "Uh...Mr. Wellington, under the circumstances—"

"It's Rachel," he said and I could hear the anxiety in his voice. "She called me, extremely upset. She and Scott loved to sail, so I took her to my boat. I thought perhaps it would help calm her but it hasn't. Regrettably, the two of you have a lot in common, and I know this is a lot to ask but..." He sighed into the receiver. "Do you think you could come to the marina? Maybe it will help her to talk to you."

Everyone has been telling me I've been too driven by my emotions lately. That the best thing for me to do would be to take a step back. But if Rachel is really in trouble...

"Detective?"

It's an unwritten rule to avoid getting personally invested in a case but I'd crossed that line a long time ago. "I can be there in about fifteen minutes," I said.

Wellington sighed. "Thank you. My boat is the *Phoenix*. We're in Slip—"

"Three. I know." I disconnected, logged off my computer, and ventured into the balmy summer evening.

The rain had tapered to a drizzle, and as I turned into the marina entrance, I noticed the sunset trying to peek through a break in the clouds. I parked in the public lot, which is about a block from the gate to the docks. I started across the lot and passed three guys checking out a shiny red Ferrari parked in a reserved space near the office.

One of them hoisted his beer bottle and called out, "Hey, babe! Wanna be our firsss mate?"

I tossed a dismissive wave and hoped they wouldn't be driving anytime soon.

Music blared from a charter boat docked on the west side of the marina. Companies often booked the boat for corporate events, and I pegged the Magnum wannabes as junior executives who'd had a little too much, too soon.

My gym shoes clumped on the wooden pier as I made my way to the *Phoenix*.

A light glowed faintly through the curtains covering the cabin picture window, and I paused to listen, but heard only the distant music and water lapping at the hulls and pilings. My muscles felt taut as I boarded the yacht, crossed the glossy deck, and slowly descended five steps to the cabin door. Wood creaked and the hair on my neck shot up on end.

Was it waves working the boat against the dock? Or footsteps?

I glanced over my shoulder and saw an empty deck. "Relax," I whispered and I took a deep breath and let it out slowly. I knocked on the polished wood door and waited, and then I knocked again and waited some more. I tried the knob and it turned, so I opened the door and called out Wellington's name as I let myself in.

The sparse illumination in the small, empty living room emanated from matching brass lamps on two end tables flanking the black leather couch beneath the window. I assumed the two closed doors on the right led to staterooms. Beyond the bar on my left, a third door was partially open, emitting a sliver of light.

I moved along the bar toward the open door but stopped when I saw three wooden-handled objects sticking out of a crystal ice bucket. I grasped one with my forefinger and thumb and lifted it until I saw the shaft of one of Wellington's commemorative ice picks. I lowered it back into the bucket and took another step toward the door, but I stopped again when I felt something under my shoe. I looked down at a single coil of rope on the floor. The same rope like I'd cut from the dock. About the same length you'd need to bind someone's hands or feet.

Is Wellington guilty after all?

When I read about Ethan, my gut told me Wellington was the killer, but after listening to him talk about his son, I'd allowed my heart to override my gut. And then Ethan's time of death didn't match the time of the phone calls, but the time could be significant for some other reason. What if he used what happened to his son to play me? What if he's using Rachel to play me now?

Listen to your gut, Benchik.

How many times had Frank Shannon uttered those words during my training?

"Rachel!" I tugged my Glock from its holster and moved swiftly to the door. I flattened against the paneled wall and reached my left leg out to push the door open with my foot. I saw a sink but nothing else. Gun out front, I poked my head in for a quick scan and glimpsed a man, facedown on the tile. With only short brown hair to go on, I couldn't tell if it was Wellington.

What the hell is going on?

I entered the bathroom and squatted next to the man. It was Wellington. I pressed my fingers to his neck and felt a pulse but he was unconscious. I felt a slight draft and sensed someone behind me. I spun in a crouch in time to catch a glimpse of dark pants before I heard a sputter. Pain coursed through my body, my muscles convulsed, and I toppled over.

— CHAPTER 40 —

I felt something cold against my cheek. *Why is my pillow so hard?* My arms flew up and down and I floated through the air. Everything blurred. Like the landscape whizzing by from a roller coaster.

My back pressed against something cold and hard, and I rocked gently, like a hammock swaying in a summer breeze.

Grandma and Grandpa. We always spend two weeks in August at their house by the lake.

I heard the swoosh and slap of waves against the hull of the aluminum rowboat. Fishing with Dad.

Why am I lying in the boat?

My head felt fuzzy—like a drunken buzz. I closed my eyes. I breathed deeply through my nose and tried to blow the air out through my mouth but I couldn't. Something covered my mouth and I exhaled through my nose. My eyes darted around as my heart began to beat wildly against my ribs. My lungs burned as I sucked in only tiny gasps through my nose.

Calm down, damn it!

I took another deep breath and held it, and I felt my pulse slow as I exhaled. Goosebumps prickled my skin. I forced myself to focus straight ahead and I recognized a faucet and then a showerhead. What the hell was I doing in an empty bathtub? I must have fallen asleep while I was taking a bath and the water drained out. But why did I leave my underwear on to take a bath?

What was I doing before this?

I fumbled my way through the fog in my head.

Desk. I was at my desk and then…What?

I heard a voice in the fog—low and slow like a 45 record playing at 33 rpm. Someone needed help so I drove through the rain to…rain…a sputter. Lightning. Was that the sputter? Had lightning struck me? Is that why I was lying in the bathtub? To take shelter from a storm?

My forearms ached, but when I tried to move into a more comfortable position, something dug into my wrists and it registered my hands were pinned beneath me.

I listened hard but heard only the swoosh and slap of waves against the boat's hull.

The *Phoenix*! Lee Wellington had called. Rachel Caruso was in trouble and he'd asked me to meet him on his boat to try to calm her down.

But where was she? And wasn't he unconscious on the bathroom floor when I arrived?

Footsteps thumped on wood as someone descended the stairs. Seconds later, the door swung open and the details of the case flooded into my mind when Jeremy Konrad appeared. "Sorry about the stun gun," he said, "but with your training, I couldn't take any chances."

Through the open door I could see across the living room into one of the staterooms. Wellington was sitting with his head down and his hands around the back of a chair. Konrad must've held the ice pick to his throat to force him to call me. That's why he'd sounded anxious on the phone—why his voice sounded strained.

I'd confided in Konrad about the unintentional bond I forged with Rachel over our husbands' murders, and I tipped my hand when I asked him to analyze Wellington. I offered plenty of ammunition for him to use against me because I'd allowed the case to become personal.

I lost perspective. I lost my objectivity. And because of it, in a short time, I was going to lose my life.

My heart pounded in my throat. "You son of a bitch!" I yelled, but with the tape over my mouth it sounded as if I were mimicking an engine that wouldn't start.

Konrad cupped his hand to his ear. "What was that?"

My eyes and nostrils flared.

"Oh, sorry." When he reached down, I noticed the latex gloves on his hands. He ripped the tape from my mouth and it felt like the top layer of my skin tore off with it.

When the sting subsided, I jerked my head toward Wellington. "Is he dead?"

"Not yet."

"Why frame him?"

"Because it's a way out." He smiled wryly. "I never intended for him to be blamed. In fact, the thought never entered my mind until you"—he pointed his finger at me—"showed up at my office last night. I thought I'd have time to eliminate more of the guilty, but you figured out the link between Reseda and Ortiz and I knew it was only a matter of time before you put the pieces together about Caitlin." He glared at me, his eyes full of contempt because I'd had the audacity to try to stop him. "At least this way, I'll be able to continue my practice."

"So how does this go down?" I asked. "I came to the boat to confront Wellington, he killed me to shut me up, and then, overcome with remorse, he shot himself with my gun?"

"Pretty much." He sat on the edge of the bathtub and wagged his thumb over his shoulder toward Wellington. "He's on the board of directors at several companies, and if he performs like the Reseda board members, he deserves to die. They had a responsibility to hold management accountable, but like so many board members, all they did was show up at the monthly meetings to collect their director's fee. Those bastards shirk their responsibility because they don't want to face hostile shareholders at the annual meeting. Trust me when I say in the grand scheme of things, his death will not be a tragedy."

What's worse? Dying? Or knowing Wellington is going to die because I tipped my hand to Konrad and gave him a way out?

Konrad cocked his head. "You can take comfort in the fact you won't have to live with your guilt for long."

My skin prickled. How could he do that? "You are so insightful." I shook my head. "What happened to honoring our loved ones by getting up every day and doing what we're good at?"

He shrugged. "I found something new to be good at."

"But why? I don't understand how someone like you can—"

"You don't want to understand because you know that if I couldn't control my anger then maybe you can't either!" His face flushed and his neck veins pulsed. He took several deep breaths until his breathing evened out. "We sat in that hospital room for twenty-seven hours," he said softly.

Twenty-seven hours. Twenty-seven wounds. "One wound for every hour," I said.

His left eye twitched a little. "I watched my daughter pray for a miracle to spare Caitlin, but then our little angel went into cardiac arrest. The doctors worked on her for almost an hour before pronouncing her dead at—"

"Three twenty-nine," I said.

He looked at me hard. "I thought I felt as empty as I'd ever feel when we buried her," he continued in a monotone. "Then my son-in-law called on what would have been Caitlin's ninth birthday and—" He sucked in a sharp breath. "Colleen told him she wanted to take a bath because she thought it would help her relax. He thought it was a great idea and he told her he'd make dinner. He poured a glass of wine for her, but when he took it into the bathroom, he found her in a tub full of red water."

It took three tries before I could swallow, and even after I did, the lump remained in my throat. My left shoulder throbbed and I shifted my weight to try to relieve some of the pressure.

Sweat beaded on Konrad's upper lip and his vacant eyes stared at some point on the wall above my head as his tragic memories enveloped him. After a moment, he blinked a few times and looked almost surprised to see me. "When I returned from Boston after Colleen's funeral, I just wanted to forget everything but..." He shook his head. "No matter how hard I tried, I couldn't get what Adriana shared in the meeting out of my mind. I was right here"—he swept his hand toward the door—"for the fundraiser to benefit mental health services, when I decided I had to know if she'd been talking about Reseda." He chuckled. "It's fitting that it will end here as well."

He reached around to his back pocket, and when his hand reappeared, he was clutching an ice pick. "I was standing at the bar, downing my third...or maybe it was my fourth bourbon...and I looked over and saw these. Lee keeps them as a reminder of his humble beginnings. I suppose deep in my subconscious I knew I'd use it to kill her, but I told myself it would be the perfect incentive to get the cold-hearted bitch to tell the truth. So I took one."

My left hand felt numb and I twisted around until my fingers started to tingle.

"I knew she'd gone to work for Legal Aid," Konrad said, "so I called her and told her one of my patients needed legal advice but couldn't afford an attorney. I told her I was near her home and asked if we could meet there. She trusted me, so she agreed." He shook his head as if he couldn't believe how gullible she'd been. "It all started out quite civilly. She offered me coffee and I confessed I'd come under false pretenses and asked if she'd been referring to the Reseda situation. She denied it until I showed her the ice pick, and then she admitted what happened at Reseda wasn't the result of equipment malfunction. She said Russell Hyatt told the senior partners the company had deliberately diluted several drugs because it allowed them to reduce costs without compromising effectiveness, but that something had gone wrong and several batches ended up as 90 percent saline. And even though they knew there was a problem, they delayed the recall until after the window period closed following the release of the quarterly financials because Hyatt and the other executives wanted to exercise a boatload of options. They wagered they could make the notification before any of the hospitals tapped into the tainted supply but—"

"They lost that bet," I said, "and Caitlin, Ethan, and three other people paid the price."

He drew in a choppy breath. "She started to cry and she apologized for not coming forward, and I may have accepted it, but then she admitted the reason she kept quiet was because the partners gave her a bonus and promised her the next junior partnership. At that moment, Caitlin's face flashed in my mind...the weak little smile she gave us before her beautiful blue eyes closed forever." Tears filled his eyes and he worked his jaw but nothing came out.

I felt my bottom lip quiver and I bit down.

This is crazy! How can I feel sorry for him after seeing what he'd done? Is it because I'd trusted him enough to discuss my deepest feelings? Or do I identify with him because of my own thoughts of revenge for Dave?

He sniffled. "Has a suspect ever told you he didn't know what happened but something just snapped?"

I stared at him for a moment before saying, "Mm-hmm."

He nodded. "I've had patients tell me that too, but I never understood what it was like for them until now. This wave of fury washed over me and…" He shook his head as if he didn't believe it himself.

"You pulled the hair dryer off the vanity and wound the cord around her wrists," I said. "You found the medical tape in the cabinet over the sink and taped her mouth so no one would hear her scream, and then you put her in the bathtub because it seemed fitting."

He met my eyes and nodded. "I filled the tub, watched the life seep from her body, and then I pulled the drain-plug and left."

"Diminished capacity," I said. "No jury would have convicted for premeditated murder."

He smiled. "Maybe if I'd stopped with Ortiz."

"Why didn't you?"

He shrugged. "I thought it *was* over, but I didn't anticipate the sense of peace I felt afterward. Week after week, I listen to grief-stricken patients talk about the people they lost. I listened to a mother describe how just one compassionate decision by Scott Caruso could have prevented her daughter's death."

"Anna Filipiak," I said.

"Mm-hmm." His head bobbed a little. "And I listened to a sister's tearful account of how her brother's life spiraled out of control and he hanged himself after Lucy Hollander's hatchet job at his company." He pushed his cheek out with his tongue. "So many of my patients came to me after falling into a bottle or turning to drugs…or fantasizing about ways to kill themselves…and I realized if I removed the cause of their pain, I could give them the same sense of comfort and peace I found. It was so much more than my words could ever do." He shrugged his brows. "I have nothing left to live for, and Ortiz's murder was enough to put a needle in my arm, so it seemed foolish not to take full advantage of the opportunity to prevent other innocent people from suffering as my family had suffered."

"Lucy Hollander was pregnant," I said.

"Collateral damage," he replied nonchalantly. "Actually, it's somewhat poetic considering that's how she viewed those who lost their jobs because of her." He rotated his right hand back and forth, examining the ice pick as if he'd never seen it before. "I suppose I should honor the facts of the case and wait until three twenty-nine tomorrow, but I don't think I can risk putting it off that long, do you?" His eyes slowly shifted to me. "It's a pity because we could've made this world a better place. You would've enforced the laws of man while I enforced moral laws." He sighed. "This will really be for the best, Val. I know you're in a lot of pain."

Wellington groaned in the other room and Konrad's head pivoted toward the door. "Sounds like your killer is coming around."

My heart started to pound with fear over what he would do to Wellington.

"I'll be right back." He held up his index finger, like he was telling a child not to fret, and he disappeared through the door.

I scanned the bathroom for a weapon.

No gun. It was probably with my clothes. No razor in the corner of the tub to cut my bindings—or his arteries. No plunger next to the toilet to beat him with. No manicure scissors on the vanity to stab him.

I'd have to fight him with the only weapon I had.

Me.

— CHAPTER 41 —

To seal the frame on Wellington, Konrad needed to inflict twenty-seven wounds. Images of the bloody punctures on Ortiz's, Caruso's and Hollander's bodies roared into my head. A chill rippled over my skin and I knew it wasn't because I was lying on cold porcelain in my underwear. I shuddered and then I sucked in a deep breath, hoping the rush of oxygen would clear my head.

Like the other murders, Konrad would probably start with my arms or legs. A head-butt could work as he leaned in—especially if he fell back and struck his head against the toilet or vanity—but with my feet bound, I'd never get the leverage I needed. In fact, if I tried to move at all as he lowered the ice pick, he could puncture my femoral artery and I'd bleed to death within minutes.

Konrad walked in. "All better."

Shit! I looked toward the ceiling and closed my eyes.

"Praying? Pfft! Don't bother. No one listens." He resumed his place on the edge of the bathtub.

The rope cut deeper into my wrists and I winced.

He frowned. "Did I tie the rope too tightly?"

I glared at him.

"I bound them because I wanted them to know what it's like to feel trapped and helpless," he said. "They had to know what it was like for me and Colleen to stand by and watch our daughters die. And they had to feel pain before they died. I told them if they behaved, I'd let them call for help and I did. I allowed them to believe they had a chance to survive just like my daughter believed she'd somehow overcome her grief and survive." His eyes glazed over as his mind wandered off to revisit one of the horrible memories that had brought him to this point. Then once again, he blinked his way back to the present. "You know, every one of them bargained with me." He smiled but it was void of amusement.

I'll be damned if I spend what time I have left begging him to— time! It was a weapon I'd overlooked.

Buy as much as you can get.

"They offered to give me every penny they had if I'd spare their worthless lives," he said. "It's funny how imminent death led them to finally find some respect for life."

"It's ironic to hear you talk about respecting life."

"Why? Because I eliminated worthless beings who were unfit to breathe our air?"

"They didn't deserve to die like—"

"They most certainly did!" Konrad shouted. "They were greedy, unethical bastards! I don't know how they could stand to look in the mirror knowing they profited from the suffering of others. To them, human beings were simply a cost of doing business…something to be written off like bad debt. They sold their souls for money, and their actions caused the deaths of innocent people the same as if they'd wielded a gun or a knife."

"So leave it to the courts."

"In a legal system manipulated by money?" He scoffed. "If this had happened in China, Hyatt would have been sentenced to death like the guys who were responsible for the tainted milk a few years back. But here?" He snickered. "We'd have been lucky if Reseda got fined. We talk about justice, but the system is corrupted. You see it every time a criminal walks free on a technicality after you've worked tirelessly to make a case…No." He made a leveling motion with his left hand. "My way is much more certain."

"Judge, jury, and executioner," I said. "Lucy Hollander would be impressed by your efficiency."

"I'm doing what you can't! And you"—he wagged an admonishing finger at me—"are in no position to judge because you went looking for Noonan even though you were ordered not to. And if he hadn't blown his own brains out, you would have done it for him!"

I wanted to shout back *You're wrong!* but I couldn't. The truth is I don't know how far I would've gone and it made me sick to my stomach.

Konrad tilted his head to the left and smiled, as if we were having a friendly chat over coffee. "It's amazing what we're capable of when we're pushed to our limits, isn't it? Life failed us both, you know. We did everything we were supposed to do. We followed the rules, tried to help people along the way, and our reward was to lose the ones who meant the most to us."

He was right—the bastard—but I fought hard to look at him without emotion and I swear I saw empathy in his eyes.

"We both know how it feels to be powerless against something to which we have devoted our lives," he said. "I've spent my life helping strangers deal with their grief yet I failed my daughter when she needed me most. And as a police officer, you were powerless to protect your husband."

Tears trickled down my cheeks and I squeezed my eyes shut.

No! I already shared too much with him. I will not show him more of my grief. Or fear.

I sniffled, and then I breathed deeply, opened my eyes, and looked up at him. "I guess I should thank you for leaving me with my underwear." I was relieved my voice sounded calm. "I imagine it's harder to kill someone you know, huh?" He lowered his eyes and I wondered if he'd actually felt some remorse. "Where'd you get the stun gun?"

He met my eyes again. "Does it really matter?"

"It does to me. I hate loose ends."

He stared at me for a moment. "A former patient secured one for me after I told him a late-night house call got ugly. He offered to get me a real gun but I told him I didn't want to kill anyone." He made a *That's how it goes* face.

A chill rippled along my spine at his cavalier attitude. "How did you know Scott and Lucy would be home alone?"

He rolled his eyes. "Stop stalling, Val."

"Hey, it's not like I'm going to be able to tell anyone," I said. "I've been busting my ass trying to solve this case. The least you can do is fill in the blanks and give me some peace of mind before you stab me to death." I shifted again in an effort to relieve the pressure on my hands and arms. "Going to Ortiz's place wasn't too risky because she was single, but Rachel Caruso and Donald Hollander could've been working a half day those Fridays and walked in on you."

He shook his head. "I saw Rachel at the Aleron board meeting the Wednesday before. I was there to discuss the renovation of a half-way house the foundation supports. We chatted a bit after the meeting ended. She mentioned how crazy it's been with the upcoming fall event, and how she was going to visit a possible venue after work on Friday. I asked about the family and she told me she couldn't wait for Beth's birthday because Scott was building a dollhouse and he hoped to finish it Friday afternoon. All I had to do is ring the doorbell. He and I had met at several events so he let me in."

"And that"—I angled my eyes toward the ice pick—"and the stun gun did the rest."

He nodded. "As for Hollander, I followed her home a few times and I saw the cab pick up her husband. I called the next day, pretending to be a friend of his from college. I said I wanted to go out for a drink to catch up, and she told me he was in Beijing through the fifteenth, but she was sure he'd want to get together when he returned."

"Did your training make you so manipulative or were you born that way?" I asked.

"A little of both, I think. And I've indulged you long enough." He propped his left hand on the edge of the tub, swung his hips around, and dropped to his knees.

My breath caught and my heart hammered against my ribs.

"I wish there were a way out of this that didn't end with your death," he said, "but I've gotten to know you well enough to know you'll never give up."

"Payton knows I'm onto you." I wished with all my heart that I'd called him at home.

Konrad studied me for a few seconds and smiled. "No, he doesn't."

"He'll figure it out."

"I don't think so," Konrad said with a shake of his head. "Cops like an easy answer and this will be cut and dry." He held my gaze for a moment and then his eyes traveled over my body to my feet. He lifted his right arm over the tub's edge and placed the point of the ice pick against my left ankle. Then he slowly dragged the tip up along my leg and over my knee. Midway up my thigh he stopped and turned the pick until it was perpendicular, and I tensed as he pressed downward into my skin.

At first it felt like the phlebotomist's needle piercing my arm when I donate blood, but then he thrust it deeper into my flesh and I grunted in my throat.

He withdrew the pick and moved his hand over the same spot on my right leg.

"Hey, Cap'n Lee!" a man shouted up on deck.

Konrad's eyes flared. I opened my mouth to scream but he clamped his hand over my mouth.

"Purrmissin to come aboard?" the man called out and several men laughed.

The Magnum wannabes?

Konrad looked at me and then at the door. After a few seconds, he pasted the tape back over my mouth, stood up, and walked out of the bathroom, closing the door behind him.

I shimmied into a sitting position and winced when the edges of the hole in my leg ripped wider. I pulled my knees up to my chest and the blood that had already seeped from the wound started to run down my leg toward my hip. I wiggled and contorted my body until I managed to slip my hands under my butt and then under my feet.

After all the times I'd resented having to push up sleeves that were too short, for the first time in my life, I felt thankful for my long arms. I gripped the edge of the adhesive tape over my mouth and pulled it away, and once again, it stung as it separated from my skin.

I started to work on my ankle binding when a single set of footsteps thumped on the stairs.

CHAPTER 42

Konrad knew how to tie a knot and I frantically tugged at the rope. It finally pulled loose and I raised my feet to uncoil the loops from the bottom. I scrambled to my knees and crawled out of the tub as the footsteps moved closer to the door.

I crossed the bathroom to the linen closet in two steps. I opened the door and sighed with relief when I found a plunger in the corner. I grabbed the handle, flattened myself against the wall, and raised the plunger, though with my sweaty palms, I struggled to firmly grip the wood. The knob turned and the door opened with a slight squeak. I tightened my grip, swung the plunger, and heard cartilage crunch when the handle contacted the bridge of Konrad's nose.

"Son of a bitch!" he sputtered, reeling back from the blow.

I shoved him back, rushed through the doorway and sprinted across the living room. I tried the knob on the passageway door but he'd dead-bolted it. The top of the door was glass, and I turned my head to shield my eyes and raised my arm with the plunger.

Konrad's fist landed squarely against the right side of my face. Stars danced before my eyes, and a split second later, my feet flew out from under me and I landed hard on my back. By the time the stars cleared, Konrad had knotted another rope around my ankles.

"I'm impressed," he said. Blood from his nose covered his top lip and chin, and he swiped the back of his left hand across his face. He glanced at the blood on his hand and glared at me. He retrieved the ice pick from his back pocket, grasped the rope around my ankles with his left hand, and started dragging me back toward the bathroom.

I wiggled as much as I could, but his grip was firm. Perspiration coated my body, and my damp skin stuck and squeaked as he dragged me across the varnished wood floor. I flexed my fingers, desperate to grab onto something before we reached the bathroom.

I felt the edge of the area rug and clutched at it as it chafed against the skin on my right elbow. Two more steps and the rug shifted, jostling an end table and sending a crystal vase crashing to the floor.

Konrad stumbled and his grip loosened, but not enough for me to break free. I barely had a hold of the rug and could feel it slipping away. Konrad tugged harder and the rug ripped from my grasp. I managed to clutch the leg of the table and it tipped and fell, length-wise.

Konrad kept dragging and the table caught across the bathroom doorway. He yanked my legs, and my shoulders felt like they ripped from their sockets, but I held tightly to the table leg. Konrad gave another strong tug and the leg I was clinging to broke off.

I raised my shoulders from the floor—crunch sit-up style—and thrust the jagged piece of wood toward Konrad. I caught him square in the ribs and he released my ankles and stumbled back against the vanity. I twisted and rolled onto my knees, gaining enough leverage to put some force behind my second swing. Like the perfect fore-hand shot down the baseline, I landed a solid blow on the left side of Konrad's head. He staggered, crumpled to his knees, and sprawled facedown on the floor.

I dropped the table leg and frantically worked to untie my ankles, casting glances at Konrad as he lay motionless—five feet away.

Maybe he'd hit his head when he fell. Or maybe he was faking it.

I gasped for breath as my heart hammered in my chest. I finally unwound the last loop of rope and scrambled to my feet. If I got within range of Konrad's hands, he could grab my ankle and yank my feet out from under me, so I stayed back and kicked his foot.

Nothing.

"Konrad!"

He remained still.

I picked up the table leg and used it as a prod, poking at him until he rolled onto his back and I saw the ice pick embedded in his chest, precisely where his heart had once been. His vacant eyes fixed on me, and he sucked a ragged breath before his head dropped to the left.

Just as quickly as it had flowed, my adrenaline ebbed, and my body turned to jelly. The table leg slipped from my hand and thumped on the floor. My head started to spin and I dropped to my knees. More blood oozed from the puncture and trickled along my thigh, and my cheek ached where Konrad slugged me.

I heard muffled voices and several sets of footsteps overhead.

Probably the Magnum wannabes on a return visit.

A man shouted, "Bedford Police!" in the passageway, and relief washed over me at the sound of Pritchard's voice.

"Benchik!" Payton called out and something struck the door with a loud thud.

I scrambled to the couch and snatched a throw off the back. Even with my hands tied, I managed to shake it open and drape it over myself. Seconds later, wood splintered and the cabin door flew open and Payton and Pritchard burst into the room.

Pritchard moved quickly to check Konrad for a pulse he wouldn't find.

Payton rushed to my side, digging in his pocket for his knife. "I distinctly remember telling you not to solve the case without me." He slit the rope binding my hands.

"How did you know where to find…Why were you even looking for me?"

"You mean because you didn't bother to keep me in the loop?" He leveled his fatherly look of disapproval at me for a beat. "After we got Matt settled at home, I called to see if there were any developments but I couldn't get you on your cell, at the office or at your house. I checked my voicemail in case you left a message—I don't know what I was thinking there."

I bobbed my head around a little to acknowledge my blunder. "I know."

He scowled at me. "So I called Dispatch to see if you called in." He paused again to flash the disapproving glare.

I held up my hand. "Okay! Enough. Next time, call for backup. I got it."

"Uh-huh," he said as if he didn't believe me. "Anyway, I got Cassidy to ping your cell phone." He glanced over at Konrad's body. "How'd you manage that?"

I told him about the Magnum wannabes who'd drawn Konrad topside long enough for me to get my feet loose and find a weapon. "Guess they were my Eskimos."

His eyes narrowed. "Eskimos?"

"Yeah. I heard this story once—I don't remember where—but it was something like 'an atheist told a religious guy he didn't believe in God because he was lost in a blizzard once and prayed for help, but God didn't listen. The only reason he made it home was because some Eskimo came along and led him back to town.' The moral of the story was God works through people, so I guess those drunks I saw by the Ferrari when I got here were my Eskimos."

Payton chuckled but the smile slid from his face when he saw the blood running down my leg. "I think you may need stitches."

"I'm fine. You see my clothes or gun anywhere?"

Payton pointed over my shoulder and I turned around. My clothes hung from Pritchard's crooked finger.

"Looking for these, darlin'?" he asked with a smile.

I reached out but he pulled his arm back.

"Don't push it!" I warned and he tossed my clothes to me. "Help Wellington, okay," I said and I went into the empty stateroom and slammed the door. I got dressed, and by the time I came out, Lee Wellington was leaning against the back of the chair outside the door, sipping from a bottled water.

"I owe you one, Detective," he said.

I shook my head. "I'm the one who got you into this."

He shrugged. "Maybe. But you also got me out. If you ever get tired of doing this job, you've got a position in my security department."

I scoffed. "I suspected you for three murders."

"You followed the leads you had," he said, "without allowing my money or connections to get in the way of your investigation. Tells me you have integrity. If there's ever anything I can do." He extended his hand and we shook. "I realize you probably need a statement," he said, "but would it be all right if I went topside for some air?"

"Sure," I said. As I watched him head for the cabin door, I recalled the acknowledgment I'd written out with my in-laws. I called his name and he turned. "I never thanked you for your letter of condolence. It was very thoughtful."

Wellington's eyes met mine and we flashed tentative smiles like people do when they don't know what else to do or say. Then he walked out and Payton appeared at my side.

"I didn't call for backup because I expected to find Rachel and Wellington here," I said. "If it occurred to me Konrad was setting me up, believe me, I would have called SWAT myself."

He looked away for a moment and looked back. "It didn't occur to you because you were working from your heart instead of your head on this one."

I knew he was right and I nodded and then I shifted my eyes to Konrad's body.

The nightmare that gripped the city for weeks is over—and so is life as I knew it.

As if he could read my mind, Payton said, "It's over, Val." He squeezed my shoulder.

I looked at him. "So why don't I feel better?"

"Because it's over," Captain Morgan said behind me.

Maybe Konrad's stun gun short-circuited my brain because Morgan's comment made no sense at all. I turned to face her. "What do you mean?"

"As long as the killer was out there, you had a diversion," she said. "Something else to occupy your mind."

How many times during this case had I zoned out even when talking to relatives or suspects? As hard as I fought it, snippets of my life and why it would never be the same had insinuated themselves into my day when I least expected. Without a case to work, what would stop those images from consuming my thoughts? My heart rate started back up.

"Congratulations on closing the case, though," she said.

I flashed an unenthusiastic smile. "Thanks."

"Oh, don't thank me, Benchik," she said with a small shake of her head. "You're going to personally catch the squad up on all outstanding paperwork. Hell, you may even wax my car."

"Cap—"

She stepped forward until her face was within a foot of mine. "You failed to follow proper procedure and went all Lone Wolf, placing yourself in grave danger. And yet your reckless behavior is what brought this case to a close. If your visit hadn't triggered Konrad's ill-advised decision to lure you to the boat and frame Wellington, there's no telling how many more people he may have killed before he became a blip on our radar. Don't ever do it again."

"Yes, ma'am." I turned for the door and the floor shifted beneath me but Payton caught my arm before I toppled over.

"Get the medics in here!" Morgan shouted.

"I'm fine," I said. "I didn't eat since breakfast and—"

"You took one hell of a jolt," Morgan said. "This time you *will* follow procedure, go to the hospital, and get checked out, or you can spend the next week on administrative duty."

—— CHAPTER 43 ——

I hate administrative duty, so Morgan's order left me with no choice but to agree to let my partner drive me to the hospital. But that's where my compliance ended.

The doctor wanted to keep me overnight but I refused. He told me I'd have to sign a waiver because I was leaving against medical advice and I asked him for a pen. Payton tried to convince me to listen to the doctor's recommendation but I ignored him, thanked him for his timely arrival, and told him to go home.

I'd gotten dressed and was waiting for my discharge papers and the CYA statement when the curtain pulled back.

Connie walked up to the gurney. "I distinctly recall telling you I hoped it *wouldn't* take another line-of-duty injury for me to see you again."

I shrugged. "What can I say? I'm a sucker for green Jell-O."

She quick-scanned me from head-to-toe and back. "What is it this time?"

"Stun gun…and a minor stab wound. I told Morgan I was fine but she insisted Payton bring me here to get checked out."

Connie grinned. "I like this new captain."

My lip curled. "Figures."

"Stab wound, huh? When was your last tetanus shot?"

"Last year, after I got snagged by a nail going over a fence. You gave it to me, and as I recall, you enjoyed it a little too much."

"Oh, yeah." Connie flashed a satisfied smile and hopped onto the gurney next to me. "I saw Greg. He told me you not only stopped the killer but you arrested the guy who shot you."

"Yep."

"So he goes away for the rest of his life, right?"

I sat swinging my right foot in silence.

"Don't tell me they made a deal," she said warily. I kept on swinging and she said, "He shot you!" Her tone was an octave higher than usual. "You're okay with that?"

I stopped swinging my foot. "I want him to rot in prison for the rest of his life but…" I snorted. "Come on, Connie. You've got to love the irony. The SOB who could've killed me ends up being an eyewitness with information we needed to stop a serial killer. I hate making deals but stopping Konrad meant more than seeing Rivera pay for shooting me."

"The greater good, huh?" She grasped my right hand in both of hers. "Cold."

"Warm heart," I said flatly. We were quiet for a bit before I asked, "You ever think about the power of love?"

"By Celine Dion or Huey Lewis?" she asked with a straight face.

I rolled my eyes. "At its best, it can guide someone to a selfless act like donating a kidney, or give someone the courage to bring a child into the—" My voice broke. Connie's eyes welled and I had to look away to keep it together.

"But at its worst, it can drive someone to kill," Connie said.

I nodded. "What happened to Konrad's granddaughter was criminal, and what happened to his daughter was tragic. He deserved some justice but…" I shook my head. "The system failed him and he allowed his rage to consume him."

The curtain opened again and a nurse presented me with a clipboard and a sapling's worth of paper to sign. I did and she told me to take it easy and left.

Connie hopped off the gurney. "Come on. I'll take you home."

I slowly lowered my feet to the floor and stood.

Connie was flabbergasted. "What? No argument?"

Truth is, I was a little surprised I managed to stand without assistance. "Believe me," I said, "the thought of crawling into bed and staying there for a week sounds really good right now but—"

"But nothing!" Connie said. "The doctor—"

"I promise I'll rest," I assured her. "But there's something I have to…something I need to do first."

She set her jaw and stared at me for a beat. "Ugh! Fine!" she said. "I'll drive you wherever you need to go."

I told Connie the address and we talked very little on the drive over. She parked in front of Rachel Caruso's house and offered to help me out of the car but I told her I could manage. I slowly crawled out, and in spite of the lingering anesthetic from the stitches, my leg throbbed as I limped up the sidewalk and rang the bell.

The door opened and Rachel Caruso peeked around it, looking surprised and apprehensive at the same time. "Detective."

"I'm sorry to come by so late," I said, "but—"

"It's okay." She forced a smile and stepped aside. "Would you like to come in?"

I knew she was simply being polite because I knew she never wanted to see a cop at her door again. I shook my head and said, "Thank you but this won't take long. I just…I have some news you deserve to hear in person. We…uh…" I never fumbled through this type of notification before, but then this case had been everything but typical from the moment I arrived at the Ortiz scene. I took in some air and let it out slowly to steady my nerves and then I calmly said, "I wanted you to know that the man who killed your husband is dead."

Her hands shot to her mouth.

I briefly explained the details because I knew firsthand that knowing who and why mattered. When I finished, her shoulders drooped and she sighed deeply, as if she'd been holding her breath since the murder. She sniffled and then she reached out and hugged me. "Thank you. Thank you for everything, Detective." She stepped back and brushed her palms over her cheeks.

"It's Val," I said, "and just because the case is closed doesn't mean the cell number becomes inoperative. Call me if you need to talk."

A smile flashed on her face and then she nodded and closed the door.

I turned and limped back to the car. I crawled into the passenger seat, put my head back, and closed my eyes. Though my news couldn't fill the void in the lonely days ahead, hearing Konrad was dead seemed to give Rachel some peace. *Maybe what I do matters after all.* I opened my eyes and gazed out the windshield.

"You enter peoples' lives at what is the darkest time they will ever face," Connie said softly. "I wonder if they realize how lucky they are to have you on their side."

My vision blurred and I blinked rapidly, hoping the tears wouldn't spill out and run down my cheeks. *I was on Dave's side and Annie's side and they're both gone. Not so lucky for them.*

For twenty-two years I'd carried the weight of what happened to Annie. And now I'd carry the additional weight of what happened to Dave. An overwhelming urge to curl into a ball and cry for a week washed over me as I realized I lacked the strength to cart it all around. I rubbed my hand across the back of my neck, trying to ease the tension, and then I confided my greatest fear at that moment. "I'm going to see him like that whenever I respond to a scene, Connie."

"You don't know that," she said. "With some time—"

"I do know that because until three weeks ago, I always thought of Annie." My mind flashed to the crime scene photo of my first best friend, a blue ribbon tied around her neck, and I cringed. "After I joined the force," I said, "I bribed the sergeant in Records with a bottle of Macallan 18 Scotch to get a look at the evidence from her case."

"Classic Val. At least you weren't cheap."

I smiled weakly. "I've regretted it ever since because instead of recalling her angelic face, smiling and full of innocence and wonder, the first thing I think of is that last photo. And because I was so pig-headed and insisted that Pritchard take me to the bank—" My voice cracked and I stifled a sob.

Connie reached over and grasped my hand. Once again, tears filled my eyes, but this time there were too many and they came too fast to blink away. She tightened her grip and I inhaled sharply and squeezed back.

"I wish it wasn't so hard for you to talk about what you're feeling," Connie said.

"Heh. Believe it or not, I used to be quite the chatterbox."

"Shut the front door!" she said.

I held up three fingers even though I was never a scout. "I missed Annie so much, and over time I learned that holding back my feelings was a useful tool to keep people at arm's length and avoid getting so close again." I leaned my head back and stared up at the car roof. "I guess what started as a defense mechanism became a habit. It was a great way to keep one foot out the door and not become fully invested in a relationship."

"Don't get close and you don't have to worry about losing someone else you love," she said.

"It was safer that way," I said. "Easier."

"Lonelier too," Connie said.

I nodded. "Until I got to college and wound up with this pain-in-the-ass nursing student for a roommate." I rolled my head to look at her and she stuck her tongue out at me. "No matter what I did to put you off, you were determined to be my friend." I sniffled. "I know it's not easy duty and I don't think I ever thanked you for sticking with it."

She smiled. "It's been worth it. I couldn't ask for a better BFF."

I flashed a weak smile and averted my eyes because I knew it was a lie. A best friend is someone you can count on to be there for you. Like Annie counted on me. But I didn't do as I was told and then I lost my temper with my mother and got grounded, leaving Annie to ride her bike alone that afternoon. She learned the truth after it was too late.

"Is there anything else you need to tell me?" Connie angled her head to get a better read on my face.

I shook my head.

"You sure?"

I nodded.

After awhile Connie said, "I'm sorry you carried that pain alone for so long."

"That was my choice, wasn't it? The curse of being an armadillo."

She chuckled and held up her finger. "I never called you an armadillo. I merely likened you to one."

"Semantics," I said. "The point is, you were right. I do rely on my shell for protection, but I hope you know how much I care and how much I love you."

Connie nodded. "I do."

It was time to get it together and I brushed my fingers across my cheeks. "I know it's late but I could really use a pizza and some *Gilmore girls*."

Her shoulders melted into the seat, and even in the dark I saw her mouth "Yes!" to herself, as if she'd been waiting for this since my nightmare began. "Shall we make it a marathon?" she asked.

"We'd be fools not to."

"I'll call Kevin and tell him we're on our way."

It occurred to me the best way to get comfortable spending time at home alone might be to spend some time there with someone who meant the world to me. "Let's go to my house."

Connie smiled her warm, bright smile that could melt ice...and always forced me to smile too. "Like I was saying, I'll call Kevin and tell him not to wait up." Then she put the car in gear and headed for my place.

ABOUT THE AUTHOR

E.V. Stephens is an avid fan of fictional crime fighters in books and on television, and this affection served as the inspiration for her debut novel. Her previous writing experience included developing educational materials, editing employee newsletters, and drafting creative communication pieces for company projects and events. She was born and raised in Chicago and still calls the Windy City home.

Ingram Content Group UK Ltd.
Milton Keynes UK
UKHW040703160323
418667UK00001B/68